THE QUIET MAN

AND OTHER STORIES

MAURICE WALSH

APPLETREE PRESS

This edition first published and printed by
The Appletree Press Ltd
7 James Street South
Belfast BT2 8DL
1992

British Library Cataloguing-in-
Publication Data
A catalogue record for this book is
available from the British Library.

Front cover image courtesy of
the Irish Film Institute.

ISBN 0 86281 307 7

9 8 7 6 5 4 3 2 1

Contents

Characters

Six men and four girls spent a night of June, during the Black-and-Tan war, at the Angler's Hotel above Lough Aonach in a certain mountainous district of south-western Ireland, and something of their life stories, strangely intermingled, is narrated in the following pages.

The six men were:

HUGH FORBES, the Small Dark Man, ex-British officer and famous guerilla leader of a Flying Column of the IRA (Irish Republican Army);

MICHAEL FLYNN, his second in command, known as 'Mickeen Oge Flynn,' unconditional republican, celibate by inclination, half priest by training;

OWEN JORDAN, doctor to the Flying Column, Irish-American and son of a Fenian;

PADDY BAWN ENRIGHT, ex-prize-fighter, known as 'the Quiet Man' because he hoped to end his days in 'a quiet, small little place on a hillside,' and was more likely to end them in a Black-and-Tan ambush;

SEAN GLYNN, gentleman farmer and intelligence officer to the IRA; and

ARCHIBALD MacDONALD, a Highlandman, captain in the Seaforth Highlanders, an old friend of Sean Glynn's, inveterate angler, and a prisoner to the Flying Column because of that failing.

The girls were:

MARGAID MacDONALD, sister to Captain MacDonald and a prisoner with him;

JOAN HYLAND, a young Irish girl, sweetheart to Sean Glynn;

KATE O'BRIEN, niece of a British major-general and as fervid a republican as Mickeen Oge Flynn; and

NUALA KIERLEY, secret service agent to the IRA, broken in the cause.

Prologue

Of the colour of amber was my true love's hair,
In face and features none to compare;
Roses red were her lips so fine
That ne'er again shall press to mine.

I

Nuala Kierley – Nuala O'Carroll she was then – was brought up over east on the Tipperary border, horse-breeding country. She learned to ride as soon as she could walk, bareback, donkeys, jennets, ponies, and, in her teens, any horse that could be held while a saddle was girthed. At the age of seventeen she was the best horsewoman in Munster – the world, if you like. That was how she met Martin Kierley.

Nuala was a distant cousin of Sean Glynn's of Leaccabuie. He used to say that he was a bit in love with her himself – everyone was – until she met Kierley; and it was then that Sean turned his eyes on Joan Hyland.

Martin Kierley was fond of horses too. Breeder, fox-hunter, gentleman-rider; handsome as damned Lucifer; tall, dark, dare-devil; good-natured besides, a friendly man, lovable – and a spendthrift: that was Martin Kierley when he met Nuala O'Carroll, and he was ten years older. And there you are! She was nineteen when she married him.

They were the finest-mated couple anyone ever saw, brilliant contrast and complement to each other: he dark and gay, she fair and inclined to be serious. It was that serious, considering, slightly frowning way she had that used to turn men's hearts to water. They were happy too – for a time – and loved each other for a longer time – and they spent money like running water. The life they led, the only life Martin Kierley could live, called for money and money and money, and they had not such a great deal to begin with. The well soon went dry. And then Sean Glynn noticed that Martin Kierley still had plenty of money to spend. Sean used to wonder sometimes.

That was during the terrible Black-and-Tan war; and there was a good deal of money going on both sides. So Sean did not wonder too much. For the young couple were in with the Sinn Fein IRA, and deeply in; and money was called for in the company they worked in.

Look now, and let it not be forgotten! Nuala loved Kierley, and she might love another man before all was done, but no man that ever drew breath would oust Ireland from its pride of place in her heart. She was made that way. A queer, fatalistic something of the woman Eire was in her, her very self. As a girl of seventeen she was in the 1916 rising, and under fire all across Dublin; and during the Black-and-Tan war – my Lord! the things she would do. But never mind all that now.

At a certain time Sean Glynn was called to Dublin. He was one of the principal intelligence officers of the IRA; a cool and daring man; but when he got a hint of what he was wanted for he knew fear. In Dublin he saw – the name will not be mentioned – a man of iron, a small, strong, mild-looking man with gentle blue eyes that would turn cold as ice; and that man talked to Sean Glynn.

'There is a leak, Sean,' said he, 'and a bad one. Men are dying and plans failing, and we must find the source – at all costs. I know the channel through which the leak flows, but not where it starts; and you – and a friend of yours – will find that for me.'

He stopped there.

'How?' said Sean. 'I don't need a friend in this – if it can be helped.'

'Listen! A certain British agent on a certain night will have a document in his possession for an hour, and during that hour he will be well guarded. At the end of the hour the document will be in the hands of a British secretary in Dublin Castle. We can get that agent any time we want – with no document on him – but the British have plenty fearless men to replace him. We must get that document in that hour before he delivers it at the castle.'

'How?' said Sean again.

'I'll tell you. We have been studying him. Hanley is his name – Captain Sir Henry Hanley, and he's half Irish – ex-British officer, middle-weight champion of his battalion, quite fearless and no fool. A strong man, and, like strong men, he has his weakness. He might be got at through a woman, but she must be some woman. She must be our very best. You'll speak to your cousin, Nuala Kierley?'

'Did you speak to her husband?' Sean put to him.

'No,' said the man without fluttering an eyelid. ''Tis not a thing you would speak to a husband about.'

'Nor to a cousin either,' said Sean. 'I will not do it, and that's flat.' Sean was not afraid of the man, but he was afraid.

That man knew what Sean was afraid of, but in Ireland's cause he never relented.

'I thought you might refuse,' he said. 'We'll put the case to Nuala herself – she's in the next room.'

And he did that, very coldly, very clearly: the hidden leak, the deaths, the failures, the risk – and the lure.

'Don't do it, Nuala,' Sean warned her. 'Don't do it, girl!'

He might as well have warned the wind. She had to do it. It was for Ireland.

'No one must know about this,' said the man, 'no one but you and Sean – and myself.' He tapped the table. 'No one in the world,' he said.

She looked at him for a long time, that deep considering look, and the supple shoulders of her slowly stiffened. She knew then why Sean had warned her.

'Very well,' she said at last, very quietly.

And then that relentless man smiled at Sean Glynn.

'You are very careful of your cousin, Sean,' he said. 'Very good! Take care of her. She and you alone are in this. Make your own plans – but bring me that document.'

II

The plans were not hard to make. Hanley, the British agent, was staying at the Rowton – the old Rowton before it was burned down. Sean Glynn took a room there too, on the same floor, but away round a corner of the passage. Nuala Kierley did not stay in the hotel, but she came there every night to the foyer or the restaurant; it was a famous resort of good society – and certain society. She was dressed for the part, but not made up. She did not need make-up. She used to sit at her own small reserved table well away in a corner, her hair shining like the palest of pale gold – whiter than gold – and a little half-shy, half-frightened daring in every line of her. Sean Glynn used to sit at a table half-hidden by a pillar and marvel at her.

She took a week to get her man, and she got him good and hard. A finely built, smooth-faced, virile, youthful man, what chance had he? He saw her – he could not help seeing her; and she looked at him, and the small fright and the small daring fought each other in her eyes – that considering, faintly perplexed, faintly frowning, wholly serious way she looked at a man. She took him like a bramble off a briar.

In three days they were dining together. She was fresh, she was new, she was making the first venture into intrigue, and she was acting neither the fear nor the daring. And he was keen – just as if the possession of the woman added the last keen flavour to the deadly risks he was taking. In a week he was completely in her toils. And at the end of that week the document came into his hands.

The two dined together that night too; and three men dined at a table near them – armed guards. And Sean Glynn knew that other guards lounged in the foyer and about the door. But Nuala Kierley did her work from within. At the end he was half drunk – more than half drunk – without knowing it.

After a time she went to her room. She had taken a room for the night, or rather, she was supposed to have, for the room was Sean Glynn's. In fifteen minutes Hanley followed.

Sean Glynn was at the end of the passage standing within a dark doorway, and, as soon as the man entered Nuala's room, he walked slowly down to the door, his hand on the butt of an automatic. He waited. He could have walked in and held the man up, but that was to be the last resort. Hanley was a daring devil, and a fight or a shot might spoil everything. Sean Glynn just waited. Inside there was a murmur of voices, the clink of glasses, then again the murmur of voices – and after that silence.

When at last the door opened softly, and Nuala's bare forearm appeared in the slit, Sean Glynn took the long envelope from her hand and went away.

The traitor was Martin Kierley.

'You knew?' the man of iron said to Sean that night.

'I was afraid.'

'So was Nuala Kierley. You know the fate of traitors? Take the wife down to Leaccabuie with you tomorrow.'

'She may not come.'

'It will be an order. She will be a marked woman in Dublin. Tell her on the way down.'

Sean took her to Leaccabuie and told her on the way. She was not surprised, but she was numb. And from Leaccabuie he took her to

Lough Aonach, where the IRA Flying Column was holed up after the Coolbeigh ambush, and where Captain Archibald MacDonald was held prisoner at the time, and where he saw her for half a minute by the light of a peat fire – and never forgot.

And then a strange thing happened. She must have got a word of warning to her husband somehow, for he escaped out of Dublin on the very day that he was to be dealt with and made straight for Lough Aonach where Nuala was. Hugh Forbes, the great guerilla leader, was with Nuala and Sean Glynn in the lounge of the Angler's Hotel when Kierley burst in.

Already he was a broken man, broken as damned Lucifer, the dare-devil gone clean out of him; but still he loved her. Surely he loved her. He grovelled. He wanted her to know it was for her he took the British bribes – big ones. And she cared for him too. But there and then she spurned him, would have nothing to do with him, would not let him touch her, would never forgive a traitor. In the end he saw that. He turned to Hugh Forbes and some manhood came alive in him.

'All right, Hugh!' he said steadily enough. 'Take me away.'

And Hugh Forbes took him away, up to the old ruins of Castle Aonach in the hills. But Hugh Forbes had a way of his own and took it. 'Look here, Sean Glynn,' he said. 'I will not have his blood on your head or on hers. The truce is coming, you say, and I'll hold him till it comes and then slip him out of the country.'

Sean warned him about the iron man in Dublin.

'Your iron man can go to hell,' said Hugh, and Hugh meant it. 'That's the place for him,' said Hugh, who feared no man.

So he held Kierley under guard. And the truce came; and on the very night of its coming Kierley escaped and, next morning, was found drowned in *Poul Cailin Rua* – the Red Girl's Pool – which is the pool of traitors. And that week the apparition of the Red Girl was seen, so they say. The man knew that life was dust, and Nuala lost to him forever. He took the only road.

And then Nuala Kierley disappeared and no friend set eyes on her for seven years.

'Then Came the Captain's Daughter'

Then came the Captain's daughter, the Captain of the Yeos,
Saying, 'Brave United Irishman, we'll ne'er again be foes;
A thousand pounds I'll give to thee, and fly from home with me;
I'll dress myself in man's attire and fight for liberty.'

———————

Chapter One

It was a fine morning that morning, and I was feeling fine too. Fine, but tired – too tired even to smoke.

I propped my weathered rifle against the drystone wall, leant elbows on the coping-stones, and let my eyes wander lazily down and across this valley that I had not seen before. It was a pleasant valley below stone-ribbed brown slopes of heather, and somehow, though six thousand miles away, it reminded me of a sheltered fold in the stony ridges behind San Lorenzo where I had once shot an Arizona white-tailed deer of nine points. I sighed in a rather agreeable melancholy. Would I ever see New Mexico again – its austere peaks, its distances, its colours? Any day, now, a Black-and-Tan bullet might find me, and my head sink on the stock of my rifle – as I had seen heads sink – and my soul go winging six thousand miles, if I had any soul to wing.

From the open kitchen door behind me, across the little fruit-garden, came the deep murmur of men's voices and an occasional high-pitched Southern Irish laugh. The remnant of the Flying Column was having its breakfast in there, and the odour of bacon and eggs made my mouth water. In ten minutes or so Mickeen Oge Flynn would be out to relieve me, but, at that, I was not feeling so very hungry after the long night march. Every tension had slacked down comfortably, and the only desire that abided was the desire to sleep: to sleep, and to wake up sleepily, and sleepily to watch life slide by softly – for a time. And I was not sorry for myself any more.

A pleasant May morning, with a soft flow of air breathing sweetness from the hawthorn and setting little white clouds drifting over the bald head of Leaccamore Mountain across the valley; and, though the blackbirds were silent, the larks were a'soar and singing; and, as an undertone to the larks' high song, there came up the green slope the drawn-out murmur of water running over shallows – a sleepy, slow, ruminative half-chuckle, half-sigh, aloof with a gentle lonesomeness in tune with a quiet mood.

There would be fish in water like that, I considered lazily: speckled trout gormandising on the May-fly, or, maybe, a clean-run salmon up from Shannon River. I could see wide pools between clumps of hazel in the valley bottom, and the young sun made bright wimplings down the long shallows. A small interest came alive in me. Myself – but I would have one good sleep first – myself and Big Paudh Moran would, like enough, be trying a cast or two in the heel of the evening.

A stoutish short man, wearing a black coat and a bowler hat, climbed over a clay fence a hundred yards below and walked up the slope towards me. He did not look dangerous, but in our deadly game one could never be sure; so I whistled two sharp notes and slipped hand to the flat butt under oxter.

'Morrow, sir!' he saluted loudly a safe distance out. 'A fine morning, thank God!'

'It is,' I agreed. 'Anything else on your mind?'

'No – well, yes, sir! I came out to see' – he hesitated – 'I came out to see Sean Glynn.'

Sean Glynn of Leaccabuie was the upland farmer who was giving the Flying Column its breakfast this morning: one of our own, a friendly man, and any man coming to see him might be friendly too. Whoever he was, he was not of the fighting line, for there was no tan on his round, smooth-shaven, perspiring face, and he wore the shop-man's clothes – not the belted trench-coat and felt hat of the columns. Only one man of us insisted on wearing a bowler hat: Matt Tobin, the thresher; and he wore it because, he said, it brought him luck. It had two bullet holes through it.

A voice spoke behind me. 'All right, doctor!' Sean Glynn came down the path between the berry bushes. 'You're welcome, John. Come away up.'

The townsman came to the hand-gate in the wall, his side-glance aware of me. 'Commandant Forbes I'm looking for,' he said. 'There's an urgent thing I have to tell him.'

I looked at Sean, and Sean nodded. 'You knew where to look, John. Hugh Forbes is having his breakfast. Come away in.'

He preceded the visitor to the kitchen door, called his name through, and came back to my side at the wall.

'John Molouney – keeps a pub at Castletown, eight miles over the shoulder there,' he told me. 'One of my intelligence squad, and as sound a man as ever drew breath.'

Sean Glynn was a young man and dark, with a college education

and no side, a man of gay and gallant spirit. He was our chief
intelligence officer in the South. Farming many acres in the valley
bottom, sheep-grazing all the moors behind us, he had obvious
business interests in every market town in Munster; and there
he gleaned information in his own quiet way and kept the lines
of communication open between the Flying Columns and Dublin
headquarters.

His voice took on weight now. ''Twas no small thing brought John
Molouney over Leaccamore so early in the morning.'

'Pity he came, then,' I grumbled. 'We are not in this place for big
things, but for a rest only.'

'God send it to ye!' wished Sean Glynn, a shade derisively. Rest
was one of the things rarely vouchsafed to the Flying Columns.

I yawned deeply. 'That a fishing river down there?'

'That's the Ullachowen.' The quiet pride in his voice made
the answer adequate. 'See that pool – the crooked one with the
blackthorn at the elbow? Only last week my friend, Captain Archie
MacDonald, landed a twenty-pounder at the tail of it. He commands
the English garrison at Castletown – Seaforth Highlanders.'

'And a friend of yours?'

'Even so, though he is one of the enemy.'

'And with a company of his kilts to guard him while he fished?'

'Devil the one – except his sister, and she gaffed the salmon as
neat as nine pence.'

'Glory be to all the patient little gods of fishing!' I gave praise,
'for this happy valley, where an officer of the enemy may catch
twenty-pounders with no one to guard him but his sister. Is she a
friend of yours, too?'

He shook his dark head and grinned at me. 'She has red
hair, but she is a darling girl all the same, and her brother
a decent man. Actually, he is one of my oldest friends. You
know, I lived in Scotland for fifteen years, where my dad was in
the revenue service, and Archie MacDonald and I were through
Edinburgh 'Varsity together. I like him – he's quiet and hates this
damned war.'

'Does he know you're in it – you black spy?'

'Not from me. He is not easily fooled, but he says nothing.'

'Foolish of him to bring a girl here.'

'My fault. He asked me if it was safe, and I said it was. He is liked
in Castletown and holds the scales even. His Highlanders haven't

put a wet finger on man, woman, chick or child – except, it might be a bit of courting amongst the girls.'

''Tis a way girls and Highlanders have,' said I.

Mickeen Oge Flynn, our second in command, came out to relieve me then and cocked his sardonic blue eye at me.

'Hugh Forbes has a pleasant bit of news for you, Owen.'

'To hell with his news!' I said, and went in to breakfast with Sean.

II

Some of the boys were still at the long white-boarded table; others, a'slouch on the rush-seated chairs, smoked comfortably; and Big Paudh Moran sat on the flagged floor, his back to the lime-washed wall, and nursed my canvas-covered fishing-rod.

'You big ape!' I snatched the rod and pinned him with the butt. 'The next time I catch your broken paws on it I'll shove it down your thrapple.'

'Jasus, Owen Jordan!' – his great hands deprecatory. 'Sure, I was only keeping it out o' harm's way.'

'Some hay-foot might step on it, sure enough,' said Paddy Bawn Enright.

Paddy Bawn was he whom we called the Quiet Man; smallish, with a trick of hunching one shoulder, and the steadfast eyes of the fighting man below craggy brows. He had spent fifteen hectic years in the States, had been one of the best welter-weights of his time, and had returned home to Kerry to seek peace on a few hillside acres; and the peace he was likely to find was the final peace of death – death in a Black-and-Tan ambush.

Stout Johanna Dillane, Sean Glynn's housekeeper – Sean was not married – bending over a bastable oven set on the embers of the peat fire, spoke in the soft Munster voice:

'Sit in to your breakfast, *mo grah geal*, an' lave be.' She laid a plate of bacon and eggs at my elbow and reached for her brown teapot.

As I ate I kept my precious rod in the crook of a knee. And I kept casting side-glances at Commandant Hugh Forbes, our famous Small Dark Man. He was sitting at one side of the big inglenook, his chair on two legs, and, as ever, his ancient felt hat was pulled aslant over his eyes. I could see only the tip of his eagle nose, the line of his mouth that was at once sensitive and grim above the broad chin. He was not smoking, so I knew there was something on his mind. The messenger from Castletown sat on his far side, sipping steaming hot tea from a mug, his brow still warm.

'John Molouney here brought us a trifle o' news, Oweneen.' Hugh Forbes's deep voice was no more than a murmur, his lips barely moved, his head did not move at all.

I did not like the way he called me Oweneen – Little Owen. There was not a man of us who was not taller than he was – and years older too – but when he was minded to put a hard task on us he used the affectionate diminutives he would use to children – us, his little ones. He was one of the very greatest guerilla leaders in all that upheaved and tortured land.

'A trifle of news, Oweneen Jordan,' he said again.

'Keep it to yourself, da,' said I, and refilled my mouth. I feared that news.

'You'll hear it, son.'

But I did not hear it for yet awhile.

The shrill of two sharp whistles came from the rear of the house, and every one of us stiffened where we sat, except Sean Glynn, who started to his feet and hurried outside; and Johanna Dillane drew in her breath and exhaled it in a moan that had a cadence of fear and patience.

Sean was back in less than a minute. 'No danger,' he said quickly, yet his voice held anxiety. 'Captain MacDonald of the Seaforths and his sister. They come up for the fishing nearly every week.'

Hugh Forbes was on his bowed legs. 'How far off?'

'Coming in off the high road – ten minutes.'

'Ever come in the house?'

'Often, for a cup of tea and a talk, but not in the mornings. There's room for ye all in the loft.'

'If we don't want a swarm about our ears. Right! Out with you, Paddy Bawn, and warn the outposts to hole up in the hayshed. Come, boys!' His eyes rested on me. 'Go on with your breakfast, Owen – a friend of the family up for the day's fishing.' He grimaced and swore warmly. 'Damn Archie MacDonald! There was never anything in his head except fishing.'

'You know him?' I wondered.

'Fine that. We were drunk together in Cairo and climbed the Great Pyramid on our ears. You've met – but no! He was never on the Salonika front.'

It was on the Salonika front I first met Hugh Forbes, that time the Tenth Irish Division guarded the retreat down the Vardar valley, and I did thirty-six straight hours with the wounded. And now we were no longer Allied officers, and Captain MacDonald was an enemy.

In three minutes the kitchen was empty except for Johanna Dillane and myself. She was hurriedly removing the last traces of the extra breakfasts, and I went on eating slowly and with no appetite.

The sound of voices came round the side of the house and proceeded across the kitchen garden to the gate in the drystone wall. A man's voice, a woman's, and Sean Glynn's – pleasant voices all. I found myself thinking that the educated English accent was a patently cultivated one, not like these, which had a softly pleasant drawl. I could hear every word.

'You are up early, Archie – and wasting your time!'

'Not a promising day – for the fishing, I mean. All right for you chaw-bacons.'

'It will cloud up after the turn of the day,' promised the Irishman, who knew it would not.

'Thought I'd give it a whirl, anyway. I may not have many more opportunities.'

'Sorry to hear that, old man. Clearing out?'

'I am. But there are still a few fish in the Scottish waters where I'm going – you remember them, Sean? – and no risk from you darn Sinn Feiners.' And then in a voice carelessly suggestive, 'And, by the way, Hugh Forbes and his column are reported – only a Castletown rumour – somewhere in the hills, Glounagrianaan or here.'

'What would bring him up here?' Sean was sceptical.

'Mischief, what else? If you do see him – Oh yes! you may see him, my quiet fellow – tell him I hope to punch his silly black head and drink one last drink with him before the hand-cuffs snap.'

'Well, oh well, soldier man!' Sean was not to be drawn one least inch.

I grinned to myself. No doubt at all but Hugh Forbes would be ready for that last drink, but this Highland officer would need to be the very hell of a good man to punch our Small Dark Man's head – drunk or sober.

'I would just love to meet the great Hugh Forbes.' That was the lady speaking.

'I'll warn him against you – if I see him,' said Sean playfully.

'They say he's fond of red hair, Margaid. Ay! red as ever was. Isn't it, Archie?'

And I smiled at that too. At that moment the great Hugh would be looking at her through a chink in the loft lattice. And why not take a peep myself? I leant across the table and lifted a corner of the window curtain.

The man was tall, lean faced, weather brown, enduring, wearing heather tweeds and a two-peaked deer-stalker; a big fishing-creel on his hip, and under his arm a trouting-rod that, I judged, would set up to twelve feet – length enough for a whale. His sister, back turned, was a slender slip of a girl in riding-breeches and knee-boots.

I had an uncanny feeling then. Suddenly I felt remote and lonely. This was a sheltered woman, and I was looking at her out of another dimension in which a terrible ideal of freedom drove us through days and nights of fear. This woman I would never know, this woman would never know me; for I was shut off from the ordinary ways of life, and there was nothing to do but fight unyielding to an end.

It might be the intentness of my gaze that made her turn round to face the house, and brought her eyes directly to the lifted corner of the window curtain. She seemed to be looking right into my eyes. Hers was the narrow type of face, broad in the brow, long in the chin, with very little colour below the clear skin. Her eyes were either very dark or had very dark lashes, and a band of dark red hair showed under a tweed hat that carried a twist of flies.

'Elizabeth Queen, alive in the flesh,' I murmured to myself.

She turned away slowly, and I let the curtain drift into place. A few more words, a parting salute, and the thump of Sean Glynn's farm-boots coming up the path. Soldier, girl, and Sinn Fein farmer had talked to each other in a tone of easy friendship.

III

Hugh Forbes and John Molouney came back to their seats in the inglenook. Sean Glynn and Mickeen Oge Flynn came in from outside; Paddy Bawn Enright sat on a corner of the table, one shoulder hunched up in that way he had; Big Paudh Moran slumped in a chair, his ox eyes fixed on me and on my rod; most of the others stayed in the loft to sleep, or moved across the yard to a cosy nest in what was left of the winter's hay.

Slowly I filled a pipe and waited.

Hugh Forbes rubbed his neck. 'A nice bit of a girl?' he suggested ruminatively.

'She has red hair, and she's Highland,' said Mickeen Oge Flynn, 'and she wants to meet the great Hugh Forbes – save the mark! What about it?'

'A sensible girl.'

In moments of relaxation Hugh had been used to expressing his intention of seeking Scotland and a red-haired wife when peace came – if peace ever came. Only a quaint fancy, we knew, a bit of make-believe to keep him and us in touch with ordinary things. But this day, strangely enough, a woman out of Scotland with red hair had almost stepped in amongst us.

'Well, well!' he murmured, and clicking finger and thumb, turned to me. 'We'll leave MacDonald be for the present – and his sister too. You heard what he said?'

'I did. Some day someone will punch your silly black head.'

'He confirmed John Molouney's news. Not good news, Owen, my son. The Seaforths are leaving Castletown.'

'Some of the girls will be sorry,' said I, match to pipe, 'and I'll have the fishing all to myself.'

Big Paudh Moran opened his mouth and shut it before Hugh's gesture.

'They are being relieved by five lorry-loads of Black-and-Tans.'

'What odds? We did not come up here to fight the Tans.' But already a depressing doubt was in my mind.

The British Military Police were nicknamed the 'Black-and-Tans' because of their uniform – black-blue tunic and khaki trews – and they possessed all the virulent fighting qualities of a black-and-tan terrier gone sour.

'We will not fight until the board is set for us,' said Hugh mildly, 'and this bunch of Tans has a lively way of doing that. They burned Ballaghford in mid-January of a snowy morning.'

'The one town in Ireland improved by a bit of burning.'

'And shot up Kilduff on Good Friday.'

'And were themselves shot up a mile outside it, and lost five men.'

'And only last month they got Paddy Pat Walsh and four of his men resting at Scartleys.'

I had no reply to that. Paddy Pat Walsh was the heart o' corn and his four men true steel, and they had been trapped and shot, no arms in their hands.

'Well?'

'Nothing!' said I, and puffed deeply at my pipe.

What hope of rest had we now, and we so tired? After three months of the hardest guerilla campaigning – ambush, sally, get-away, and night-jumps of forty miles – our leader, Hugh Forbes, had pulled what was left of us, twenty fighting men, right out of the war area into the quietness of these hills. Wise in war, he knew when men had had enough. We had been getting careless, reckless, selling lives too easily, and Hugh had said:

'All a matter of nerves, children. There are so few of us against so many, we dare not die too easily.' And then his deep voice had grown wistful. 'It is so easy to die, and be done with it all.'

And here we were now, hoping for a quiet month amongst the hill-farmers; fishing a little, sleeping deeply, gathering a fresh store of munitions, experimenting with land-mines cunningly contrived out of railway buffers, girding ourselves for a fresh sally to the endless and careful fighting that might last not only our lives but the lives of children still at breast. That is how we in the South viewed that war. It would go on and on and on, against a foe terrible in his steadfastness, until we were dead – or until we were free.

Hugh Forbes was talking to me with suspicious mildness.

'We were talking it over before you came in, and – well! one of us will have to go down and look the Tans over.'

'And establish lines of communication,' amplified Mickeen Oge Flynn, who never beat about any bush.

'Tie all our knots for us, and, like enough, get a bullet in his belly before he's done.'

I looked sideways at Sean Glynn. He was our intelligence officer and the man for the work. He shook his head.

'Sorry, doc! I'm off to Dublin tomorrow. Headquarters work – and no safer – but I'd gladly exchange with you.' He frowned. 'I have to set a woman – of my own blood, too – at a man to get at another man and a traitor – whoever he may be.' There was something deadly in his quietness.

Hugh smiled at me, that devilish, half-wistful smile of his that got round a man.

'We thought you might volunteer for Castletown – maybe?'

A mouthful of smoke stung my throat, but I swore as I strangled and gestured furiously round the room.

'I haven't asked them, son,' said Hugh. 'They're mostly from this side of the country, and marked men at that. Let a spy put an eye on one of them in Castletown and –' again he flicked his finger and thumb.

'Look at it this way now! You are a stranger in this territory, and though you possess all the qualities, except the good ones, of a spavined mule, you sport a mild front – like most of you Yankees; a sort of hand-dog, youthful, half-clerical austerity, for all that you are a seasoned old sawbones. If we borrowed a black coat and a Roman collar from Father Ryan, devil a Tan would look crooked at you.'

I pointed a thumb at Mickeen Oge Flynn. He had the lean, grave face of an ascetic, and, before the cold fire of his patriotism had driven him out to war, had spent three years reading Divinity at Maynooth College.

'I don't mind,' he said quietly. 'I'll go.' He was more intensely republican that Hugh Forbes himself and was afraid of nothing in this world or the next.

'You've a face would hang a dog in Castletown,' Hugh told him. 'You'll go, Owen?'

'I will not,' said I firmly.

'You'll have your reasons?' He was milder than ever.

'I have. I'm going fishing.'

They all laughed at me except Big Paudh Moran and Hugh Forbes.

'A fair half-reason. Let's have the other half.'

'I'm afraid.'

And again they laughed at me.

'No reason at all, small son. Fear is part of our life.'

'But I'm a coward at heart and would let you down in a tight corner.'

'We'll risk that. What else?'

'I'll tell you, pig-head. Who instituted the rest-places for the spent columns?'

'We did.'

'You did. And this is one of them. Look now! Start trouble here, and Castletown has flaming roofs. Ambush the Tans on the hill-road, and, in reprisal, this house and every farmhouse along the rim of the valley goes up in smoke. There's reason for you. And we'll say nothing about the shape we're in.'

'All that is on my mind, Owen, and heavy on it, but,' and his voice hardened, 'we will do our work where we can and how, and,

when the time comes, no place – or man – can shirk the sacrifice.
You'll go?'

'An order?'

'No, this is a volunteer's job, and you may well be afraid. You'll
have no arms on you, and your life will be on your sleeve for any
Tan to pluck.'

I pushed back my chair and lifted to my feet. 'All right! I'll go –
on one condition.'

'One condition?' He threw back his head. His voice was stern.

'One condition.' I was as stern as he was. 'If you guarantee to flay
Paudh Moran alive the moment he breaks the only greenheart tip I
have left.'

Something lit behind the dark eyes. 'That puts you one up on me,
Yankee. Right! The guarantee is given.'

'Skinned I will be too, be Jasus!' lamented Big Paudh.

I glared into the big lad's face resentfully, but his ox eyes were
mildly beseeching, and his round cheeks twitched.

'There! You'd find where it was hidden, in any case.'

I thrust the rod into his hands, and his great palms caressed the
canvas cover.

'Jasus, Owen! I'll be mendin' it.'

'A coupla flies now – and a bit of a minnow,' suggested Paddy
Bawn, the Quiet Man.

It was too late to take back the rod, and, in the end, they had my
cast-box and fly-book too.

Chapter Two

I

I leant my elbow on the high, zinc-covered counter of John Molouney's bar and drank my tankard of brown stout slowly and with satisfaction. Everything was fine now, and I hadn't a taut nerve in my whole body. For my work was done to the last tight hitch, and I was going back to the column at Leaccabuie within an hour. I had such a feeling of well-being that I should have known it portended an unpleasant few minutes.

Fifteen days in the jaws of Castletown, and no breath of suspicion had ever blown on me. But indeed, the very least breath would have blown me sky-high. Danger there had been, but danger just round the corner; and one man, though he did not know it, helped to hold that corner for me: Captain MacDonald of the Seaforths, the fisherman of Ullachowen. He still remained in Castletown with half a company of his Highlanders, and the soldiers, ever on good terms with the citizens, would not stand for any rough work by the new military police.

So we leant over the counter – John Molouney, two other trusty men of the town and myself – and went over the final knots of our secret lines. No movement, no rumour, but would be known to our column within three hours; and at the given word trees would be felled, culverts blown up, telephone-lines cut, the quarry isolated for the final bay. All was set, and I was free until that final issue was joined.

I remember that, as we leant there together, I was feeling sorry for these three men of Castletown who took their lives in their hands day after day in order that the Flying Columns might operate effectively.

And then danger jumped us.

'Put them up – up with them!' the harsh alien voice snapped.

Our hands went up like one man. We were trained to get our hands up quickly or into action quickly.

'About turn – jeldy now!'

We came about, but we were careful not to do it drill fashion.

A big man in the uniform of the military police – khaki slacks, blue tunic, Glengarry bonnet – filled the doorway. He poised a long-barrelled revolver level with his shoulder, and, like the head of a snake, the high-sighted muzzle moved swayingly from side to side.

'Committee-meeting heads together – eh? Staff murder meeting – what?'

'Not at all, sir,' protested John Molouney warmly. 'Only a story I was telling.'

'You Sinn Feiners are good at that. Come outside! You too, Molouney! Come on, you! Keep your hands up!'

He backed out, a little uncertain on his feet, and we followed. My uncontrollable heart was beating high up in my breast. If this was an organised raid and not the usual bit of rough horseplay, I was as good as dead. Outside he lined us up, our backs to the window and our buttocks against the projecting wooden bar that protected the plate glass. A quick glance up and down the street showed me a citizen here and there dodging into doorways, and two other Black-and-Tans lounging and laughing on the side pavement not twenty paces away. It might be just horseplay after all.

Across the street, on the steps of the only hotel in Castletown, stood a tall man in the undress uniform of a Highland regiment and at his side a slender young woman in grey.

I considered the man who held us: a tall blue-chinned fellow, with hollow dead-white cheeks and eyes blazing a black devil. He was half-drunk and his nerves more than half-shot – a man on the brink of a blow-up. I understood that man. I knew the insides of him, for I was as like him as peas in a pod: tall and black and strung, and I knew that I had nerves.

That man, set to subdue a people not easily subduable, had been subject to months of constant strain. There was nothing of the traditional ebullience about this people, no wild flare and quick quenching. It was a people quietly inimical, wearing submissiveness as a mask, bearing abuse calmly, biding its own time, choosing the ground on which it would fight, and then fighting carefully, wilily, toughly – not dying easily like the brown races. The strain of waiting, the strain of watching, the deadly explosiveness below the deadly calm, had brought this man to the breaking-point. At this moment he felt in his bones that we were four Sinn Feiners hands-up before him, and he knew that nothing he could do would force an admission or an explosion from us. That was our code. He would risk his life to make one of us explode into action.

'We are watching you, Molouney,' he warned, 'and we'll get you – good and hard.'

He faced me closely. 'You've been going round with him. Who are you?'

John Molouney at my side answered for me, 'Me cousin, sir, a clerical student out of Mayooth.'

'Shut up, you –!' The back of his hand smashed on my friend's mouth, and John merely blinked and lifted his hands a little higher.

'A – Shinner, you?' He persisted in using one repellent adjective.

I remained silent.

'No dumb insolence, – you!' The word could be used as a verb too. 'You are a Shinner?'

'Not guilty.'

'You – liar!'

He thrust the muzzle of his weapon against my shut mouth so that the flesh ground against my teeth and blood tasted salt on my tongue.

In his half-drunken state I might have wrenched the gun from him. I had the will to do so, the angry urge on the verge of action. And, having done so, I might, on the odd chance, fight myself clear of the town; but these three good men lined up with me would be dead within the minute. So I held my hands firmly above my head and kept my fingers from crooking.

Over the Black-and-Tan's shoulder I saw the Highland officer step down to street-level from the hotel porch.

'A – Shinner, that's what you are.' Probably he sensed what was in my mind and kept on baiting me. 'A clerical student drinking beer in a – pub! More like a – Yank to me! One of Forbes's spies – what? You shoot in the back, don't you?'

'No.'

'Bah! You – Irish liar!'

The last shred of his control snapped suddenly, and he struck me a drawing blow on the side of the head with the long barrel of his gun. The felt of the black clerical hat broke the force, but a sharp pang stabbed my temple, and a blackness leaped across my sight and was gone.

To prevent my knees from buckling I brought hands down to the wooden bar at my back.

'Hands up, you –!'

'Easy all!'

II

The voice was quiet but authoritative.

The Black-and-Tan whirled on his heel, weapon lifted, and found himself face to face with the Highland officer, Captain MacDonald, the fisherman of the Ullachowen.

'What's this, Garner?'

'Shinners – IRA killers, Captain.'

'You know?'

'Whispering, heads together – in there.'

'That all?'

'Molouney is under suspicion – and this fellow –'

The officer was close to him now. 'You're drunk, man. You can't treat men this way.'

'The –'

'Not while I command.'

His voice was still quiet, but I could sense the hot Scots devil behind it.

'I will deal with this, Garner.'

'They'll plug you in the back.'

'They have had many opportunities. Go back to barracks! Do you hear? I'm in command here. Go!'

Possibly this man Garner was a decent enough citizen in ordinary life – law-abiding and weak too. He could not stand up to the held strength in the soldier's tone and bearing. He hesitated, then his shoulders slumped and as he turned away, his gun fumbling into thigh-holster, his face was abased and the madness out of his eyes.

His two companion Black-and-Tans treated him with laughing contempt. For a little while they stood and watched us, intently, dangerously, storing us away in their memories, then swung in line and marched quickly up-street towards their barracks.

Captain MacDonald looked us over consideringly, a quizzical half-smile on his lean Scots face, and his hand smoothing down his chin.

'Well? You fellows may be Sinn Feiners – very probably are.' His smile broadened. 'Whispering, you know, is bad manners and worse policy, but scarcely a crime.' He nodded quickly. 'Get under cover – and stay there.'

'Thank you, Captain,' said John Molouney, and wiped his bloody mouth.

My three friends disappeared through the saloon door, but I hesitated to take my hands off the steadying bar behind me. I felt a thin trickle down my temple.

'Ah! he got you,' said the soldier. One hand was firm on my shoulder, the other careful at my black hat. 'Yes! the foresight nicked you. Damn brute! Small, but – blood enough, anyway. Come along, young reverend! I want a closer look at this.'

I cursed myself inwardly. The quicker I got away now, the better.

'Nothing at all, Captain MacDonald,' I protested, and held my shoulder against his pull.

But his firm hand took me across the street to where the young woman in grey still stood on the hotel steps.

'Puncture above the temple, Margaid,' he told her. 'We'll have a look-see.'

She was as prompt and as impersonal as her brother.

'I'll get my outfit. Take him up to the bathroom.'

In the bathroom he threw a towel over my shoulders, bent my head over the wash-basin, and sloshed water over the side of my face from a big sponge.

'You should avoid bad company – and public-houses, reverend sir,' he said ironically.

His sister came in quickly, a first-aid outfit already half-unrolled in her hands.

'That's not the way. Leave it to me, Archie.'

She thrust a wooden-seated chair against the backs of my knees, and her fingers were light at my brow.

'Sorry to trouble –' I began.

'I like this. VAD nurse for two years.'

'Fond of a bit torture,' said her brother.

The careful snip-snip of scissors, the dab of iodine, the pull of plaster, the manipulation of bandage, all followed the trained technique. As a doctor I knew that. She was very close to me as I sat, and there was some faint pleasant touch of perfume all about her; and, sometimes, I saw deft fingers and, sometimes, the small sympathetic twist of a mouth. And there were golden gleams in her dark red hair.

Though she was smartly efficient, there was something excited in the dark blue eyes below the lashes that were almost black. And yet, she treated me quite impersonally, just as if I were a hurt puppy. Again I experienced that curious feeling of being remote from her and remote from her world. I did not like it. Her impersonality nettled me. That is why I spoke.

'Sorry to distress you.'

'Oh! This is nothing.'

'Your hands tremble?'

'That's only temper.' And then she exploded on me. 'Are all you Irishmen cowards?' I surely had drawn her.

'Every last one of us – same as other men.'

'Ay, faith!' said her soldier brother, and chuckled. 'Glad you don't boast Christian meekness.'

That made her madder. 'I would rather be shot dead than bullied like that,' she cried, and whipped bandage firm.

'I had that choice offered, surely.'

'And you chose to be bullied.'

'It was not given me to choose the desirable,' said I.

'Ho-ho!' This was the soldier. 'What do you mean by that, young man? Clericals don't usually appreciate that desirability – unless they be saints.'

'A man I know,' said I, 'says that death is the easiest choice to make.'

'And where did he find that out?'

'In the Great War.'

'He would know.' He smoothed his chin with a slow hand and looked at me speculatively. 'I wonder who said that?'

I could have bitten my tongue off. Hugh Forbes was the man who had said it, and this man knew him; and Hugh had some pet phrases known to all his acquaintances. I rose to my feet and scrubbed my blue jowl with the towel.

'Garner might have some reason in his madness,' said the soldier doubtfully. 'Men of your cloth don't usually resort to beer-shops.'

'Where else would a man get a drink on a warm day?'

'A clerical student?'

'Did you ever know one to look coldly on a tankard of brown stout?'

'Just so!' He laughed, and then put a question, carefully casual, 'You are an Irishman, I suppose?'

'Spent my youth in the States,' I told him, knowing that he had caught my touch of Western drawl.

The girl was looking at me curiously.

'Where have I seen you before?' she murmured musingly, no longer quite impersonal.

'Been about town several days,' said her brother.

'No – not here. I seem to remember – the eyes.'

I could have told her that there was a pane of glass between us that time, but, instead, I reached for my hat.

'If you will excuse me.'

'You are getting out of town, young man?' suggested the soldier.

'On my way, captain.'

'And stay out.' That was an order by a British officer.

They went with me as far as the porch of the hotel and saw that the street was clear before they let me go. From the foot of the steps I looked up.

'My thanks.' And then a thought struck me. 'Some day I might show you where a good fish lies.'

'You fish?'

'Trying the Ullachowen this evening.'

'Ah! now I remember,' said the girl.

'Stick to fishing, reverend sir,' said the brother in satirical warning.

I looked him in the eye then. 'You are a MacDonald,' said I, 'and there were MacDonalds before you, son of a great race – and the heather was not always above the myrtle. Somewhere you took the wrong turning.'

I pulled my hat aside over the bandage and marched down the street. And I felt her eyes on my back. I would not see her again.

Chapter Three

'H-s-s-t! Listen!'

Hugh Forbes's strong whisper went down the line, and a thrill went with it. From miles away, through the still noon air, came the staccato purr of the big cars.

Hugh focussed his glasses on a distant hill-slope, and I, even with the naked eye, could see a white signal wink.

'They come.' His deep voice boomed. 'That's for the turn at Boland's Cross.'

We were where there was no drawing back now. For a moment there was a hollow place in my breast where my heart should be, and then the old accustomed feeling came a'crawl: the fear that I might show fear.

I looked along the line of men manning the peat bank, and I envied them. Paddy Bawn Enright and his friend Matt Tobin of the bowler hat bent, heads together, over a Thompson gun, and there was only a live interest in their faces. Paddy Bawn had too often faced the tension of the squared ring ever to show any in his steadfast eyes, and Matt Tobin, hat on the back of his head, went over the mechanism of the gun as if it were a part of his threshing-machine. Others were bedding down their rifles in the heather and taking tentative long sights. Mickeen Oge Flynn looked across at me and smiled his friendly, sardonic smile – indomitable fighting men, every one. Only, here and there, eyes had gone strangely bleak, and the bosses of firm cheek-bones stood out rigidly under drawn skin.

'Jasus, Owen!' whispered Big Paudh Moran at my left shoulder. 'Haven't we got them where they live?'

'And die,' murmured Hugh Forbes at my other side.

Big Paudh, ordinarily a simple, ox-eyed, wondering soul, following me round like a corpulent shadow, was now serenely calm, full of a benign confidence. Here he was master of his task. He had propped two long sods of dry peat a foot apart in the heather, and his well-kept rifle pointed between them down the slope. Before the storm broke, his big head would cuddle down, his left hand move far out below the guard, and, no matter how long and how desperate the fray, his machine-like and deadly precision would never falter.

I looked aside at our leader, Hugh Forbes. His face, too, before the issue was joined, was characteristic. He seemed to be pondering some particularly perplexing problem and to be desperately, forlornly unsure of any solution. His rifle was propped against the peat bank before him, and he looked down at the capped ends of the wires he held in each hand. His voice was dejected.

'Dammit! Maybe I shouldn't do it.'

Always had he said that, and always was it done.

'Why do it, then?' I gave back in formula.

He lifted his head and looked over his shoulder at the scattered line of farmhouses showing their thatched roofs above the curve of the slope that, beyond, dipped into the verdant valley of the Ullachowen. Only yesterday I had killed a clean-run salmon down there, and now, this still summer noon, I was set to kill men – or be killed.

'Smoking walls and black rafters!' rumbled the deep voice.

'And the fishing ruined for Owen Jordan,' added Mickeen Oge.

'To the devil with him and his fishing!' Hugh cursed mildly, and slung his binoculars to the front.

'True for Mickeen Oge, all the same,' said Big Paudh in my ear. 'The fishing'll be gone all to hell.'

'And you with it, likely.'

'What harm? Man, Owen! there was a bull of a trout rose to me twice below the sally bush – you know the place. The tail of him made a wallop like a barn door.'

'You never told me, you thief.'

'An' me keepin' him for meself. I'd a got him but for breakin' the tip. Whist! Paddy Bawn spliced it for me afore Hugh found out. Don't be tellin' him. Whisper! If I don't come out o' this, try him with a brown nymph well sunk – an' strike like a sledge.'

'Come out of it or not,' I warned, 'if I catch you near that sally bush I'll drown you.'

'An' me the fool to tell you.'

'Christ!' Hugh's voice exploded. His elbows were propped in the heather, and the reflection of the eye-pieces of the binoculars made circles of light on his cheeks. 'There's a woman in that leading car.' He twisted aside and thrust the glasses at me. 'Take a look!'

The big Crossley lorries had at last come into sight round the curve of the road a mile away, three of them in a close line. They were coming at a moderate speed, not in their usual reckless rush, and I had no difficulty in picking them up. Every lorry was fully manned: fifteen men to each, and every man a proved fighter. Two to one against us. Yet we held them in the hollow of our hands.

On the wide driving-seat of the leading car were three people. One was a woman.

'Yes!' I told Hugh. 'Captain MacDonald and his sister.'

'Oh, the damned fool!'

The problem was Hugh Forbes's, and his only; and, in the doing of what he considered his duty, Hugh could be coldly ruthless. There was nothing I could say or do, and my heart might beat as heavily as it liked. I shut my mind away and looked over the rifle-sights across the valley. It was a bare and shallow valley, with low curves of heather swelling up to the horizon and bare black patches of peat that swallowed the sunlight; in the damp hollows the canna, the white bog-cotton, hung on its stalk; one distant hillside drowsed under the hazed golden glory of the whin; and the high piping of a hill-lark lifted above the roar of the approaching cars. But, below and behind all sounds, a brooding quiet lay heavily on that shallow valley.

One hundred and fifty measured yards below us, the brown moorland road swept in a wide curve, dykeless, ditchless, entirely without cover. Here and there rotting posts that once had carried wires leant at all angles, and on the backs of two of these, two hundred yards apart, scraps of white paper were pinned. Only we knew the deadliness that lay concealed between these two scraps.

Hugh Forbes's deepest voice boomed sternly down the line, 'Let no man fire till I explode the mines. Let no man fire till then.'

The contact-wires were ready in his hands. Was he going to do it, then? None of my business. I was only third in command after Mickeen Oge Flynn. But my heart hurt me with its beating.

There was the leading car now. I did not let my eyes rest on the woman. The second car was close behind, and I looked at that; fifteen men close packed, Glengarry bonnets rakishly atilt, rifles pointing to the sky. They were singing in that car, a gay song with a marching tune – one of our own songs that used to keep our feet moving in the long night marches:

> Eileen Oge, and that the girl's name was;
> Through the barony her features they were famous.
> And if we loved her, who was there to blame us?
> For wasn't she the pride of Petravore?

The leading car was on the withinside of the first scrap of paper and it was slowing down. It was slowing down. And slowly it came to a halt directly below us, the other cars close behind. Dead in the middle of our trap.

I shut my mind close down, drew in a deep breath, and looked along the rifle-sights. A blue tunic perched and was steady on the fore-sight.

'Low, down hill!' came Big Paudh's rumbling advice. 'An' don't jerk the pull.'

II

Captain MacDonald and his sister alighted from the driving-seat. I was not looking at them, yet I could see. There were the fishing-creels being slung on shoulders; and the sound of voices but not the words; and the engine went with an impatient roar as it accelerated.

And then the cars moved, slowly, slowly, gathering speed and gathering speed, and, still gathering speed, roared and disappeared round the curve of the valley.

Captain MacDonald and his sister – Margaid, he called her – came up the slope on the narrow path that wound in the heather.

Again came Hugh's warning voice, but it was stern no longer.

'Doggo! Lie close!'

I crushed my face in amongst the twisted stems of bog-myrtle and did not feel the hurt; I pressed my body close to the breast of peat to still its trembling.

Hugh's palm came gently on my shoulder. 'We owed that for your tough Yankee hide. God's hand was in it, maybe.'

'And Hugh Forbes's hand as well,' murmured Mickeen Oge Flynn, 'and not such a bad instrument in the hands o' God.'

I never looked up till I heard Hugh's lifted voice.

'Morning, Captain! A bright day for the fishing? Step down this way.'

The Captain, his sister behind him, was stepping down the brief slope to the bottom of the peat bank. His face had assumed the soldier's mask to hide his astonishment – or something much deeper – and his voice was finely cool.

'Good morning, Forbes! Glad to meet you again – even at a disadvantage.'

Hugh, planted on wide-set bowed legs, head forward, looked at him underbrowed. We knew that attitude. Something was going to give in a minute.

'The rumours were not so far out after all.' The soldier was halted now, hand irresolute.

'No – not very.' Hugh's voice was still even. 'Not a safe territory for a lady, is it?'

'Safe enough till you came.'

And there Hugh exploded.

'Blast your stone face, MacDonald! Have you no more respect for your sister than to take her riding in a Tan lorry?' The sweeping gesture of his hand directed the other's attention to the situation.

I don't think the soldier realised till then what he and his sister had escaped. He looked and saw: the appraising eyes of fighting men, the rifles bedded in the heather, the shelterless road open to sweep of fire, the contact-wires projecting from the peat bank. The mask of his face could no longer hide the shock; his jaw lengthened as it fell. And then he did a nice thing. He turned to his sister at his shoulder and laid a hand on her arm.

'Please forgive me, Margaid,' he said urgently. 'I was a criminal fool.'

'That's better,' said Hugh Forbes.

The other turned almost impulsively.

'Thanks, Forbes, but – I deserve to be shot.'

'Just about,' agreed Hugh grimly.

'Get on with it, then.'

His foolish words shocked the girl. Up to now she had been curious, interested, no more than excited, not seeing what the eyes of her experienced brother saw. But was this really an ambush? Was her brother in the net and in danger? Were the horrific stories of the terrible Flying Columns true? I saw the intake of her breath, the widening of her eyes; she seemed to shrink within her riding-breeches. Hugh Forbes saw too.

'Don't be a damn fool, Archie! Is this your sister?'

'Yes. This is Hugh Forbes, Margaid.'

She smiled a shade wanly, holding her brother's arm, not yet able to trust her voice.

'Up for the day's fishing?' went on Hugh easily. 'Faith, we have often watched ye at it, and once – you may remember, Miss MacDonald – you expressed a flattering desire to meet me.' He could be as courtly as the devil, this small dark man.

'I remember,' she murmured, and her eyes came across to me. Till then I did not know that she was aware of my presence.

Her brother looked at me, too, and nodded briefly.

'Exactly! I might have known. How's the head, reverend sir?' There was still a strip of plaster above my temple.

'Thick as ever,' Hugh answered for me. 'One good turn deserves another. But he is a doctor of medicine, not divinity.'

'A doctor?' half-exclaimed the girl.

'One of those low Yankee degrees. But we are wasting your time.'

Captain MacDonald glanced over his shoulder to where Mickeen Oge Flynn and Paddy Bawn had quietly occupied the path leading to the road; then he rubbed his long jaw – a habit of his – and looked up at the zenith.

'Not much use trying the Ullachowen under that sky,' he suggested casually. 'I think we'll try that hill-burn a mile or so back the road.'

'If I were you,' said Hugh smoothly, 'I'd wait for the evening rise on the Ullachowen.'   .

They looked at each other warily, like fighting dogs in no hurry to come to the issue that was unavoidable.

'Perhaps you're right,' agreed the soldier.

'And I would like to talk to you – of old times – while you are wasting foot-pounds of energy.' Hugh nodded towards me. 'At the same time, Owen Jordan here might show Miss MacDonald where a good fish feeds.'

'Jasus!' I heard Big Paudh's whisper.

'As you say,' agreed Captain MacDonald.

III

That afternoon's fishing was no more than an excuse. We fished some indeed, but, except for a few small trout and more than enough of tantalising parr, we caught nothing. Captain MacDonald, moreover, could not concentrate very well on the work in hand, or rather, he was concentrating too much on what might happen next. He had no illusions about his position, and he knew that Big Paudh Moran and Paddy Bawn Enright, sort of playing at gillies, were with us merely as his guard.

Mickeen Oge Flynn joined us late in the afternoon, and, as previously arranged, I then undertook the task of getting the girl out of earshot. We were to leave Captain MacDonald to be reasoned with by Hugh Forbes and his second in command.

The sun was westering down into the wide mouth of the glen, and the feeding-time of the big trout was at hand. Margaid MacDonald was fishing out a long run, throwing a nice cast off a nine-footer, and keeping a straight line out of the water; and, like all good anglers, she was still fishing carefully after vain hours. I worked down to her shoulder.

'Care to try for a big fellow, Miss MacDonald?'

'Are there any, Mr – Doctor Jordan, isn't it?'

'Yes. Up the river.'

'Far?' She was not sure of us wild men for yet awhile.

'Round the corner. A fish another fellow was keeping for himself.'

She got my tone of confidence at once. 'Lead me to him,' and there was mischief in her smile.

So, she and I, with Big Paudh Moran at our heels and Paddy Bawn paralleling us along the bank, moved up the stream a quarter of a mile; and I think that her brother was glad to see us go.

We halted at a fine sweep of pool, where a sally bush leant over at the breast of the curve on the other side. The slow current made a ripple amongst the trailing branches and curled into a small backwater under a clay bank. I pointed across.

'An' wasn't I the damn fool to tell him!' came the anguished voice of Big Paudh.

'Over there – with flukes like a barn-door,' I told her. 'We'll try him with a heavier fly. What have you got?'

I went through her fly-book, stocked mostly with Highland killers, too gaudy for our heavier streams, and chose her a double-hooked blae saltoun with scanty hackle and thin wing.

'A bottom feeder, that fellow,' I explained as I tied the fly on at the tip. 'Nymphs out of the egg, and we need weight. Let your fly sink and strike hard at the first touch.'

'I know.'

She slipped into the gravelly edge of the pool and began making tentative fly-wetting casts, lengthening her line as she went deeper in.

'Careful!' I warned. 'You'll be over the top.'

'Felt a trickle already,' she called laughingly.

I went and sat on a low green bank back from the pool, and Paddy Bawn came and sat at my side. Big Paudh stood out on the gravel, one hand scratching perplexedly behind his ear. We watched her silently, thinking our own thoughts.

She was a supple, finely strung girl in her riding-breeches and brown blouse; and the sun, shining up the valley, brightened a lock of the red hair that had escaped from under her tweed hat. A small and lonely bit of a girl set here amongst us in a tortured land, fishing carefree in a false peace! Her brother was a dashed fool ever to bring her here. His was a peaceful area, indeed, thanks mostly to his own understanding of the breed, but that understanding should have told him that the peace was a false one and might shatter at any hour – as it was shattered now, though this girl did not know that yet.

I was sorry for her then, and with that sorrow came a strange small wave of feeling that was almost tenderness. We must be careful of this girl. Whatever happened, we must set a wall of safety about her – kindness, gentleness, the saving salt of humour – and she must not know anything of the fear and wearing effort in which we lived day and night.

Paddy Bawn's thoughts must have been running on the same lines as mine. 'A nice bit of a girl, sure enough!' he murmured. 'God bless her! Maybe her brother'll have sense after all.'

'The Scots are a pig-headed breed.'

'Sticky! They'd go to hell for a friend. I mind once over in Pittsburgh – his name was MacRae –'

The girl laid down a nice fly dangerously close to the trailing branches of the sally, and the current took it deep and sure to the edge of the backwater. I saw the point of the rod jerk.

'Strike!' I urged under my breath.

And she struck. But alas! What with light rod, double-barbed hook and heavy water, the strike lacked firmness. The rod leaped and curved half-circle, and a wide fluke came out of the water and threshed under.

'You're into him. Point up!'

But the point came up of itself with a jerk, and the cast looped out of the water and tangled. That was all.

'Oh, damn!' cried that girl with all her heart.

And on my feet, stamping the gravel, I forgot the lady in the angler.

'Thunder! That's no way to strike a big fish. Come out of it, woman!'

She looked at me over her shoulder, eyes wide and mouth a little open.

'Jasus, Owen Jordan!' came Big Paudh's shocked protest. 'That's no way to talk to a lady. Have you no bloody manners at all?'

'Sorry!' I said. 'I forgot.'

And there she threw back her head and laughed a laugh that was rueful enough but had no pique in it. She waded slowly out of the pool, her line trailing in the water.

'Remember – in Castletown – you promised to show me a good fish? Are you sorry?'

'I am sorry I was rude.'

'Not very rude – for an angler. But my rod was a bit light, wasn't it?'

'True for you, miss,' lied Big Paudh.

'No use trying again?'

'Divil a bit!' said Paudh hurriedly. 'He'll have a puss on him for days.'

'Next week, perhaps,' I promised her.

'But I am going away tomorrow. This was to be our last day on the Ullachowen. Oh dear!'

'You used stronger language half a minute ago.'

She laughed. The little tension or suspicion of the afternoon was suddenly gone. So! She was going away next day. And her brother? Her brother, even now, was having things put before him by Hugh Forbes and Mickeen Oge Flynn – and tomorrow was a long way off.

'Do you know,' said the girl, 'I could do with a sandwich, and Archie – my brother – has my packet in his bag.'

Big Paudh slung his wicker creel to the front. 'Johanna Dillane above filled a paper bag, miss, and two bottles of milk.'

'You darling man.'

We sat on the green bank, our feet in the fine river gravel, and ate sandwiches companionably, for the girl insisted that we share with her. Big Paudh watched her diffidently and schooled himself to take ridiculously small bites instead of his usual snap and gulp; Paddy Bawn, after the continent fashion of the fighter, merely nibbled at his sandwich and stared across the width of the pool as he chewed. She, unconcernedly, arched back her neck to the tip-tilted bottle, and the milk gurgled as she drank. She had a lovely, long neck, and one might have a childish urge to smooth the velvet of it with a finger-tip.

'Don't get your tongue stuck,' I warned her.

'Teach your grandmother,' she gave back, and a little pearl of milk trickled on that firm chin – a longish chin, and obstinate, as I know.

And there I began to rewonder at the quirkiness of life. An hour or two ago we had been strung to kill, and here, now, we were lazying in a valley of peace – though it was a false peace – and making a girl out of another world feel at ease. And tomorrow? Tomorrow I might be at the other side of the new moon.

And the girl began to wonder too. Her jaws moved slowly, and she looked all about her, strange speculations behind her eyes; and somehow I was able to look behind those eyes and follow the wonderings in her mind.

The sun shone brilliantly up the valley, and the shadows of the scattered trees were long and dark on the green carpet of the grass; over the high brown crowns of the hills the sails of the clouds of evening were scattered widely on the blue; across the river and back again a swallow zig-zagged on fleet wing; and above the lonesome, aloof wimpling of the water the thrushes were beginning to tune up for evensong, and a solitary green linnet kept piping its one run. A valley set apart for quietude, surely. That was the very thought in her mind. And she sighed.

And from the valley the girl turned to us, quiet men all, quiet as this valley below the hills; and the wonder deepened in her eyes. One by one, she looked us over; ox-eyed Paudh Moran, diffident with shyness, strong-browed Paddy Bawn with the immobile face and steadfast eyes, myself of the black-avised, lean American seriousness. Were we men of the Flying Columns, the terrible men, and was she sitting with us unafraid? She was not afraid. In that secret place of womanly intuition she knew that we were men no woman need fear; she felt that in blood and bone and mind there was a sibness between herself and us. We were men who held our hands from killing because of a woman? I could follow every turn of her mind. Her eyes opened at me.

'Was that really an ambush – back there?'

Because of what was in her mind I prevaricated.

'Just an observation post.'

'And you had hundreds of men posted.'

'You saw all there were of us.'

'But the Black-and-Tans – the police – are terrible fighters. They speak of the hundreds.'

'Faith! an' they do so,' put in Big Paudh.

Paddy Bawn chuckled. 'I mind myself and Matt Tobin, just for devilment – we had a pint or two taken, it could be – and we couldn't do much harm in the dark. Anyway, the two of us held up a lorry-load of Tans a whole night at Monreddan Chapel, firing a shot here and there and letting a screech out of us to wake the dead. And next morning we were two columns, or maybe three, and twenty of us toes cocked – according to the Tans.'

'Ay, faith!' agreed Big Paudh.

'If we had hundreds, or, rather, equipment for hundreds,' I began.

She threw a hand out impulsively, persuasively. 'But what chance can you have – what hope?'

'We often wonder.'

'England – Britain is so resolute, pig-headed, if you like. In all her history she has never been the first to cry enough.'

'Once,' said I, 'where I come from.'

'Oh, yes! You are an American.' A trace of contempt was in her tone. 'Why do you fight here?'

'England is the one nation worth having a whirl at. My father taught me that.'

'Poor teaching.'

'The finest in the world. My father spent ten years in an English prison – he was a Fenian. You are not English, are you?'

She stamped an impatient foot. 'But how long is this – this folly to go on?'

'I couldn't tell you that,' said I mildly. 'But my grandsons will continue the fight – if necessary.'

'What?' she cried in complete surprise.

'My wife,' said I, 'will rear sons to carry on.'

'You are married, then?'

'I am not. But –'

'That fellow!' Big Paudh was as nearly derisive as he could be. 'He wouldn't look at a girl, an' she Grecian Helen, as the song says.' He chewed ruminatively. 'An' coortin' a damn pleasant occupation, an' no harm in it. Paddy Bawn, do you mind purty Grania Grace beyant in Grianaan, with her heart in her eyes an' she peepin' at the lad here?'

'Shut your big mouth!' Paddy Bawn advised him firmly.

Margaid MacDonald looked at me curiously, some new speculation in her eyes, and that speculation I could not follow. Then she smiled, and a gentle mocking was in the voice that followed every falling cadence of Paudh's soft brogue.

'Grania Grace! What a lovely name! An' she peepin' at him out of lovely eyes, no doubt. An' he wouldn't even look at her?'

'You people shouldn't speak with your mouths full,' I admonished them sourly.

Big Paudh swallowed hastily and nearly strangled; and the girl threw up her chin, after a fashion of her own, and laughed with an odd merriment.

'Big children of fighting men!' And then, 'Is your great Hugh Forbes without a wife, too?'

A thought struck me. 'He talks of going to Scotland for a red-haired one.'

'To Scotland?'

'Why not? He says the finest red hair comes out of the Highlands, and,' my eyes on the sun-rich band below her hat, 'I am inclined to agree with him.'

'Splendid – splendid!' she clapped her hands, and a touch of colour came nicely to her face.

Big Paudh took a little time to get the drift. 'The first dacent thing he ever said in all his life!' he cried then.

'And no more than the truth,' said Paddy Bawn, who would one day swallow his words.

'Propaganda!' she laughed. 'You are trying to make a Sinn Feiner out of me.'

'It might be in the blood of you,' I told her, 'and in your brother's too. Here he comes now to answer for himself.'

IV

Captain Archibald MacDonald, Hugh Forbes and Mickeen Oge Flynn came round the curve of the pool, and, judging by his face, the British officer was depressed and a little angry.

Hugh was serene as the evening. He looked us over as we rose, the sandwich papers scattered at our feet, and nodded his black head.

'Truckling with the enemy.'

He came directly to the girl and bent a little over her.

'Tell me, Margaid MacDonald, are you as pig-headed as your brother?'

'I couldn't be, could I, Mr Forbes?' She smiled at him.

'It would be hard for you, *mo colleen dheas*. Listen! We are merely suggesting that he go back to Castletown and forget everything and everyone he has seen today. Quite simple, isn't it, seeing that he is leaving the country tomorrow?'

Her answer came without hesitation. 'But he could not do that. He is a British officer.'

'You might be your brother's sister after all – I don't know yet. Look now! Take your own case?' His great voice half-coaxed her. 'Your memory – not so good sometimes?'

'It could be very bad – oh, but –!' And for the first time, I think, an inkling of the hard reality of the situation came home to her. She and her brother had seen enough to spoil all our plans, and this was a country at war.

There was dismay in the look that went round us circle of men; and when her eyes came to me they looked deep into mine for one piercing second. Then she gazed on the ground, and the colour that had come slowly to her cheeks ebbed more slowly away. I knew then that she was in awe of her own thoughts, and that her thoughts were those of a woman and not at all of the problem set before her.

Still in that dark muse she went to her brother and took hold of the lapels of his coat.

'Archie, I am afraid.'

'Nonsense, Margaid!' He slapped her shoulder lightly. 'Nothing to be afraid of.'

'But you do not understand. How could you? I am afraid to stay here – I must – I want to get away. Home, Scotland. Something – anything might happen. Oh, but –!' She could not explain any more. 'Could I?' She turned quickly to Hugh Forbes. 'You would not harm my brother?'

He was almost rude. 'Hell, girl! Nothing you can do or say, nothing the whole damn British forces can do, will bring harm to your brother from us. You may make your choice freely.'

She did not choose for a time, and then she sighed resignedly, almost forlornly.

'No. I cannot promise anything. I am British too.'

Hugh held up two thumbs before her eyes. 'You and your brother – and pig-headed stands. Very well, Britons! You are now prisoners.'

She nodded, and put him a final question. 'Prisoners? Does that mean – prison?'

'No, my dear.' There could be wonderful depth to his voice. 'We'll keep you with us. We will spread green rushes under your feet and put our hands under them so that you may step softly.'

She looked down at her riding-breeches and knee-boots. 'But I have nothing to wear.'

Hugh laughed. 'Briton first, and woman behind all! Your suitcases should be up at Sean Glynn's now.'

'You are unwise, Forbes,' said Captain MacDonald, his voice not hiding his irritation. 'You would serve your cause better by letting us go and then clearing your men out of here.'

'The game has to be played where the board is set. You ought to know that, MacDonald.'

'And the board will get kicked over on you. This whole valley will be combed out by search-parties – soldiers, too. You can never hold us.'

Hugh threw his hand wide. 'Here is the valley of the Ullachowen, and there my own Glounagrianaan running down to the sea, and over there the glen of Garabhmore, and beyond it Lough Aonach and the valley of the Dunmore – bens and glens and water, and islands in the water. We'll hold you, Briton.'

'I'll escape in spite of you, by God!'

'Let God choose. You are going to have the time of your life.'

But the girl said nothing at all.

Chapter Four

It was the second night after the ambush at Coolbeigh Bridge in Glounagrianaan, and the second night was always our worst. As this is not a chronicle of the Black-and-Tan war, I will say nothing more of that ambush than that we cut off a lorry-load of Tans, had two men killed, three wounded, and a third bullet hole through Matt Tobin's bowler hat. Thereafter we jumped twenty miles to Big Michael Flynn's place at Lough Aonach, where our prisoners were held for the time.

Big Michael Flynn was Mickeen Oge's uncle, and he ran the Angler's Hotel above the lough. It was one of the least unsafe of our hide-out places, for it was ten miles from the nearest railway station at Castletown and the mountain road between had been trenched in four places so that no military lorries might surprise us while we rested. Of course, there were no anglers in residence, nor had there been any for two years, since not even the most hard-bitten sportsman cared to risk his skin in that unrestful land. Captain Archibald MacDonald, our prisoner, had the pick of the finest fishing in the world.

We lay about in the lounge, a wide low-beamed room with a great open fireplace wherein a peat fire smouldered out of white ash: and that red glow was the only light. There was Hugh Forbes, Mickeen Oge Flynn, Paddy Bawn Enright, Captain MacDonald, his sister Margaid, Kate O'Brien and Joan Hyland. Outside the open French window Big Paudh Moran leant over the veranda rail and kept in touch with the sentinel posted at the gate of the drive.

The two Irish girls, Kate O'Brien and Joan Hyland, were companions for our female prisoner. Dark Kate O'Brien, as fervid a republican as Mickeen Oge Flynn, was the niece of a British major-general; and Joan Hyland, tall and fair, was Sean Glynn's sweetheart. Sean was still at headquarters on his dangerous secret service work, and his sweetheart was keenly disturbed about him, for she knew that more than one intelligence officer had gone up to the heart of things in Dublin and had never come out alive.

Most of us were in wicker chairs in a wide circle about the hearth, but Hugh Forbes, in his own characteristic fashion, lay full length on a glass-topped table by the wall, his hat under his poll, pipe aside in his teeth, and silence on him like a pall. We were all silent. And the summer night, fallen softly outside the wide windows, was silent too; and Lough Aonach, a quarter mile below us, spread out its wan and lonely pallor below the silent hills.

The second night after an ambush was always our worst night. That inescapable reaction after a fight was then at its peak; our nerves gone all slack. Oppressed, depressed, wondering what it was all about, no longer sure of ourselves or even of our cause, we just slumped there in the lounge and waited for something to take us out of the black mood. And we were hopelessly silent.

Big Michael Flynn, an immensely corpulent man moving on light feet, came in through the bar-door and proposed putting on a light.

'No-o!' said Hugh Forbes down in his throat. 'Let the dark hide us.'

'Very well so, *agrah*! I will bring ye in a drink in a small while, if a drink will be any good to ye. Mickeen Oge, put a coupla sods to the fire and tell 'em a story. Tell 'em a ghost story, Mickeen Oge.'

That was it. We were waiting for Mickeen Oge Flynn. A strange mixture, Mickeen Oge. A fighting man and half a priest. Some austere force in his make-up brought him back to balance before any of us: and then he became our spiritual comforter, restoring the resiliency to our minds and setting our cause before us like a light.

We waited, and from outside, across the fields, quiet under the balmy night, came the double call of a corncrake, and that rasping cry was as lonely as the hoot of an owl.

Margaid MacDonald turned in her chair near me – it was a habit of hers to sit there – and spoke in a low voice:

'A night for ghost stories – they are all about us.'

'No,' said I. 'The IRA and the Black-and-Tans have laid all the ghosts.'

'Don't you believe in ghosts?'

'Tonight I don't believe in anything.'

I felt a gentle touch on my arm, and her voice murmured, 'It will be all right, *a laochain*' – the old Highland childish endearment, and I felt a queer little moan rise in my throat.

'We have a famous ghost here at Lough Aonach,' came the softly

ringing voice of Kate O'Brien, 'up at the old castle. We call her the
Red Girl – and she is fatal to all renegades.'

'Let her rest, Kate O'Brien,' admonished Hugh Forbes. 'She is
the forlorn and tragic one, and brings trouble with her always – as
we know.'

Captain MacDonald did not speak at all – quiet and understanding man, this Highland officer. Whatever his own feelings
at a disaster to his own side – but, like most Regular soldiers, he
had small respect for the Black-and-Tans and was sick of the whole
business – he respected the mood that weighed on us. He sat there
quietly amongst us, making no sound, no stir, asking nothing of us,
waiting for the equalisation of the currents.

Then Mickeen Oge spoke. 'Paddy Bawn here has a ghost story
worth telling.'

'I have,' agreed Paddy Bawn. 'The best ghost story in the world
– my father told it to me – and it is a true story.'

'Tell it, Paddy Bawn.'

'No, Mickeen Oge, you tell it. You've heard it often enough.'

'Really it is a simple story – wistful, maybe,' explained Mickeen
Oge, 'and the truth of it has been proved beyond doubt in time and
space. Myself a lad, I knew the woman it happened to; old and happy
she was when I knew her, for she had the memory of that night sixty
years before still about her.'

And while he spoke, the small tongues of flame, licking about
the peat, lit and dimmed on our still faces and set our shadows
wavering on walls and beamed ceiling.

II

Her name was Ellen Oge Molouney – said Mickeen Oge – and
unhappiness was about her like a cloak. She stood it for as long as
she could, and that was no short time, for the Molouneys come of
a good stock and their breaking-point is long drawn out. But that
breaking-point did come at the bitter end, and then she did the
only thing she could do; she ran away. As broken spirits have done
all down slow Time, she set her face towards that place where her
mother was.

She was only fifteen years of age: a tender, shy, sensitive, small
girl, with blue eyes and black hair and a mouth made for smiling
and for grief. And, furthermore, she was only bond-slave to her own

grand-uncle, Red John Danaher of Browadra Farm, on the banks of
the Castlemaine River. Bond-slave! Servant-girl! One and the same
thing in those times, which were the Bad Times, when the poor,
our forefathers, wasted all God's time in keeping body and soul
together – and made a bitter bad job of it; when millions worth
of cattle and corn were exported to England, and the poor starved
on rotten potatoes.

'Stop there, Mickeen Oge!' Hugh Forbes interrupted him. 'Stop
there! We here tonight suffer and Ireland suffers so that in future no
child shall starve while beasts fatten. Go on now, my jewel – you've
lifted the heart in us already.'

Red John Danaher was a terrible man and a devout Christian: a
big, raw-boned man with sandy-grizzled hair, rugged cheeks and eyes
cold as the Blasket sea in November! He was carefully considerate
of his beasts: his thirty milch cows were the best milkers in the
parish; his horses the sleekest; his fat pigs never weighed less than
two hundred pounds; and by Michaelmas his geese were tripods.
But for man-servant and maid-servant he had no consideration at
all. He worked them to the bone fifteen hours a day and took evil
care not to feed them into slothfulness. 'Pamper them,' said he, 'and
asleep they'll be over spade and hook and *skeogh*; a lean man and a
lean dog does the best work.' And God knows! His big sheep-dog was
as lean as a January bush and loved him – like a dog. For breakfast
his servants, five men and two maids, had squares of *paaka* (maize)
bread and skim milk; for dinner, leather-skin spuds and sour milk;
and for supper, a thin porridge of oatmeal and Indian meal. And
on that diet they worked hard and all the time, for there was some
terrible insane force in John Danaher that made men cringe and
women fear.

Consider now how small Ellen Molouney, sensitive and finely
made, suffered exposed to that force. Look! If she fell wearily
asleep across her *sugan* (rush) chair during the nightly rosary,
her uncle's voice came out of its unctuousness to rasp at her;
if his eyes rested on her, her spine shivered; if he came into
the kitchen at mealtimes the bite choked her, and if her hand
was stretched out to dip the potato in the salt, the potato dropped from her nerveless fingers. Ay! even strong men sat back
from the table hungry when Red John Danaher watched them
eat.

Ellen Oge could stand work and she could stand cold and she was used to hunger; but, made as she was, she could not forever stand fear and loneliness. At long last she ran away.

She chose a night in the first week of the hungry month, July; a fine, clear summer night, with a full moon quartering across from south to west. At the stroke of twelve she slipped from the side of Maura Purtaill, who, open-mouthed, snored, threw on her few clothes – a short red petticoat, a shapeless winsey frock, buttoning from neck to waist, and a spotted handkerchief tied over her lovely black head. She did not put on her shoes, but over toe and heel and slender leg she pulled a pair of black *lopeens* (footless stockings). Her only shoes – small, square-toed, hand-made shoes, with a strap to cross the instep – and her spare clothes she tied in a small bundle, and she was ready. She owned nothing in all the world but that small bundle.

She was as quiet as a mouse – quieter than a mouse. Her hard heels barely rubbed the steps of the ladder from the loft down into the big dark kitchen where the peat coals were smoored below the raking of ashes. She worked back the wooden bolt of the back door against her thumb, the latch made but the slightest click, and she was out in the still and balmy summer night. The moonlight, across the big yard, shone on the whitewashed wall of the long byre, and that cold light made her shrink and tremble for she had to venture across the open to reach the back gate. But she gripped her lower lip with her teeth and made the great essay – on tiptoe, very carefully, but not hurriedly; and the windows behind her were like eyes.

And then, the raw-boned yellow sheep-dog came out from a corner below a hay-cart and barked. He barked only once, and then trotted across the yard, tail waving.

'Go to bed!' she whispered urgently, her heart in her throat. 'Back to bed, Jack!'

Too late. One small bark was enough to rouse Red John to enquiry in those desperate times when hungry people were driven to steal. The friendly dog had not reached Ellen before an upper window jarred open.

'Who is it?' Quiet enough his voice. And then, 'Is that you, Ellen Oge?'

She stopped in her tracks, all the young life draining out of her. The power of that terrible, quiet voice held her against all desire.

'Go back to your bed! Go back to your bed!' He did not call her, as he was used to, a *rashpeen*, an *oinseach*, a *sthreel* (a weakling, a fool, a slattern), but his voice under control had the quality of iron. He knew what Ellen was about. Well he knew. But he did not want anyone else to know.

The window closed down, and, the instant it was closed, Ellen up with her light young heels and ran for the back gate. And the dog ran with her.

Red John Danaher came out at the back door, barefooted, in his shirt and trousers, and the yard was empty under the moonlight. He said no word then, but his hard feet carried him fast across the yard. Out in the *bohereen* he halted and, little finger in mouth, blew three short, sharp whistles. The sheep-dog knew that whistling by painful experience. In one minute it was back and cringing at its master's feet, and was rewarded by a sidefooted kick in the ribs.

'Up now!' Red John pointed a finger, and the dog gazed at him, intelligence in its eyes. 'After her, Jack! Steady now – steady, I tell you!'

Poor small Ellen Oge Molouney! There was no place where she could hide from that friendly dog and that terrible man – no place but one. Running across the second field from the house, she heard her grand-uncle's whistles and saw the dog leave her. She knew what that meant and ran all the faster. Northwards she ran, for northwards was her home, at distant Ballydonohue beyond Listowel. And that was all she knew about that road – that long and weary road that crosses the humped shoulder of Slieve Mish and winds along the bare flanks of Glanruddera down to the Feale Bridge at Listowel. We know that road in the dark, and our blood is spilled on it.

Once only had she travelled that road, and now, in the light of the moon, she would venture it again with the help of God. Northwards she ran, then, terror lending wings to her heels, and that terror, blind as terror is, led her straight into a trap.

The Castlemaine River, beyond Browadra Farm, made a deep and narrow loop, and she ran directly into the bottom of it. She raced up the high bank and stopped. There was the river, deep and still, below her, and the moonlight, shining on it, made it polished black steel. Quickly she saw the trap she had landed in and turned to race along the embankment. And then the dog barked not two fields away, and running back along the curve of the loop meant running into her grand-uncle's hands. She looked wildly about her.

'Mother Mary – Mother Mary – Mother Mary!'

Close to the water, down the sloping bank, grew a stunted bush of alder. It was the only refuge that offered, and she slid down to it and threw herself close to the twisted trunk. Head and shoulders were hidden below the branches, but anyone coming along the bank could not fail to see her slender legs. Her eyes were over the very brink of the river and could look into the pool beneath them. And there her eyes looked.

It was deep water, and there was no hope of crossing that way. But it was clear water too, and the moonlight pouring slantwise showed every pebble on its gravelly bed. It was clear and cool and calm and inviting – inviting as sin. For the Devil must still get his due while the soul is still clothed in flesh, and his temptings will come at all times and in all places. There behind her was the dog's bark coming nearer, and now she could hear the man's voice urging it on. And down below was the quietness of the pool – the endless quietness of the pool. Oh! but it was quiet down there. No voice could ever rouse her, no anger ever touch her, no fear overwhelm her. The pebbles were as brown as warm amber and they winked up at the moon; pleasant it would be to lie among them and gaze up at the high far stars and have no fear, no grief, no loneliness any more – ever – ever – ever.

She was already slipping when the dog's bark and the man's voice stopped as if they had been snapped across. And instead there flowed to her across the night the pleasant sound of a careless whistling: a round, mellow, easy-going whistle that was at the same time touched with a strange sadness. The tune was the *Lon Dubh* – the *Blackbird*. You know it. A dance tune, one of the hard long dances, and besides it is the only Irish lament for the Stuart kings. Skilly dancing and skilly whistling it calls for, and this whistler knew every turn and every grace-note. Gay it was as a brave man who puts hope behind him and is not afraid, strong as a cause which is lost often and held ever, wistful as a man who has known beauty. And here and now it held Ellen Oge Molouney from slipping.

She drew back, sat up and looked at the embankment above her. The whistler was coming along the top of it at his slow ease: a tall man, wearing an old white hat and frieze body-coat, a hurley stick under his arm, his hands in his pockets, walking with a slight limp – not a limp that was a hindrance, but one that gave a pleasant roll of shoulder and swing of head. He halted up there, not in surprise but with a sort of careless ease, and threw up a hand in a pleasant, happy gesture.

'Good night, *a colleen*!' Deep and kindly his voice.

'A fine night for a ramble, thank God?'

'Good night, sir!' whispered Ellen.

'Is it fishing you were now – or, maybe, a bathe you had in mind?'

'No, sir. I was going home.'

'Home!' His voice was vibrant. 'Home! A good place to be going on top o' the world. Home I would be going myself – but sure, the night is young and we are in no hurry.'

At that he sat down, his feet towards her, and took a clay pipe from his waistcoat pocket. He dunted the head of it into a hand to loosen the dottle, and she heard the thud and rasp on his hard palm.

'Come away up and sit down,' he invited, 'and tell me the road you'd be going.'

And she climbed the bank and timidly sat near him; and he blew through his pipe, and made no move to touch her lest she be frightened. For the time her terrible uncle seemed in another world.

Slowly he cut his tobacco, slowly ground it between his palms, and, like a man thinking leisurely, filled the well-used pipe and shook the dottle ash on it. And he talked to her with a gentle carelessness that gave her confidence.

'And where is the place you call home, *colleen oge*?'

'Ballydonohue, sir – at the other side of Listowel.'

'To be sure! Surely! A nice, handy walk. And you know the road?'

'Not well, sir. 'Tis that way.' She pointed to the long flank of Slieve Mish where, in the cold brilliance of the moon, the white houses twinkled on the dun of the hill.

'Well now – well now! And I going that way myself. Wait you till I get this going, and I'll convey you a piece of the road. Ballydonohue? 'Tis well I know it, from Pubil Dotha to Trienafludig, from Galey Cross to Cnucanor.'

'Do you, sir?' And then she volunteered, 'My name is Ellen Molouney.'

'A daughter of Norrey Walsh's, maybe?'

'Oh yes, sir! Do you know her?'

'Long ago – long ago.' He looked down at her uplifted face and smiled in his deep-set eyes. 'You have her brow and the very turn of her chin. Ay! and I knew your uncle, Shawn Alsoon of the chapel – but it was long ago, girleen, long and long ago. Wait now, till I light up, and we'll take the road, the two of us.'

She saw his face clearly in the red glow of the tinder: a kindly, humorous, strong face, with deep-set eyes and a scar running from temple to the angle of the jaw.

He rose to his feet. 'Come, *a weenoch* – my little one!'

She rose at his side. 'I am afraid, sir,' she began tremulously; 'My uncle –'

He reached his hand to her and she took it – a firm, dry, warm hand.

'Do not be afraid, *mo leanav, mo leanaveen oge.*' His deep voice crooned and was sorrowful that she, so young, should know fear. 'Nothing in this world or the next will harm you tonight. Come, now!'

And they went along the top of the bank, hand in hand, the tall man limping gallantly, and the little maid moving lightly at his side.

At the swing of the loop Red John Danaher stood at the foot of the embankment, and his dog crouched between his feet. Ellen Oge pressed close to her protector, and the two hands tightened in each other. But John Danaher never moved. He was as still as carved stone, and his wide-open eyes were as blind as granite. And, when the figures of man and maid had vanished into the night along the bank, the red man was still rooted in that one spot. And in that spot his servants found him in the morning. For many days he spoke no word, and, when speech at last came to him, he said no word of what he had seen or felt. But whether he was better or worse, only God knows.

Ellen Oge Molouney, all her days – and they were many – kept close about her the memory of that walk through the July night. It was as happy as walking in a king's garden with a king's son, and love in the songs of birds; as long and as short as a fine story and it well told; as pleasant as May morning and the blackbird lilting his one tune; it was as quiet as that June hour before the sun sets into the solitudes of the gloaming, stealing gently; it was as unhurried as a noneen opening in the dew; as timeless as a dream.

She could never tell the roads they came to or the places that she saw. Indeed, they came to no made roads at all. Their feet moved over dewy grass where the gossamer was like pearl threads on the green; along hedgerows where small birds saluted them with drowsy cheeps; under tall, straight trees, standing to attention column by column, where the rays of moonlight striking through were finer than white silver; along small streams that came out under dark bushes to gurgle and gleam at them over clean gravel. That is all she remembered of that journey in the night. In the distance dogs barked or howled forlornly at the moon, and the white houses glimmered along the hillside. But they themselves moved in a world apart, in a dimension of their own, using time and space to suit the content that filled them. And no cock crew.

They were in no hurry. Often they rested by stream and hedgerow, and the tall man talked to the little maid, softly, gently, with a tenderness beyond all tears. He told her tales she knew and tales she did not know; and he got her to display her artless young heart that he cherished with a pride finer than the pride of all victories, all glories, all defeats. But alas! The night went on, nevertheless, and happiness will not abide forever under the sky. The moon was setting and a vivid whiteness streaming up in the north-east when, at last, they came out on the open road above the Feale Bridge. And there the tall man stopped Ellen Oge, his hand lightly on her shoulder.

'There, then, is the Feale River, girleen, and that is Listowel town beyond on the slope. You know where you are now?'

'Oh yes, sir! That's Cnucanor Hill in front of us.'

'Here then we part.' His voice was deep and low. 'The dawn is here, and we cannot keep cocks from crowing, for the cocks have to crow in every dawn. You will have to hurry now, Ellen Oge.' He ran his hand gently down the nape of her neck and gave her a little push between the shoulders. 'Run, *a leanaveen*! your mother will be waiting for you.'

Lightly, then, she ran down on to the bridge. And away out on the island farm a cock crew, and his clarion was as keen and as sad as the horns of fairyland. At the middle arch she turned to wave farewell. The road was empty. The whole hillside was empty – empty. The desolate dawn-light showed the emptiness of all life, all hope, all fear – even all despair. But not to Ellen Oge Molouney.

Listen now! The distance she had come was forty odd miles as the crow flies, and she had done it in less than four hours. Whatever else is true, that is true.

Wait ye! That morning her mother, Norrey Walsh, rose at the dawn, a full hour before her usual time. She built up the fire out of its rakings, put on the kettle to boil, laid the table with two cups, a fresh soda loaf and a pat of new butter; and she chose two of the brownest eggs and put them in the skillet, ready for boiling. And then she went out into the morning, and there was the sun rising over the

Drum of Glouria; and there was her daughter Ellen running to her round the last twist of the *bohereen*.

She was a quiet woman always, and not effusive. She only put an arm round her little one's shoulders. 'I knew you'd be here early, Ellen Oge. Last night I dreamt of you, and you on the road. You'll be killed an' all with the tiredness.'

Ellen Oge snuggled into her mother's side. 'Sure, it was only a step, mother – just beyond there.'

'Forty Irish miles, girl. You got a lift, maybe?'

'No. But, mother, how could it be that far? Sure, I only left after the dead of night – and the sun only up now.' She went on with a rush. 'And oh, mother! wait till I tell you about the grand man showed me the way as far as the Feale Bridge. I was – I was frightened of my Uncle John, and he came along the bank of the Maine River and him whistling the *Blackbird*!'

'God save us all!' said her mother, and then quietly, 'What like of man was he, colleen?'

'Maybe you'd be knowing him, mother. He knew you and Uncle Shawn – long ago, he said, long ago. And, oh dear! I forgot to ask his name. He was a man would reach up to the collar-brace there, and he had a limp in one leg – but he could lep the moon. And a hurley with a lead boss, and, oh! he had a great big scar one side of his face – there. Would you be knowing him, mother?'

'God rest his soul, daughtereen! He was your own father.'

'My father – my father that's dead?'

'These fifteen years, Ellen Oge. But, dead or alive, the Molouneys can take care of their own. Thanks be to God.'

III

Hugh Forbes was the first to break the ensuing silence.

'We will wear them as a shield upon our arms, as a shield upon our hearts, for Love is stronger than Death,' he murmured deeply. 'Our dead, too, will take care of us, if we do not fail them.'

The silence grew deeper and in it could almost be heard the feet of the dead – our dead. No symbolism had been implied in the story but the wandering girl, the wandering woman – the Irish knew her as the woman Erin, under many names. Something moved about us, someone whispered, or something – I think, now, it was Margaid MacDonald in a lucid resignation.

'The secret place in your heart no woman can touch – but the woman Erin.'

I cannot explain the overpowering clairvoyance that held us, as if we knew finally and for all time, and were set there waiting for what was to come.

And upon that sense of expectancy came the footsteps.

When Big Paudh, our sentry, shoved open the French window and the cloaked woman came in, we were held as in a trance. By her carriage she was young, and the long, dark blue hooded Irish cloak made her face a pale oval. A sod of peat flickered and flamed, and before she could turn from it I saw that that face was of extraordinary pallor and, to us at the moment, of unearthly beauty. And her hair at the edge of the hood was paler than pale yellow.

Immediately behind her was Sean Glynn, but I think no one looked at him until he spoke.

'God save all here!' It was the customary salute, but his voice was beyond mere bitterness.

'God save ye kindly!' Mickeen Oge's voice, by contrast, was kindly warm.

Hugh Forbes was sitting up on the glass-topped table. 'Ye are welcome. How did ye come?'

'Across the lough,' said Sean. 'This is Nuala Kierley, Hugh. She is tired.' He turned to Big Michael Flynn. 'You have a room ready, Michael?'

'I have, *agrah*.'

The woman turned to the big man. 'I will go to it, please.' Her tone was low and entirely without colour.

'Very well so, *acuid*. Come now!'

She had not been one minute amongst us, but she left a dumbness behind her and a new weight on our minds.

I found myself looking at Archibald MacDonald. He was half-turned in his chair, his eyes on the door by which the woman had disappeared, and, as I looked at him, his shoulders shivered as if a cold breath had blown over or in him. And at that moment I knew that, whereas we had been under the spell of our own imaginings, he alone had looked upon the woman herself and sensed her brokenness.

Sean Glynn pulled himself out of the slough and came across to the fireplace. 'Sorry these scoundrels caught you, Margaid,' he said. 'The English papers are making a sensation of your disappearance.'

'They would,' she murmured.

He looked at his friend, Archibald MacDonald, but that man seemed still to be staring at something within his own mind.

'Any news from Dublin?' asked Hugh Forbes.

'A good deal. There is some real talk of a truce at last – it may come soon. But it will come too late for one man.'

'Bad as that, Sean?'

'It could not be worse – worse than any of us imagined, Hugh.'

Hugh turned down a thumb.

Sean nodded. 'Any day – today – tonight.'

'Does Nuala Kierley know?'

'She does – now.'

'My God!' said Hugh Forbes.

And there I remembered why Sean Glynn had gone to Dublin: as he himself had said, to set a woman of his own blood at a man to get at another man who was a traitor. Was Nuala Kierley that woman? Who, then, and where was the other man this night? We had no mercy on an Irish traitor. A shiver went over me as it had gone over the Highlandman.

I looked at Sean Glynn. He was looking into the red heart of the fire, and the wavering light of it washed over his set and rigid face. This was not the cheerful man we had known, the light-hearted gallant man who took life and even love gaily. And there I noticed that not once since he had entered the room had his eyes rested on the fair girl who was his sweetheart. It was not the moment for cheerful greetings, and a man does not carry his affection on his sleeve, but Sean had made no difference between Joan Hyland and the rest of us – in a sense, indeed, he had almost noticed her less, as if held by a pitiless embarrassment. The girl must have observed this too. Her eyes were on him intently. He refused her eyes. But she said no word.

His voice lifted almost angrily. 'Is there a drink in this house at all?'

Mickeen Oge's chair protested as he kicked it back.

'Make it deep, Mickeen Oge.'

I could see that there was a bitter taste in his mouth. Sean Glynn had been through the mill. Margaid MacDonald at my side knew that too; uncannily she had sensed the undercurrent that was in our minds and speech. But she was not sorry for Sean Glynn. For the woman was she sorry. Suddenly she leant forward in her chair and accused us, her voice queerly strained.

'You are not human. You have no mercy on woman. You would use her – use her – use her – buy and sell her, body and soul.'

'Never her inviolate soul,' said dark Kate O'Brien quietly.

And I had a selfish thankfulness that I was only a plain fighting man after all.

Chapter Five

I

'A bonny river, the Ullachowen!' said Hugh Forbes. 'Are you going fishing with Margaid MacDonald?'

'Like to go yourself?' I queried back sourly.

'I might then – and be damned to you!'

'By the way, Hugh,' Mickeen Oge enquired sort of casually, 'are you still thinking of taking that trip to Scotland – for a red-haired woman? I haven't heard you mention it for some time.'

'I wonder now,' mused Hugh quizzically, 'if that there mountain ever thought of coming to Mahomet?'

'A volcano topped with a red flame,' said Mickeen Oge. 'But who is our Mahomet? Hugh Forbes, or – it never could be Owen Jordan?'

'To hell with that fellow!'

'Amen!' said I. 'He is a damn fool to be listening to ye.'

The three of us were leaning on the drystone wall of Sean Glynn's kitchen garden, and, down below us, the translucent heat haze of the afternoon had settled sleepily into the bottom of the valley.

It was getting on for mid-July now, and the last time we had been here was late May. In the seven or so weeks between we had marched and fought and counter-marched the full circle, but not yet had the game been played to a finish. We had dealt most thoroughly with one lorry-load of Black-and-Tans at Coolbeigh Bridge in Glounagrianaan; we had skirmished for two days with a company of Highlanders over Garabhmore Mountain and back again; we had blown up culverts, trenched roads, burned barracks; and now we had closed the circle for the final round by what was left of us with what was left of the enemy in Castletown. And we were very weary.

I turned to move away from the wall, but had not taken a stride before Captain MacDonald and his sister Margaid emerged from the kitchen door beyond the garden. Behind them came Big Paudh Moran draped with fishing-tackle, and Sean Glynn brought up the rear.

'We're for trying the evening rise, Hugh,' called our prisoner as he came down the path towards us.

'To be sure, Archie. A guard – or the usual four hours?'

'Oh! your damn guard disturb the fish and argue like hell. I'll take four hours with Sean Glynn.'

'Very good! The boys have taught you to swear nice and handy.'

'I'll drown him in *Poul Tarabh* if needs be,' said Sean.

Captain MacDonald looked hale and hearty, apparently without a care in the world. For seven weeks he had had the time of his life, as Hugh Forbes had promised: the pick of the best fishing waters in Munster and plenty of time to try them – early in the mornings, late in the long summer evenings, and, in secluded areas, at any time he pleased. And neither God nor the Devil had helped him to escape. Very early on he had discovered that if he wanted to fish he had either to be subject to a particularly strict guard or give an implicit understanding to return to the column within four hours, and on good fishing water he always took the four hours. The relations between himself and his captors were little short of brotherly, and he spent most of his time warmly arguing with them on every subject under the sun.

Sean Glynn looked more like a prisoner than his friend, the Highland officer. Sean was set and serious, no longer debonair. He had rejoined the column at Lough Aonach, bringing broken Nuala Kierley with him; had brought her to his own place at Leaccabuie some days later, kept her there for a week, and then she had gone away – where no one knew. And now he was back with us, but his nerve had not come back with him. He was drinking more than he should, and that was a bad sign, for, in our game, drink and life did not go long together. And it was plain to every one of us, his friends, that he was avoiding Joan Hyland. There was trouble there, but whether it was because of Nuala Kierley or not, we could not be sure. One thing I did know: Nuala Kierley was a woman who might change the mind in any man, and the change might not be for good.

Hugh Forbes turned to Margaid MacDonald. 'Take four hours, Margaid?' He had a friendly way of using her Christian name that, for some reason, did not appeal to me.

She looked us over one by one and shook her head frowningly. 'No – I'll want a guard.' Never once, strangely enough or naturally enough, had she been given parole.

'Little irreconcilable!' he half-teased her. 'And who is going to guard your guard?'

Margaid MacDonald did not look hale or happy. For a month, up to that night at Lough Aonach, she had seemed to enjoy the life; the rambling ways, the unconventional living, the new experiences, the care of fighting men; and she had a fine, pleasant way of criticising us for our good, as if she had business with us. But then, and quite suddenly, she had sobered down and seemed to shut herself away in some secret chamber of her own; growing queerly listless, despondent, losing all interest in us. And she no longer criticised anything. She was thinner too, her eyes sunken a little, and her face, that never had much colour, had now no colour at all. But her chin remained obstinate as ever – obstinate and dour to withstand patiently some ill of the mind.

We were worried about her. Only the previous night we three leaders had decided to run her up to Dublin at the first opportunity, and from there slip her across to her own Highlands. And yet we felt that it was not the physical hardship that was wearing on her. We had been very careful of her comfort, taking her across country by easy marches, using a dog-cart for night work when the roads were open, feeding her on the best that the country offered, and giving her the companionship of pleasant girls at every resting-place. But the despondency on her – a queer kind of hopelessness – had only settled deeper down. She was as gloomy – well! she was as gloomy as myself.

Hugh Forbes brought his hands smartly together. 'Fine! I have the evening to myself. I'll guard you.'

She smiled at him, as she always did. 'No, Hugh! I want to fish this evening. I'll take Paudh – and Owen Jordan.'

He turned his back to her, facing me, one eyebrow down and a sardonic sympathy about his mouth.

'A woman has to have her own way in some things. I can't help you, small son.'

II

So we went fishing.

Captain MacDonald and Sean Glynn went off by themselves down the river; Margaid MacDonald, Paudh and myself worked upwards. And, though she had come out to fish, the girl did very little fishing. I did none at all. I handed my rod over to Big Paudh, and he went hurriedly round a corner to some choice pool of his own.

I sat on a low grass bank, my feet on fresh-water sand, smoked slowly and watched the girl work down a long run. She had a nice supple action of the wrist, and the taut readiness of a strung bow. The sun swinging down into the mouth of the glen shone all about her and set a curl aflame, and the strong flow of the stream ridged up her knee-boots and made a pleasant gurgle.

She fished the run out, caught two sizable trout and came slowly back by the margin of the pool as if she intended going over it a second time. But, opposite where I sat, she halted, her back to me, and for a full minute looked up at the bulk of Leaccamore, whose swelling brown breast was faintly brushed over with the early budding purple of the heather. Then she laid her rod carefully along the gravel and came across to me. She sat down within a yard, loosed the wicker creel off her shoulders and leant an elbow on it.

'Thought you came out to fish?'

'Time enough.' She nodded towards her rod. 'You try it.'

'No. I'm tired of fishing.'

'I am tired too,' she agreed simply.

And the two of us – poor simpletons – sat there moodily contemplating the evening glory washing over the breast of the great hill that changed not from its immobility under any caress of sun or wind. I could feel her melancholy.

'I am sorry you are unhappy,' I said at last.

'Who said I was unhappy?'

Instead of answering that half-sullen question I said, 'It will not be long now.'

'Until you kill or be killed?'

'More than that. There is talk – more than talk – of a truce.'

'There is always talk.'

'But since King George's goodwill speech in Belfast – of all places – it is certain that secret negotiations are going on with the leaders in Dublin. Any day now there may be a truce – and you free to go.'

'And you?'

'If peace comes I'll go back to New Mexico.'

'To marry that wife?'

'What wife?'

'The wife – you remember – the wife to rear sons to carry on.'

'Oh, that! All foolish talk.'

'And pretty Grania Grace that Paudh –'

'To hell with her!' I exploded ungallantly.

'Don't you like her?'

'Nor any other woman,' I lied bitterly. 'I hate every bone of them.'

'And they hate every bone of you,' she gave back, her eyes suddenly blazing at me.

'I know that.'

'When did you find out?'

'It's plain enough,' I said heavily.

She turned away from me then, leant both elbows on her fishing-creed and cupped her chin in her hands.

'I hate this awful country.' She barely breathed the words.

'So do I – sometimes.'

'Yet you would die for it?'

'Hate goes with that too,' I half-tried to explain.

'I know.'

'Tell me,' I asked, another thought in my mind, 'has anyone been unkind to you?'

'Unkind? You are all so kind and gentle – and unhuman.'

That left me floundering.

'Don't you see?' Her voice a monotone, she was explaining to herself as much as to me. 'I am shut out. I am a prisoner, yet I am shut out. Everyone is kind, considerate, very careful of me, but I only touch the surface. Any urge coming from within myself beats vainly on that cold chivalry – cold as ice within. I am an alien amongst you. You know, at the beginning, I actually half-intended playing Delilah to some Samson; but you men are possessed, obsessed, lost in one woman only – Eire, the sorrowful one. All other things – even passion – you touch carelessly, at a passing whim, as you go by. Oh! This is a terrible land for a woman.'

'We buy and sell her.'

'I will not be bought or sold.'

'Who is trying to?' I wondered.

'No one, of course. That first day I was afraid of myself and – all of you. But there is no need to be afraid any more now.' And then I barely heard. 'It has gone beyond fear.'

Her head was turned away from me, her chin in her hands, and her shoulders made no movement, but I saw the slow tears trickling down her wrist.

'Could you not let me go away, Owen Jordan?'

'It will not be long now, girl,' was all I could say, and, by way of comfort, I leant forward and gently touched her shoulder.

She shivered under my hand and jerked her shoulder away.

'Don't touch me,' she cried fiercely.

That hurt – hurt like hell.

'Sorry. I didn't know you disliked me so much.'

'Sometimes I hate you.' She jumped to her feet, her face still away from me. 'I'm going down to see what Paudh is doing.'

She went, her feet strangely uncertain in the shingle, down by the pool, and left her rod lying on the gravel.

I sat on where I was.

She had, surely, given me my quietus. And why not? I tried to be philosophic. I was not the sort to attract a woman. I knew what I was. The odd pup in Mother Nature's litter, and that soulless mother would never miss me if a Tan bullet found a billet. And yet, I sardonically mused, I might, by some perversity of luck, carry on to a crabbed and lone old age. Lone? No! Men were my friends. With men I had a fellowship. Out in New Mexico I had good friends: Gene Rhodes, the lovable one; Long Sandy Maclaren on the loose foot; Art O'Connor, my partner. And the men here in the South would not forget me either, though I might be six thousand miles away. Big Paudh Moran, faithful as a hound; Paddy Bawn, holding to his ideal of quietness; Sean Glynn in the toils; Mickeen Oge Flynn, whose austerity no woman might break; Hugh Forbes, who held us lovingly in his strong hands. Hugh Forbes? I wonder! Could it be against the Small Dark Man's iron that Margaid MacDonald had broken herself? Had she discovered that his whimsical ideal of a red-haired woman out of Scotland was only a shield to some secret urge of his own – perhaps the terrible urge for Freedom.

'Oh, hell!' I exclaimed. 'Don't think about it.'

I threw myself on my back and gazed up into the deeps of the sky. I was weary, weary – but I could carry on. High up, a thin feather of cloud drifted aloof in the blue abyss, and the edges of it were already touched with the rose of evening . . . I would make myself as aloof as that small cloud.

III

The blunt toe of Paudh Moran's service-boot woke me out of a dream wherein I held a child's hand.

'Where's the girl gone to?'

I sat up and yawned deeply. 'She went down your way a minute ago.'

'An' she came back your way – a good half-hour ago.'

I was on my feet then.

'Good God! She's gone.'

Her basket was still on the bank, her rod on the gravel, but she was gone. Escaped! I knew it – knew it with a certainty that was psychic. There was no need for me to stare up and down the course of the Ullachowen, though I did that. Half a mile below I could see her brother and Sean Glynn moving along the top of a bank, but there was no Margaid MacDonald anywhere. She had come up from Paudh, found me asleep, and there was her opportunity . . . But first, she had made me careless by wounding me and getting me to nurse that wound . . . And now she was on her way to Castletown, the only place she could go to.

'She's up at the house, I bet you,' said Big Paudh hopefully.

'Bet the devil!' I caught his shoulder. Now was the time to think quickly, and think not at all of what escape meant. 'How long, did you say?'

'Half an hour – good.'

'Up with you and warn Hugh Forbes.'

'An' if she's there?'

'Whether she is there or not, you are to come back up the Ullachowen as fast as God'll let you – right up to Castletown or until you meet me.'

'What'll you be doin'?'

'Trying to head her off.' I swung him round and gave him a staggering push. 'Off with you!'

And he went lumbering up the slope to Sean Glynn's house half a mile above. In spite of his size and weight, he was quick on his feet and incredibly tough-winded.

The Ullachowen flowed in a deep arc round the base of Leaccamore Mountain, and along that curve, eight miles away, was Castletown. The chord to the arc, right over the high shoulder of the hill, shortened the distance by three miles, but the going was the roughest; knee-deep heather, hidden boulders, eroded chorries. The fugitive would never choose that road. By the river she must have gone, and, with hawthorn fences and barbed wire, that was no easy road either. Give her two hours at her best pace and allow for her half hour's start – could I do it? I chose the road over the hill.

I splashed across the shallows thigh-deep and faced the bulging breast of Leaccamore.

I did not spare myself in that race. I was weary enough before I started, but I was tough too, and drew on all my reserves. I took only one brief rest, and that on the crown of the ridge, looking two miles down on Castletown. The huddle of purple roofs was already in the shadows of the gloaming, but the gilt cross on the spire of the Catholic church gleamed in the last rays of the sun, and round me, where I panted in the heather, flowed a tawny red glory.

I looked along the curve of the Ullachowen far below me, but no figure moved there in the slowly gathering twilight. I did not mind that, for she would keep out of sight among the hazel copses as much as possible.

When, at last, I again splashed across the river I was so leg-weary that a twisting stone under my feet brought me to hands and knees in the water. I scrambled up and out on a broad embankment, and there were the backs of the houses of Castletown not a furlong away. It is a strange fact that most Irish country towns turn their backs to running water. Higher up the river a massive stone bridge spanned the stream in three fine arches, and a wide, well-trodden promenade path led to it from where I stood.

Castletown seemed a town asleep, though night had not yet fallen. Only, here and there, a thin blue spiral of smoke drifted from brick chimneys. No couples strolled along the pleasant river walk, no loiterers leant over the parapets of the bridge, no amateur gardeners worked in the vegetable patches behind the houses. I knew the reason, of course. The curfew was in force by the police, and the citizens had to herd indoors with the set of sun.

There was no sign at all of Margaid MacDonald. If she had beaten me to Castletown there was nothing more I dare do; if she was still down the river, I had better head her off as far from the town as possible. I stood in full view of the bridge, and if a Tan patrol crossed over, the bullets would come singing round me. Moreover, I was aware that the river bank was outposted at night, and even now a sentinel might be set at any point downstream. That risk I had to take.

Some distance below me a band of larches gathered in about the path, and I used the last of my wind to reach their shelter. I ran tiptoe on the grass edging, and my feet made no sound.

Just inside the larch grove a rustic seat was set close to the path, and in the far corner of it a woman sat. A man stood close over her, one foot on the seat at her side.

The woman was Margaid MacDonald. The man was a big fellow in the uniform of the Black-and-Tans. His rifle was propped against the back of the seat, and the butt of a long Webley showed from a holster hanging at his thigh.

She was in the corner of the seat, pressed close in, fear and anger in her eyes, and her breast surging. He was like a cat with a mouse, in no hurry, leaning towards her, not touching her; and the context of his speech was not to be mistaken.

'But where is your brother, then?'

She shook her head desperately.

'No!' he said. 'Don't you know that no one denies the police?' There was no mistaking the suggestiveness in his tones.

She saw me then, over his shoulder, and I knew that she was glad to see me at that moment. She made no sign, no exclamation, and that showed her quality; but the leap of light in her eyes warned him. He turned head, whirled on one heel, and his right hand dropped towards thigh-holster. But I was quicker as I leapt.

'Up with them!'

The automatic muzzle was against his stomach above the belt, and his hands were in the air like a reflex action. We knew each other at the same instant.

He was the fellow Garner who had clouted me that day outside John Molouney's saloon. And, as then, he was half-mad or half-drunk.

'You *were* a Shinner, you swine!'

My breath whistled through nostrils, and my arm was a stiff bar pressing against him. His dead-white, lined cheeks twitched, and a madness lit behind his black eyes.

'Shoot, damn you! Shoot!' He expected no mercy.

'Keep them up!' I had seen his hands clench.

'Go on – get it over! I am sick of it all.'

I knew I could not hold him, but I could not kill him there before the girl. Quickly I decided to give him the butt, but he forestalled me.

'I'll make you.'

His left hand struck down at my wrist. I should have pulled the trigger then, yet I did not. I suppose, at the back of my mind, I was vain of my strength and felt I could quickly master this

half-drunken, wholly rotten madman; and possibly some vindictive
inner devil wanted to repay him with a little manhandling. My left
hand grasped his right wrist before he could reach his gun, and we
came together breast to breast.

And there I realised my mistake. He was stronger than I was, with
the false and frenzied strength of madness. As we strained there, my
right hand already wrenched out of range, I looked over his shoulder
at Margaid MacDonald, still in the seat corner.

'Get out! Too strong. Get out!'

And then I was on the ground under him. I braced myself and
held on; and he held me down and lifted head over me. He knew
he had me, and I knew it, but I hoped for a little second wind to
give the girl time to get away.

'I'll settle you this time, you –' I felt his right arm strain.

The mind will sometimes drive the body to its best even though
the body revolts. The ugly word he used before the girl made me
nearly as mad as he was.

I do not remember much of the next minute or two, but, presently,
I was surprised that I was doing not so badly. Oh! but I was tough.
I was still under him mostly, but once my shoulders, jarring into the
crutch of a root, gave me leverage to get a knee up and hard into
his diaphragm. That helped to even matters. And, after a time,
I discovered that he was not so strong, or that I was growing
stronger.

And then, and suddenly, the life that he had lived came home
to him. He went loose as a rag, and I rolled him over, wrenched
hand free, smashed into his face three times, jerked his gun from
its holster, and came to my feet over him. I gave him a rude
boot-toe.

'UP!'

He came to his hands and knees and then swayingly to his
feet.

'Get out!' I thrust his own gun hard against him.

His fury over, the madness had gone out of his eyes. He was no
more than a poor, done man with a sagging bloody mouth, very
much afraid of death.

'Get out!' I prodded him savagely.

He turned and lurched out of the trees and up the path.
I watched him for a little while, thrust the guns away, and
turned round.

IV

Margaid MacDonald was still there, on her feet now, but still shaky, as much after the real fright she had got as after her flight. She made an effort to pull herself together and smiled wanly.

'He nearly licked you,' she said, her old critical spirit not dead.

'You might have stood on his ear for me,' I told her.

Somehow, I was no longer winded or weary. A latent reserve had come into action, and, though my breathing filled the whole cavity of my breast, I was feeling fit and tough. I walked straight up to her.

'We'll be going back now, Margaid MacDonald.'

And, shaking her head with desperate emphasis, she would not meet my eye after one startled glance.

'It is not safe here – not for a moment,' I urged.

'I am not going back,' she said with forced calm.

'But –'

'Don't you see? I dare not go back.' She was no longer calm. 'Can't you see?'

'Very well,' I agreed. 'Give me your word.'

'Please – please, Owen! Don't ask anything of me – I'm afraid.'

A little anger mounted in me.

'Woman! what is there to fear?'

'Oh! I don't know. I must go away.'

'Come, then! Let us go at once.'

She stared at me hopelessly. 'Not kind, only reasonable. Not merciful, only just. You did not kill that man, but you showed him no mercy. And now – Very well! I will not go with you.'

'Then I will have to carry you,' I said hotly, and I was more than a little angry now.

Something suddenly furtive in her glance told me that she contemplated flight; but my hand was firmly above her elbow before she could move. At once she whirled to free herself, and I had to use a second hand.

'I will not go – I will not go.'

And I had to hold her. She was as supple and strong as whalebone, and, in order not to tear her blouse, I had to grasp her within my arms. And I grasped her closely – in spite of any will of mine. My arms tightened, and she threw back her head and stared at me. A white-hot rage surged in me.

'You don't like me to touch you. No? Very well!'

And I brought my mouth down on hers and held it.

She went limp in my arms, and I lifted my head.

'Oh! you brute!'

'Exactly!' said I, and forthwith picked her up and strode furiously down the path between the thin, tall trunks of the larches.

She made not the least stir in my arms, and, though I never looked down at her, I knew that she was staring up at me. I kept my eyes on the path ahead. I felt unnaturally strong, and I was so mad that I scarcely knew what I was doing.

We came out on an open field, and I fixed my eyes on the black bulk of a hawthorn hedge on the other side. It looked far and far away in the lessening light of the gloaming, but I clenched my teeth and made for the shelter of it. And to hell with aching arms!

I got there, arms numb and back breaking, and was about to stand her on her feet when, with a heart-stounding crash, a big figure half-leaped, half-tumbled between two bushes.

'Hell!' I exclaimed, and dropped her. She sat at my feet.

'Jasus!' cried Big Paudh Moran.

A second figure crashed through the hedge. It was Paddy Bawn Enright.

They panted like hounds.

'Mother o' God! Is the darling girl hurt on us?' cried Paddy Bawn.

'No – sulking! It will be your turn to carry her next.'

She scrambled to her feet. 'I'll walk.'

'You're nothing but a bloody pagan, Owen Jordan,' said Paudh with conviction.

It took us more than two hours to get back to Sean Glynn's, and, during the last hour, the girl was glad to hang heavily on Big Paudh's arm. She took not the least notice of me.

And, as we went, the big bell in the Catholic church at Castletown started ringing, and, when the air drifted from that direction, shouts came faintly to us down the valley.

'The alarm?' whispered Margaid.

'Och! the Tans up to some divilment,' Big Paudh told her. 'Never you fear, they won't venture a mile out o' town in the dark.'

Paddy Bawn, at my side, looked at me quickly, and I nodded.

'I might get to my quiet place after all,' he murmured.

We had both the same thought in our minds as to what the ringing might mean.

It was full night when we got back: a bright summer night with the moon three parts full above the shoulder of Leaccamore. As we came over the last rise we saw lights in all the windows fronting the farmhouse, and the kitchen door was wide open with light splaying out across the garden. This was unusual and careless, for where the Flying Column holed up no light was shown. And as we came nearer there reached our ears the lively jigging of a melodeon and the stamp of dancing feet.

'Jasus! Hugh Forbes must be out of his mind,' cried Big Paudh in a voice of awe.

Hugh himself met us at the gate in the drystone wall.

'Apollo and his laurel bush!' he cried at us gaily. 'Haven't ye heard the news?'

'We heard the bells ringing,' said I.

'Ay, the truce has come. John Molouney brought out a wire from Dublin an hour ago. Peace, my children, peace!'

And that was that. All that had happened this evening – waste effort! Oh, damn! From very far away I heard Margaid MacDonald's voice.

'Where is my brother?'

'He went back in the car with John – and Sean Glynn. They were in a state about our little runaway.'

'Could I get to Castletown tonight, Mr Forbes?'

And after a long time Hugh's voice, very quiet. 'Yes! he will be anxious, your brother. I'll get Paddy Bawn to tackle the pony; but come ye away in now and have a bite of supper.'

v

They went up the path between the berry bushes, but I stayed where I was, my hand on the wooden gate. After a time I closed it from the outside and moved down the wall to where a wide plank made a bench across two cut stones. There I sat down and looked into the valley of the Ullachowen, faintly pearl in the summer night, with the moon making silver gleams on the long runs between the pools; and all the great hills stood up black and stark below the moon. The dance music coming from the house only touched the surface of the quiet, and a land-rail craking in the meadow was part of it.

This episode was over now – snapped clean across, not to be resumed in this world or the next. I would not see Margaid MacDonald again. Better so. Her coming and her staying and her going were only small incidents in the terrible Black-and-Tan war – and that war was only an incident in itself, and now done with. In a year, or ten years, or twenty years, life, damn it – life would go on as usual. That was life's way. I would go back to New Mexico – I would take Big Paudh Moran along – and there I would ride a horse and mend broken collar-bones and go deer-shooting with Sandy Maclaren and Mose Lynn and fishing with Art O'Connor, but – but I would never rear sons to carry on . . . And even of that I could not be sure . . . And at the end no trumpets would sound for me at the other side.

A shadow on the ground roused me out of that deep muse. Margaid MacDonald stood looking down at me. I rose slowly to my feet and was sorry that she had come.

'Hugh Forbes sent me out to say good-bye,' she said in her low voice.

'Good-bye, Miss MacDonald.' My hand dare not move to her. 'I am sorry I insulted you.'

She was close to me, looking up into my eyes, and did not say a word for a long time; and in the wan light of the moon her face was heart-stabbingly fragile, delicate – lovely.

'Why did you hold me – kiss me – like that?'

A question put simply, and simply answered. But why? What was the use in baring myself? Anger leaped in me again.

'No!' I stressed. 'I am not sorry. I'm damned if I am! I would do it again – this minute. Woman! can't you see – can you not see what you have done to me?'

She turned away from me and sat on the bench – quickly, just as if her knees had suddenly weakened. I glowered down at her.

'Sit down here,' she said gently and touched the bench at her side.

Again, what was the use? She was kind, kind of heart behind all, and would seek to lighten my offence at this end. Well! we might as well get it over. I sat down glumly. And she sat very still, gazing out across the valley and the hills and the whole small, wide world, her head up – poised in a pride greater than the pride of kings.

'I should have known back there.' There was no sympathy for my hurt in her voice, that carried pride too. 'When you warned

me – with that man. And you know, though I was cursing like a
trooper under my breath, it was rather pleasant to be carried in a
man's arms. Awful, wasn't it?'

'Hellish!' said I.

'I wonder! Do you care very much?'

'Not so much,' said I angrily. 'I'll get over it in a day or two – or
twenty years.'

'Was that why you were like a bear with a sore head for a whole
month?'

'You bit off a few noses yourself.'

'Queer, wasn't it? And you couldn't reason from cause to effect?'

Paddy Bawn's voice lifted from the kitchen door. 'Miss MacDonald
– Miss MacDonald!'

'In a minute, Paddy Bawn,' she called back.

'The pony-trap is waiting to take you to Castletown,' I reminded
her.

'The trap is down,' she said calmly, 'and you and I are inside. I
am not going.'

'No?'

'No. Listen, you poor stubborn simpleton.' She laid her two fine
hands on my shoulder and drew my head closer. 'Let me whisper
in your ear.'

That whisper is a secret of my own.

In about a minute Hugh Forbes came out and found us sitting
there.

'My poor craythurs!' said he pityingly.

'Thank you, Hugh,' said Margaid.

'Thanks, say you? And botheration, I says! I waited five minutes
in there, all on tenterhooks; I waited ten and up and had a drink
to myself; I waited twenty and then cursed the pair of you high up
and low down – and I off and sent Paddy Bawn into Castletown to
tell Archie you were safe here. And is it thanking me you were? And
look at me with the stony wet road to Scotland still in front o' me,
and, maybe, no red-haired woman at the end of it.'

'You'll find her,' promised Margaid.

'You can't be lucky always,' said I.

'He is just hungry for his supper, Hugh,' said Margaid.

And that is *my* story.

Over the Border

Over the Border, might he ride there tomorrow,
Over the Border, for surcease of sorrow,
Yet hides he here grim within his own Border
With drink to woo sleep and drown Love's disorder.

———————

Chapter One

I

It might be that I would not have visited Sean Glynn at all but for the east wind that buffeted me day after day down the length of Edinburgh's Princes Street. My Highland blood had been thinned by three years in the tropics, and that keen breeze off the German ocean kept searching me through and through, until, Christmas still a week ahead, I decided I had had enough of it and to spare.

Moreover, I was lonely in Edinburgh. My only sister, Margaid, was married to Doctor Owen Jordan at a place called Alamagordo in New Mexico, I don't know how many thousand miles away; and the salmon-angling season would not start for another six weeks. I had had a letter from Margaid that week. After four pages detailing the activities of a two-year-old son with the appalling name of Patrick Archibald Jordan, and the ignominious failure of her husband and Big Paudh Moran to hit a sitting deer – 'Jasus, ma'am! he was like the side of a house an' horns on him like a holly bush'– she finished as follows:

Do you never hear from Sean Glynn of Leaccabuie – you haven't mentioned him in your letters for ages? Owen is a bit anxious about him. Hugh Forbes in a non-committal way merely writes that 'the lad is sound in health and making money by the farm' – as if that was all that mattered – and Mickeen Oge Flynn hasn't written since he escaped from the internment camp. Has Sean married that lovely girl Joan Hyland, or did that bad Kierley business come between them? Do not forget to answer all my questions. You generally do forget, and you generally will until you get a wife to do your letter-writing for you – as I do Owen's. What about it? You know, Owen has written his account of the way I came to take pity on him. I shall send you a copy as soon as I get round to type it. Such vanity! By the way, Art O'Connor, Owen's partner, is visiting the old country next year, and you may run across him – he is a fisherman too, and that peculiar type, the Americanised Irish-man, who makes fun of the Celtic twilight – and needs a lesson. . . .

A wife! To the devil with a wife! Why must women be always at the marrying? But presently I found myself thinking that Southern Ireland was not such a bad place in winter – good cock and snipe shooting – salubrious – palms down to the sea and all that! Mightn't be such a bad idea after all; and I could be back in time to try the Red Craig pool on the Findhorn.

So I wired Sean Glynn after the manner of the very close friendship that existed – or had existed – between us:

Would like to spend Xmas in Munster – get someone to ask me.
                                    Archibald MacDonald.

And his laconic reply:

You are asked to Leaccabuie – come right over.
                                    Sean Glynn.

I did not like that laconic wire. For the Sean that I had known so well would have spread himself even on a telegraph form: damned me for an Albannach, deplored the shortage of turkeys and good malt whiskey, warned me to bring my own cartridges – number eight for cock – advised me how to cheat the customs, and decided to meet me in Dublin for a night's jollification.

Still, I went right over, and I know now that it was not a bad thing that I did. But I might have hesitated had I been aware of the weariness of the train journey that lay between me and Leaccabuie. True, I had been over that road once before, but that was in a troop train during the Black-and-Tan war, and there had then been enough risk to keep me interested. Accustomed to the sea, I thought little of the run from Glasgow to Dublin: merely went to bed after striking the swell of the Clyde estuary and woke up next morning in a kicking sea off the Bailly lighthouse outside Dublin Bay. Nor was the rail journey from Dublin to Ballagh Junction particularly wearisome; the train was steam-heated, a Pullman car attached, and there were not more than three stops. But after changing to the local line at Ballagh the journey seemed without purpose or end.

Outside the windows there was nothing in the winter landscape to hold the eye across the grey-green fields that curved and folded to a dim and rainy horizon; and the short winter day was already falling into night before the hills of the south-west began to roll in on either hand. All that I could see was that there was more than a sprinkling of snow on the bald heads of them. There was a station every three or four miles – and the miles strung themselves out to nearly three figures – and at every station the train halted and dallied and did a little clamorous shunting. As far as I cared to notice, scarcely a passenger got on or alighted, yet the train was met at every station by quite a number of people: young men slouching under the dim oil-lamps, pairs and trios of girls strolling waist-clasped up the line of carriages and looking in – not peeping – with level and appraising glances. Very cool and calm and pretty girls most of them were, smiling rarely; and the slouching young men under the lamps took absolutely no notice of them.

I was not aware of much salubrity within the first-class carriage, supposed to be heated by a flat, lukewarm foot-warmer, but luckily I had a whole compartment to myself, a fur-lined coat and a couple of rugs, so that I was able to recline at full length, smoke strong tobacco and take speculative stock of things. And I thought mostly of Sean Glynn, for, let the truth be told, I was disturbed in my mind about him and I knew that, sooner or later, I was bound to seek him out and see for myself.

II

Sean Glynn was the best friend I ever had – and is, though I have many splendid friends – yet I had not had a line from him for something like two years. Sean had spent his youth in Scotland and he and I had gone through Dollar and Edinburgh University together; we had camped and fished and shot – with a little poaching on the side – all over the wide province of Moray; and both being of Gaelic stock, we came to know the contour of each other's minds. Then I had taken up soldiering as a profession and gone to war; and Sean, on the death of his father, had given up freelance journalism and returned to his native Ireland and to farming on a fairly extensive scale. And then he, too, had gone out to fight for an ideal of freedom: not for Britain, but against all that England stood for in Ireland.

After the Great War my regiment had been sent to Munster to help the Black-and-Tan police subdue the Sinn Fein IRA – a wholly rotten job, rottenly planned, rottenly conducted and rotten in ideal, and every honest soldier felt rotten about it. By a coincidence not too strange, my company of Seaforth Highlanders had been sent into Sean Glynn's territory, and there we had resumed the old acquaintanceship. Outwardly a peaceful farmer with business in every market town, he was at that time one of the principal intelligence officers of the IRA in the South, but I was not supposed to know that. I had no evidence, of course, but, knowing Sean Glynn, I knew that he would be in the thick of things. I will say nothing here of how my devotion to angling led to my capture by the great Hugh Forbes's Flying Column, and the lively two months that ensued for Margaid and me before the truce set us free – she to marry Owen Jordan, I to go to India with my regiment.

The last time I had seen Sean Glynn was at Castletown railway station where he had come to say good-bye. There was a gloom on him that day, there had been a gloom on him for many days, and, by way of lightening the atmosphere, I leant from the carriage window and said, 'You'll be a staid old Benedict next time I come over – what?'

'Oh! To hell with women!' He laughed sourly.

And I had agreed with him most heartily, though I was surprised at his explosion, for he was, at that time, engaged to marry Joan Hyland, a pretty neighbour of his.

And then had come the brief enquiry into the particularly bad Kierley scandal. There were horses and wine and song and women, and apparently a good deal of tainted British cash, in that affair, for the Irish make a thorough job of scandal and treachery when they take a hand in these things. Sean Glynn was in it, and deeply in. There was evidence that Nuala Kierley and he had stayed in the Rowton Hotel in Dublin one night, and next day had gone down to Sean's farm at Leaccabuie, where the woman had stayed a week – I saw her myself at Lough Aonach Hotel by the half-light of a peat fire, and my blood had stirred in me. And at the end of that week her husband, Martin Kierley, was found drowned in the Red Girl's pool at Lough Aonach. The subsequent enquiry emphasised the scandal rather than anything else, for neither the English nor the Irish authorities wanted to show their hands in the affair. Anyhow, the enquiry had been stopped short, and no action taken.

I had been at our depot at Fort George at the time, pre-paring for India, and I wrote Sean a note of congratulation or commiseration; and after a longer time than usual had a brief acknowledgment:

Thanks for your congratulations. They are not quite deserved – and you seem to know that, you old blood-hound. You are right, my son! I am done with women – every last one of them. The Glynn is a dying breed, anyhow. I had five uncles, yet I am the last of the Glynns. But I will take my own way of dying – God and the devil willing – a long time hence, and I will not let any woman kill me either, by God!

And that was the letter of the man who had been engaged to marry young Joan Hyland when Ireland's fight had been won.

It was the last letter I had received from him. I had gone out to India, and, though I had written him at least three times, I had never drawn a word in reply.

And now I was coming to Leaccabuie to see with my own eyes what was wrong, and that something was wrong I was certain. I had only two facts to work on – the Kierley affair and Sean's break with Joan Hyland, and these might be inextricably mixed together – but, whatever the facts, something had befallen him that changed his humorously sane outlook on life, made him cast aside love, ignore every friendship, set his feet on a new and strange and dangerous road. If necessary, I would walk with him on that road, for a man has to do anything he can to help a friend . . . and if I could do no good I hoped to do no harm.

So I mused as the jolting little train moved staccato-wise into the heart of the high hills.

III

The guard popped his head in at the door.

'Leacca, the station after this, sir.'

'Thank the Lord!'

'To be sure – to be sure,' he agreed pleasantly, and banged the door as if in a desperate hurry to start his train. And then I heard his voice addressing the station-master. 'An' what he'll find at Leacca to thank Himself for bates me.' The two receded chuckling, and in another five minutes we resumed our journey.

Sean Glynn was not at Leacca station to meet me, though I had wired my train from Dublin; and that small neglect hurt in spite of all my reasonings on the way. I stepped out on the dimly lit flagged platform and peered up and down, and as far as I could judge there was no one there to meet me. I felt a twinge of forlornness then. For that small, dimly lit station was no more than a halting-place in the wilderness, and in the darkness all round was no sign or loom of habitation. Yet out of that darkness folks had come like moths to the light. Three or four men slouched carelessly about the arched station entrance below an oil-lamp, and two girls, arm-fasted, walked by and examined me with cool remoteness.

I tucked my rugs under an arm and walked back towards the guard's van, and the men at the entrance watched me as I approached. Perhaps it was some kinship of race that made an inner sense aware that they did not regard me as a mere chance traveller, that they were interested in me, that they were aware of my identity and destination. But I was not perturbed, for I had been long enough in the South to know the breed. And, somehow, that sense of awareness lifted me out of the slough of forlornness.

As I came abreast of the group a man pushed his way unceremoniously through and lifted hand in a half-military salute – a middle-sized man in riding-breeches and leggings, with good shoulders under rough tweed.

'Major MacDonald?'

'Yes.' I halted, facing him.

'I have the car outside, Major. Sean Glynn sent me in to meet you.'

'Why, you are Paddy Bawn Enright?'

'I am, sir.'

We shook hands warmly.

I knew him at once – his deep-set blue eyes under heavy brows, and the set, queerly immobile face of the fighting man. He had been one of Hugh Forbes's Flying Column, and one of the best; and his friends used to call him, half derisively, half affectionately, 'the Quiet Man' because, after a dozen or so hectic years as a prize-fighter in the States, he had returned home to look for a quiet place to settle down in – and had not found it. Had he found it yet?

'And how is Sean?' I did not emphasise the enquiry.

'Good, sir! Fine – just fine! One minute, if you please, and I'll get the baggage.'

He turned and went off quickly, a wiry, active man with one shoulder hunching a little. And while I waited I smiled to myself.

Oh yes! I knew the breed. Paddy Bawn, sent to meet me, had stood behind the group at the entrance and watched me walk down the platform, re-establishing the mind-picture he had of me, finding out for himself if the years had changed me. Perhaps the years had. And another thing, when he informed me that Sean Glynn was good and fine, he also told me, by some subtlety of mind acting on speech, that my friend was neither one nor the other.

He returned with a kit-bag in either hand and a gun-case under an arm, and we went out under the arch to the station yard. The men at the entrance moved readily aside, and one of them said in a friendly way, 'You're welcome back, Major. Safe home to ye!' I no longer felt an alien.

I looked for the motor-car. There was none. The car was the Irish jaunting-car, or 'side-car' as it is called in Munster, and the light from the station entrance showed a fifteen-hand pony in the shafts, a tousle-maned beast with astonishingly clean forelegs. It was bridle-held by a small urchin and stood as quiet as an old sheep.

'That's the boy, Jurreen! She didn't try and run on you?'

'Faith, and 'tis me wouldn't let her, the bastard,' piped Jurreen confidently.

While I climbed on to my side of the swaying car, Paddy Bawn stowed the luggage behind the dashboard and then came and deftly fixed the rug round my feet.

'Hould her, you devil, Jurreen!' he warned as he sprang up on his own side, but the mare did not even flick an ear.

'Here, lad!' I called, and felt for a shilling.

'Thank you, sir – and God spare you!'

'Hup, mare!'

And I gripped the front rail. But the mare turned quietly and walked sedately out of the station yard into the darkness. The car had only a single right-side light, and that one of those ancient patterns of candle-lamps. All round and close about us was the blackness of the winter night, and the dim candle-power no more than hinted that our way led into a tunnel of trees arching over the road, and that the road was uphill.

The mare paced along stolidly, and there was no breeze, nor any sound except the muted crunch of rubbered wheels and the regular clippety-clop of iron-shod hooves; and I noted, not for the first time, that the sound of a horse walking is not easily distinguished from the sound of a horse in a hand-gallop. We seemed to be in no hurry. I leant an elbow on the cushioned well of the car and spoke to Paddy Bawn.

'How far is it to Leaccabuie? About four miles?'

'Four miles, sir – and a hang-over. Soon as the girl here gets past the rise of the hill she won't be long.'

I liked his voice, strong and a little thick, with its occasional quaint touch of Americanese.

'I am sorry that Sean Glynn is not so well.' I spoke as if the knowledge were old.

'Well? Faith! he's as lively as a trout – an' you'll see that for yourself, Major.'

There was no doubting the sincerity of his tone. It told me what I wanted to know – that physically, at least, Sean Glynn was sound enough.

'Do you live at Leaccabuie?'

'Sort of land-steward to Sean Glynn, for the time.'

'I see. And what about that quiet place – you know – that quiet place you were on the lookout for?'

Paddy Bawn leant across and spoke confidentially.

''Tis waiting for me, Major – 'tis waiting for me this long time, but it wasn't convenient for me to leave Leacca. Still an' all, God is good! and – I'm damn glad you've come, Major.'

'Yes, Paddy Bawn?'

'You're needed,' said Paddy Bawn.

And that is all he did say. He wanted me to reach my own conclusions. But to me he had implied very clearly that some duty or loyalty kept him at Leacca, and that he looked to me to act the part of some providence.

And then we came to the top of the rise and out into the open; and the mare livened up. Paddy Bawn, who had no whip, merely flicked the reins, and she let herself go smooth as an eel. I know something about trotting horses and pacers, but that unkempt mare surprised me. I couldn't see her action in the dark, yet I knew it was not the high-kneed action of the show ring, but that long, low swoop with the reach at the end that eats up the miles. I tucked in the rug, pulled up the collar of my coat and let body go with the easy swing and roll that is so pleasant in a well-balanced side-car.

'She is good,' I called across.

'Not that bad. She's done Leacca station in fifteen minutes and a hurry on us.'

'Not in the dark?'

'Och, the road is as safe as a feather bed – barrin' an ould devil of an ass on the ramble.'

Presently, I noticed that the night was not what one would call cold – not cold with the searching rawness that comes off the North Sea, but with the brisk sharpness of sea-water in June weather. And out in the open I could use my eyes. We were swinging westward along the northern crest of a valley that opened out wide and deep below us and was speckled plentifully with specks of light. Across the valley was the loom of a great hill, and, on the summit of it, the wan glimmer of snow below a star-spread sky of extraordinary green. Cloud islands sailed that green and gave one a weird perspective of a mystic translucent ocean in a dimension of its own.

'Quite a population down there,' I said.

'Good land all down the Ullachowen Glen. 'Twill be a rale purty sight tomorrow night when the Christmas candles are lit.'

'Christmas candles?'

'To be sure. Haven't ye the likes in Scotland?'

'No-o. I don't think so.'

'Glory be to God! Christmas Eve, comin' on night, wax candles – the length of your arm – are lit by the man-of-the-house in every window. All the night long, and not one of them quenched before first Mass on Christmas morning. 'Tis to light the Mother of God and she in her need.'

And I contemplated in imagination that valley and hillside illuminated in every window all through the dark of the winter night to ensure that the Mother – any mother – any woman – should not go shelterless in her need.

In less than twenty minutes we swung in through an open gateway and up a lifting roughish avenue, swerved past the bole of some big tree, and curved into the wide cobbled yard of Leaccabuie House – a long, flat, two-storied façade below a thickness of rye thatch, with a broad arched door at the head of three curved steps. I remembered that comfortable house.

Paddy Bawn had the door open before I was well alighted.

'Leave the baggage to me, sir. Come away in.'

The room I entered through that door was hall, living-room, kitchen all in one. It was long and wide, but not too high, with a flagged floor and a ceiling heavily beamed, and from each beam hung a flitch of bacon finely smoked and glistening with salt. A big turf fire burned on an open hearth at one end, and at the other an enclosed stairway led to the upper floor. A black oak dresser, loaded with blue and brown delf, gleamed in the light of a swinging brass lamp.

My friend Sean Glynn was not in that room to welcome me. There was only a comely, middle-aged, black-garbed woman who rose from a chair at the fire-side. I remembered her too: Johanna Dillane, Sean's housekeeper.

'Ah! Major, sir! You're welcome. Sure, 'tis fine to see you again – an' the bad times forgotten. Take off your coat now – an' you famished with the cold that's in it, and the hunger. Mr Sean is above in the room waiting for you.'

We shook hands, and her eyes were busy searching into me. She scarcely gave me time to say a word, but led me to a doorway within a covered entry to the right of the fireplace, ushered me through and shut the door behind me.

I stood within the door and looked at Sean Glynn.

Chapter Two

I

Sean Glynn sat at the fireside end of his dining-room table, and he was the Sean Glynn that I had always known. I had expected to find him gone shabby and careless, flaccid, his mouth out of control; but there he sat, clean-cut and keen as ever, his mouth firm, his eyes brilliant and steady. By his right hand on the table-cloth stood a half-full tumbler.

'Archie MacDonald, his own self,' he said quietly, with the old, slow enunciation I remembered so well.

He sat there calmly and did not even smile. A spark of anger leaped in me. But luckily the dour Scot is stronger in me than the hot-tempered Celt, and no cold welcome could make me turn back now. I steadied myself in time.

'Changed days, Sean!' I said in as quiet a tone as his own. 'Am I not welcome?'

'Changed days surely, Archie! But you are welcome all the same. I have a lump in my throat – damn you and it!' And he smiled in a way that told me, roll time and tide, the old liking would never die. It was all I wanted to know.

He pushed back his chair and rose to his feet. And there I noticed that he steadied himself for a moment with his spread fingers on the cloth. There was, however, no trace of tip-and-balance in his walk as he came across the room, and his gaze met mine steadily, and perhaps a little challengingly. But, again, I noticed something. The brilliance of his eyes was clouded by a faint haze – not a drugging – just that small dulling and dazing that is caused by only one thing – malt whiskey.

Sean Glynn was of the black Gael; not too tall, but built for endurance; deep-chested, light-limbed, aquiline-faced, his eyes so deeply blue that in the lamp-light they looked black; a cool, strong, formidable man. And yet?

'I looked for you on the quay at the North Wall of Dublin?' I said.

'And I was not there.'

'I looked for you at Leacca station?'

'And I wasn't there either.'

He turned to the table at his side and traced a long ellipse on the damask with a finger-tip. 'Two hundred and fifty-two acres, two roods and ten perches plantation-measure of arable land, and fifteen hundred acres of mountain and moor – that is my domain, the border within which I abide, and outside that border I will not move for god, dog or devil –'

'Man or woman?'

'Here within my borders you are welcome, Archie MacDonald – and you ought to know it.'

The small first tension slacked, and I glanced at the table.

'What have you in that decanter?'

'My poor fellow – and you famishing.' He went to the table-end and poured three fingers into a glass. The decanter neck clinked the crystal rim and drew a piercingly sweet note. 'Water or soda? Water for good whiskey always. Try that.' He lifted his own glass.

'*Slainte!*' I toasted. It was good whiskey.

He put down his empty glass – half mine was left – walked to the door, and opened it.

'Johanna, is there anything to eat in the house?'

'In a minute, sir – in a minute.'

He looked at me over his shoulder. 'You're lucky. Come and have a wash. There's a smut on the end of your Scots nose – and it had to be nicely aimed.'

And that was how I arrived and was made welcome at Leaccabuie.

II

There was grouse and woodcock for supper. The grouse season had expired a fortnight before, but the game tasted none the worse for that. The night drive had put an edge to my appetite, yet Sean, who apparently had had more whiskey than was good for him, ate as heartily as I did. Before we sat in he invited me to another drink, and, though I refused, replenished his own glass; and during supper replenished it once more.

'You seem to know that is good whiskey,' I remarked.

'I'm no bad judge.' He lifted his glass and looked through the sunny amber of it.

From what dripping cell, through what fairy glen,
Where mid old rocks and ruins the fox makes his den,
Over what lonesome mountain, *acushla mo croidhe* . . .
Are you come to me – sorrowful me?

And there is more of it,' he finished with abrupt satire. 'No, I haven't taken to poetry-making – though that is by a sad man and a poor Irishman.' He mocked me. 'Your glass is empty?'

'Not yet.' I was afraid of the insidiousness of that whiskey.

'Very good! 'Tis not your vice. You know there is one thing a man must have?'

'Three, I was taught. Faith, hope and charity.'

'Men have dispensed with these – and lived. No! A man must have a vice or be damned all his brief days.'

'And have one and be damned in the hereafter.'

'Your Scots Calvinism.' He laughed.

He was on a subject leading my way and I held to it.

'Easy enough to choose a vice, old boy. Plenty of them.'

'Not so many worth while. Look! The making of books, the racing of horses, the singing of songs, the love o' woman – and this.' He clicked his glass with a finger-nail, and it answered with a note of curious sweetness.

'You are not writing a book by any chance?' I enquired.

'The Lord forbid!'

'Keep a horse in training?'

'A hound or two.'

'You are a rotten bad singer, I know.'

'Well?'

'Oh, nothing!'

'Squeamish to ask about the love of woman? I have tried that too.'

'Don't boast, Sean. You may not have exhausted that subject.'

'Think so? Once a woman went through my two hands and she was broken, like you'd break a rotten stick. Yet she wasn't rotten – by God! she was not rotten. And another could not see through the humours and jealousies to whatever verities there be. Sounds personal? But what the hell do you know about women anyway? Let us stick to this fail-me-never,' and he flicked his glass with disintegrating satire.

'You must be damn sorry for yourself.'

But he only laughed, and at me.

'No use, brother; we know each other too well. But don't rush your fences. Take your time and look about you, and find out the sort of life I live before – before you reach conclusions.'

'You work, I suppose – or does Paddy Bawn do all that for you?'

'He does his share and I do mine. This night I'll go to bed as late as you, but I'll be out of it the morrow's morn before you. There is a bawn of sixty milch cows, and you can tell me if one of them is badly cared for. My work. Man, I do not set foot in this room until nightfall.'

'And then?'

'Work, a book, a pipe – smoking, reading – smoking, reading – and this my vice, and it is adequate.'

'Work, a book, a pipe, a drink in reason – these alone, and sleep thereafter.'

He moved his head slowly from side to side, and one hand ground into the other. 'That's it – that's it, surely! Sleep thereafter. And every night I have to bridge the abyss.'

'No one to talk to? Why the devil do you hedge yourself in with this border of yours?'

'Because it is too easy to go outside.' He looked at me steadily, and his mouth had a quirk very near contempt. 'Because, day and night, myself and you and every other damn fool urge me to go outside. And I promise you that, when my grip loosens and I want to be found dead in a ditch within six months, I'll just step across.' He went on. 'As for men to talk to, there are many, but a limitation of subjects in this free island where we are afraid to talk about things worth talking about. There are two good men who come to see me once a month or so, and you know them both: Hugh Forbes of Glounagrianaan, and Mickeen Oge Flynn of Lough Aonach – and they would talk the leg off a pot. They are coming over to see you Christmas evening. Hugh, you know, is married now.' He grinned at me. 'Finished with your questions?'

I grinned back. 'For the time.'

'You Scots are all the same. You must have a reason for everything, and you pursue it till it is cold and inhuman. Why not take me as you find me and damn the consequences? But if you do want a reason, I'll now provide you with one of the best as ever was.'

'Well?'

'A glass of punch as punch should be made.'

'There's a man in Bombay, and one in Simla, and another in Aden, and ten from Torquay to the Kyle of Tongue, and each one of them holds the only secret for making punch. I have it myself.'

'And fine too. You try mine and I'll try yours, and you can watch me at my compounding. Reach me that kettle there. Here are the tumblers, and we'll put one lump of sugar in each and two cloves – only two – and a spoon to keep the glass from shivering when we pour in the boiling water – that way. Now we'll place the slice of the thick of a lemon on top of that, and – reach me that grip-quart, that black one; 'tis a blend of my own – for punch only. Grain whiskey and malt and just a flavouring of mountain-dew. Now watch! We let the spirit trickle over the edge of a spoon – gently, brother, gently – so that it floats above the lemon. See? Is that enough? Another quarter of an inch. There! Another small taste. That's it now, and no heap on it. Look at it, Archie! The hot water below, the whiskey on top and the lemon between – and you leave it three minutes to temper before you stir. Can you wait three minutes, my dry soul?'

'I can.'

'Sometimes I can't, and more's the pity. But tonight I will. A drink for two lone men this Christmas weather, and a reason by its lone self.'

It was my turn to laugh. 'No use, brother,' I half-mimicked him. 'We know each other too well. But I'll accept your reason for the night.'

'You'll have to.' He reached for his glass. 'It is my turn now, and you'll talk, talk, talk – and anything you say will be evidence against you in the great book of Gabriel. Do you mind, Archie, the time we camped out above Loch Linnhe and decided over our Carlsberg that we were two grand talkers, and woman the very devil?'

He had a way with him had Sean Glynn. He had his armour on, and, because he knew every turn of my swordplay, I could not touch him. I was baffled but not beaten. For if his vice – or his trouble – was no more than this sordid one of drunkenness I was not yet done with him. That vice kills, and the death is a shameful one. And yet? A man who worked all day and drank all night might, must, have some trouble of soul to make the night dreadful. My mind fastened on three things: a woman broken in his hands, a woman that failed him, and drink to drown memory. Halt there! I would put no name to these women yet awhile.

III

Let it be said now, sadly or in pride, that I am not a drinking man. Yet I did not go to bed sober that night. But I was more sober than Sean Glynn, thanks not to a hard Scots head, but to the fact that Sean had many more drinks than I had. And drunk – plain drunk – as Sean was, he never lost his power of speech and clear thinking. He sat deep in his chair, and his speech came slower and slower – the only sign of effort – and with a marvellous concentration of will he twisted through all subtleties to a reasoned conclusion, and pursued speculation to the brim of fancy; and, as well as I was able, I kept pace with him after the manner of old nights.

Somewhere in the house a deep-lunged clock struck twelve slow strokes, and with the last stroke there came a tap at the door, and Paddy Bawn entered.

Sean turned a slow head. 'White Patrick Enright, my black devil! Has the hour struck, *achara?*'

'Twelve hard wallops.'

'Want a drink?'

'With the Major in the house I'm tempted – what would you say yourself?'

'You'll not get it.'

'You're a hard man, Sean Glynn.' He turned to me. 'You see, Major, it was one of my small shortcomings across in the States. I was a hard man to train, and rye whiskey slowed me down till a lad came along and put the Indian sign on me. So I came home.'

'Two pints of porter at fair or market,' said Sean, 'and one bottle of Paddy Flaherty whiskey tomorrow for Christmas – and I'll break every bone in his body if he takes more.'

'I wonder,' I half-queried, half-hinted, 'could I safely break every bone in someone's body?'

'Maybe you could,' said Sean. 'But we'll have to go to bed now. One of the rules of the house – and Paddy Bawn could lick the two of us.'

'Do you live by rule?' I was sarcastic.

'I do, strangely enough – every anchorite has to.'

He placed his hands on the arms of his chair, but failed to draw himself to his feet. 'I can't do it tonight either,' he said sadly.

Paddy Bawn came to his side, and looked across at me with

questioning eyes. In answer to that query I lifted to my feet and held there.

'Oh! you hard-headed Scot!' envied Sean. 'You will always make harbour under your own steam.'

Paddy Bawn reached a hand across his master's shoulder and under an arm, and Sean came to his feet. There he swayed, and his dazed, yet brilliant eyes focussed me. 'You have done a foolish thing, Archie MacDonald,' he admonished me. 'I know your vice, and it has not yet come to you; but if you are wise you will leave this empty, empty house and not stop running till you have no wind left.'

'I was never good at running,' I replied, 'but I will run if you will run with me.'

He made a long ellipse in the air with a heavy hand. 'Two hundred fifty-two acres – you know – my border march, and god, dog or devil –'

'Or woman either?'

'The devil sweep all women!' cursed Paddy Bawn warmly. 'Will ye be coming to bed now?'

I followed them out into the kitchen, where the light was turned low and the peat fire smoored and the big clock ticked slowly and desolatingly, and up the old stairs that had creaked under so many feet for a hundred years. And that ancient house was full of loneliness and want.

And we went to bed.

Chapter Three

I

It was clear dawn when I woke, and before I was right awake I knew I had a head, and when I was full awake I knew I deserved that sort of head. It was Paddy Bawn's knocking at the door that roused me. He came in bearing a tray.

'Morning, sir! Johanna Dillane thought you might like a mouthful – tea it is.'

'The decent body!' I sat up in bed. 'So long as it's wet.'

The tea was hot and strong and reached the right place. Paddy Bawn crossed to the wide, low window, jerked the blind, and flooded the room with the soft winter light of morning.

''Tis goin' to be a great day. There was a piece of a shower back o' cockcrow, but the sun has a sound look. I bet you the cock will be among the sallys at Killerseragh.'

I groaned. 'Safe enough from me. Tell me, Paddy Bawn, was I drunk last night?'

'Not you, Major – but you had drink taken.'

'Sean Glynn had drink taken too?'

'A lie like that would damn your soul,' said Paddy Bawn.

'Sober, was he?'

'Drunk as a blind fiddler.'

'Ah! I see your nice distinction. Sleeping it off, I suppose?'

'Sleep, says you! He is up this hour, into his cold bath, and out in the bawn – a whole morning's work behind him already, with the milk measured and the lorry off to the creamery.'

'Jove! A tough fellow!'

'Tough! tough as a woodbine gad!' And then: 'But the gad breaks with the dint of time – an' we haven't all the time in the world.' He came and took the empty cup from me. 'A drop o' cold water, and you'll be fit for a mower's breakfast.'

I did not care to ask directly if drunkenness was Sean Glynn's nightly state. I put it another way.

'Will I have drink taken tonight, Paddy Bawn?'

'And tomorrow night as well,' he answered my thought. His black brows came down. 'Can you refuse?'

I made no boast. I just shook a dull-aching head. 'There is something wrong with this house.'

'There is,' he agreed. 'Everything is wrong with this house.' He went across to the door and looked at me across his shoulder. 'There is a want in this house,' he said, 'but the house is not to blame. May the devil sweep all women!'

He cursed with a cold fierceness and banged the door behind him.

II

I got out of bed and crossed to the window giving on the valley that, last night, had been a purple trough speckled with stars. The builder of Leaccabuie House had had an eye for landscape. It stood on the brink of the valley, and, from the low drystone wall of the kitchen garden, the ground fell away in smooth fields to where wound the strong stream of the Ullachowen, whose wimplings I could see, and the very pool where I had landed a twenty-pounder in May of '21; and beyond the river the valley lifted steeply into the brown stone-ribbed bulk of Leaccamore Mountain that, high up, carried a lean backbone of snow under the thin sky of winter. Right and left, valley and slope were dotted with lime-washed houses, each in a clump of orchard, and the green round these dark clumps was the green of emerald. And over all shone the clean, cold brilliance of the young winter sun.

'This is the place,' I thought, 'where swack men should thrive, and broad-breasted wives rear strong children. Oh! this lovely and forsaken house!'

I had a cold plunge, dressed quickly, put on heavy boots, and went downstairs into the hall kitchen. Johanna Dillane, by the side of the new turf fire, was busy over her black bastable oven, and I thanked her for the morning tea.

'One does be often having a drouth before breakfast, Major,' she said. 'Mr Sean is beyond in the stall – out by the big door there, sir.'

The big door opened directly on an immense square of yard, half-cobbled and half-concreted. Away at the back was the long line of farm-steadings: byres, stables, barns, all evidently in first-class condition. Two finely feathered red setters and a lovely fawn grey-hound bayed at me from an archway and came across unhurriedly to investigate. I knew enough about bred dogs to no more than flick finger and thumb, and they at once greeted me as one of the privileged.

Voices came through an open door on my left, and I looked into the flagged living-room of the farm-hands. Some six or eight men and maids sat round a deal table and were busy with eggs and bread and butter; and there was the pleasant odour of strong – but boiled – Indian tea.

Paddy Bawn at the head of the table called across, 'He's over in the stall, Major, the door next the arch.'

I stopped his move to rise. 'Don't trouble. I'll get him.'

Inside the big stall – or byre – the sweet flavour of milk and hay and cattle greeted me; the smooth, leanish backs of milch cows made a long vista of red and dun, and there was a faint munch and rustle of leisurely cud-chewing. Through an open door leading from the haggard came a great, slow, blind fork-load of grey-green hay, and gaitered legs moved behind and below it; Sean Glynn's bare black crown peeped above.

'Mind where you're going,' I warned as it came down on me.

'Ha, slugabed! Out to earn your breakfast?'

He turned in amongst the cows, spread the hay in the feeding-trough, and came back to where I stood, three-pronged fork at the trail.

We examined each other critically.

'You look bad.' He shook his head mockingly. 'It'll take me half an hour to work the dry feeling out of your bones.'

'Pity you don't look as bad as you feel.'

And, indeed, one would have to look closely to make a near guess that Sean Glynn was after a hard night. His face was neither fish-bellied nor flushed, and his bare neck was smooth and firm with muscle. Only a certain small fading in the blue of the eyes and a faint pencilling below the eye-sockets told their story; and the hair above his close-set ears could no longer hide the grey.

We went out into the hayshed, where a three-pronged fork was placed in my hands, and for the next half-hour we were busy at the fine warm work of fresh-foddering the cattle and tidying their beds.

'We'll let them out for a breath of fresh air after breakfast,' he told

me, 'and then have a wallop at the woodcock. Paddy Bawn tells me
they're in.'

That half-hour rid me of the morning-after chill, and, when the
men slouched across the yard from breakfast, I was glad to lay aside
my fork and lead the way to Johanna Dillane's plentiful table. The
dining-room was freshly aired, the heavy mahogany shone, the white
damask gleamed under its ware, the peat flamed redly on a clean
hearth, and decanters and glasses had disappeared; there was no
stale flavour of whiskey punch and smoke in the spacious room. A
visitor, not knowing, would have thought this an orderly, comfortable
house, and the owner of it a sane man.

III

Later that day, Sean and I, with the red setters, went after the
woodcock in the sallys a mile behind the house and, shooting better
than we deserved, got ten brace. Sean was the better and steadier
shot and occasionally wiped my eye with his second barrel.

Well into the afternoon we took a circle on the turbary behind
the sallys and failed to get within range of a flight of wary grey-lag
geese. I remembered this country: the low rolling moors with the
grey hill-road winding through, not unlike Nairnshire at its best.

I pointed across. 'That's where I spoiled your ambush?'

'And got laid by the heels.'

'You got your grouse over there?'

'Yes. No use for snipe – too dry.'

'Let's try it – for a spare old cock.'

He hesitated. 'No. I never shoot over it now.'

My Scots stickiness would not be denied. 'Is it not within your
border?'

He frowned at this – my first daylight reference to his obsession
– and then he laughed. 'It is too near my own border – if you want
to know.'

That was a useful hint. It was on the tip of my tongue to ask him
who lived on the other side, but I refrained.

'What you want,' I half-taunted, 'is a high wall.'

'It would serve if it were high enough.'

'You mean to keep trespassers – including myself – outside?'

'No. To keep me inside.' He looked at me. 'Don't worry at it, old
chap – but you will,' he said with dry humour.

Night was falling and rain from the Atlantic pelting us before we got home, and I was glad of a change of clothes and one stiff whiskey – whiskey of a subtle serenity that might draw to itself any lone man with a shadow on his soul. And after dinner we talked and smoked, and, with a slow, dignified inevitability, Sean Glynn got drunk. But this night I remained wary and resolute and took no more whiskey than a normal man should take, just enough to light up the mind and loosen the trammels.

I merely touched the border of that realm in which Sean Glynn sported, where he attained wisdom without effort and grasped problems with certainty, and recognised that one thing mattered about as much as another where all things mattered little. And though he did get drunk, he retained his wonderful, slow clarity of mind and speech, a marvellous, fearsome concentration that was, somehow, admirable and dignified – and to be envied. A temptation to any man.

Midnight struck, and Paddy Bawn, that faithful, quiet man, entered with the last stroke. And Paddy Bawn had drink taken. His face was chalk-white, his deep-set eyes shining, his jaw muscles ridged and rippled as if he were grinding his teeth in a temper. But he was in the best of humour.

'Just the half of the bottle, Seaghan Glynn, *a chara* – just the dead half and devil the taste more – and the other half tomorrow night, if God spares me. But wasn't it the great pity I forgot to drink the Major's health?'

'If that be so, White Patrick Enright – and, though you may not have drunk his health, certain it is that you did not forget' – Sean's voice was richly slow – 'still and all, if healths must be drunk, drunk they will be in three small tumblers of punch.'

'And why would they be small,' Paddy Bawn wanted to know, 'and plenty hot water there in the kettle on the *greesoch*?'

Between them they compounded three glasses of punch, and they were not small. This was the *deoch an doruis* – the drink at the door – and I made no objection.

Sean, calling on a final reserve of force, lifted to his feet and steadied there. And Paddy Bawn raised his glass; his eyes gleaming, his mouth bitter and strong, holding himself like a steel blade. 'To Major MacDonald of Scotland, tested and true,' he toasted. 'And here's to ourselves too – the three of us – three lone men in a lonely house, and may there be a Glynn in it always!'

We drank that toast and laid down our glasses.

'Go to hell, Paddy Bawn!' cursed Sean, and sank into his chair.

'If so 'tis ordained, to hell I will go, but if I were you –' he paused.

'If you were me?'

Paddy Bawn's mind leaped beyond my reach. 'If I were you, Sean Glynn of Leaccabuie, I would go to hell my own way, and it would not be much different from your way.'

Sean Glynn lifted a hand in salute. 'I knew I could hide nothing from you.'

'As a mere Scot,' I said derisively, 'to me it seems that your road to perdition is too easy.'

'Maybe it is, Major, maybe it is,' agreed Paddy Bawn, and his eyes were friendly. And then they hardened and locked with mine. 'Hold you your ground,' he besought me. 'Stick to it, true man!'

He strode across to one of the windows and pulled aside the blind. 'Come here now, and see all the candles burnin'!'

All up and down the great valley below us, and all along the slopes of the hills, every window was illuminated. It was a night of velvet blackness under a blackness, and gazing down into that valley gave one a nightmare feeling of gazing down into the bowl of some strange sky.

'There you are now,' said Paddy Bawn, wistfulness in his voice. 'Every window shining and every hearth swept clane, sweet bread on the table and new milk on the dresser – the way no woman, an' she in her need, will suffer as the Mother o' God suffered.' His voice changed and grew bitter. 'And here we are looking down on it all, and all we have within the four walls is a barren woman and three hard men. We'll be goin' to bed now.'

But outside in the hall-kitchen two tall waxen candles burned in brass candlesticks before an unblinded window, a new fire flamed on the hearth, and a linen cloth on the black dresser was laid with food and drink.

Sean swayed against Paddy Bawn's shoulders and came to a halt.

'Will you be for quenching them, man o' the house?' Paddy Bawn's voice grated. 'Say the word, and in spite of the fires o' hell I'll blow breath on them.'

Sean looked at the pale flames of the candles and shook a heavy head. 'No, Paddy Bawn. We'll not hurt Johanna Dillane. Leave them

– leave them. Never will any woman be guided by these candles to this door.'

'God is good!' said Paddy Bawn.

'Oh, obstinate breed! And I wanted them there, Bawn – I wanted them. But am I not telling you that no woman dare ever come to this house in any need? I took a woman for the need of my cause, and, with my eyes open, I broke her – broke her – and where is she now – and what does she sell? And another woman – was she wise? Bah!' He shook himself clear, and with a single sweep of the arm knocked both candles over; and at once the red flames of the peat took possession of the room and set our shadows posturing grotesquely on the walls.

'Take me to bed, Paddy Bawn.' Sean's voice was drained of all emotion. Without a word Paddy Bawn's strong arm went around his master's shoulder.

IV

Upstairs in my room I snicked up the blind for another look into that illuminated valley. In order to get a clearer view I was about to turn my lamp low when I happened to glance along the widening path the light made across the kitchen garden below the window. Goose-flesh ran up my thighs and over my body.

A woman stood just within the edge of the light at the open hand-gate in the drystone wall – a tall woman wearing the hooded Irish cloak. She was looking up at my window, and I saw the black wells where her eyes were, and the white gleam of her chin; and then she stepped back and aside into the darkness outside the wall and was gone.

The lift of the head, the quick movement, all showed that she was in the vigour of youth. Once before I had seen a woman in a half-light wearing an Irish cloak. That was at Lough Aonach, and the woman was Nuala Kierley, and that time, though I only saw her for a minute, and she never looked at me, something stirred at my roots. I had not that feeling now; after the first eerie little shock I was merely curious as to who this woman might be.

I put my light out and peered across the dark of the kitchen garden. If she appeared in the gateway again I would see her against the light in the valley. Nothing happened.

After a long time I went to bed. Some woman was interested in Sean Glynn's house – or in Sean Glynn. Did she need him, did he need her? Had she seen him knock the candles over? I was a damned interfering Scotsman, and I would keep on being that.

Chapter Four

I

Paddy Bawn and I went snipe-shooting on Christmas Day. I tried, almost to the point of anger, to persuade Sean to come with us, but the snipe moor was beyond his borders and he would not be moved. This border-keeping began to obsess me too. I had a growing desire to drag him outside to see what might happen and had some illogical notion that he would be rid of his trouble if I could once break down this obduracy of his.

I was brutal enough. 'Don't be an ass,' I told him shortly. 'Get your gun and come along.'

For the first time I drew a flash from him. 'Oh! go to blazes!'

I was nettled. 'Very good! But let me tell you one thing first. Before a man can do what you are doing he must think a hell of a lot of himself.'

'So he must – so he has to – blast it all!' And he turned on his heel and left me.

The snipe moor was on the other side of the valley, round the western flank of Leaccamore where it faces its brother mountain Barnaquila across the great glen of Grianaan. There Paddy Bawn and I spent two or three brisk hours and, though I am not a deadly shot at snipe, made a very fair bag, thanks to the abundance of game, the admirable work of the setters, and the quickness of Paddy Bawn to knock over the bird I had missed. Parts of the peat moss fairly frightened me, for there appeared to be no more than a tough, but thin, skin over an unplumbed morass. Small red-edged pools, floating the broad leaves of the bog-lily, were all round us; and, as we picked our way between, the moor quaked and little tremors ran across the pools.

'Divil a bit of fear,' said Paddy Bawn, 'barrin' you step in a bog-hole.'

'Plenty to step in.'

'Begor, ay! They have no bottom, them holes. They go down to – what do you call that place t'other side o' the world?'

'The Antipodes?'

'That's it. Dinny Byug Rua fell into one two years come Shrove Tuesday – the day he was to be married – an' 'twas the last seen of him. He didn't want to marry the woman anyway – and they say he fell in. And then his sister Maura had a letter from him from New Zealand where he came out. She says so herself, and she goes to the altar rails once a month, but you can take it or lave it.'

'A high dive that – or was it a long jump?'

'A bit of a jump, I'm thinking – like this one.'

We had come to the hedged fence of the road here paralleling the bog, and Paddy Bawn took a short run and a flying leap between two bushes.

Immediately there followed a really frightful clatter of iron-shod hooves – exactly as if Paddy Bawn, in mid-air, had developed four shod feet, and, on alighting, had started to prance and buck all over the road. And then came a woman's voice calling aloud. I jumped on the fence and forced back a trail of briar to Paddy Bawn's side. He was not prancing – and not even cursing.

II

I saw the blue-clad figure of a woman, short hair blown upright, swaying in a lady's side-saddle, and, under her, a young chestnut horse rearing and pivoting and struggling to get its head.

I dropped my gun on the grass edging of the road. The heart of that cyclone was no place for a woman.

'Get hold of him!' I cried.

'She's safe as a house,' said Paddy Bawn.

He was right. That young woman was quite adequate to the work in hand. She was welded to that side-saddle, and her gauntleted hands, down on her mount's shoulders, held his neck curved into his breast and brought his head round to us time and time again, and her voice was not calling out in fear but half in chiding, half in soothing.

The chestnut horse was young, but he was kindly grained and well broken and, forced to face the object of his fear, soon grew manageable. His rider relaxed her grip and, one hand patting his shoulder and her voice crooning, 'Now, boy, now, boy – there now, boy!' she brought him close up to us, his eyes still wild and his nostrils quivering. She looked directly at Paddy Bawn and laughed with an unhappy bitterness.

'I suppose you wanted to break my neck, Paddy Bawn?'

'I did not, then, Miss Joan – not for a piece yet, anyway.'

There was a bleak humour in his voice that made me look at him. He had lifted his old deer-stalker and now he stood stiff as a ramrod, his strong-boned face unsmiling, and his eyes unflinching. There and then that Irish fighting man was no other than one meeting a not-to-be-despised enemy.

'Thank you, Paddy Bawn.' She smiled faintly, appreciating some hidden meaning. 'How are you keeping?'

'Good, miss – fine, fine.'

'And Sean? No one ever sees him now.'

'Not a hair out of him!' And then with sudden bluntness, 'And small credit to you, Miss Joan.'

'I would hate you to be easy on me, Bawn,' she said quietly.

'I won't, either,' said Bawn hardily.

Her eyes had only touched me, as it were, up to now, but here she looked directly at me and smiled frankly.

'Captain MacDonald?' she said. 'Do you not remember me?'

'Miss Joan Hyland of Janemount, Major MacDonald,' Paddy Bawn introduced us.

I had lifted my hat and now I bowed. 'I remember Miss Joan Hyland very well.'

'I am glad to meet you again – Major MacDonald.'

'I am glad too, Miss Hyland.'

Three years ago, when I had first met her, she was no more than a pretty slip of a country girl. Now she was a mature woman and wise and sad. She was that entirely Irish type, rather broad in the face, her eyes blue and long-lashed, not so much broad-set as deep-set; and her cheek-bones, though finely formed, giving some undefinable Scythian flattening to the whole face. This flattening was emphasised by a slight downward curving of the nose-tip, a curve that, carried farther, is seen in the old tragic Greek masks.

We looked at each other, and thoughts and conjectures were jumbled in my mind – the potent charm of that woman, Sean Glynn hiding within his own border, the things Paddy Bawn had said and implied. She must have had similar thoughts.

'You were Sean Glynn's best friend,' she said. 'He was always talking about you.'

'I have heard Sean Glynn speak about you too, Miss Hyland – but not for a long time.'

'I am the last one that he would speak about now,' she said quietly.
'Well, I must be going. Good evening to you both!'

A touch of heel and a lift of reins, and she left us to watch her.
The chestnut ambled smoothly on the grass edging of the road, and
the figure in the saddle swayed easily with shoulders straight. Her
fine fair hair waved and fluttered, and the white nape of her neck
showed above her collar.

'The devil sweep women – every last one of them!' cursed Paddy
Bawn familiarly, and there was excess of bitterness in his tone.

'You do hate that woman, don't you?'

'Hate? I do not then.'

'You sound darn like it,' I said in surprise.

'Hate is the last thing I have in my mind for her. Any hour of the
day or night I would spread green rushes under that one's feet – in
the house of Leaccabuie.'

'You blame her then – not Sean Glynn?'

He scratched his head under his hat. 'I dunno – I dunno at all.
She has a damn foolish ould blether of a mother.'

'There was more than a lover's tiff in it, Paddy Bawn?'

'There could be. If we don't be hurrying, Hugh Forbes and
Mickeen Oge Flynn will be in the house before us.'

But I wasn't quite finished with him yet, and as we walked on I
remarked casually, 'Perhaps I was too hard on Sean?'

''Tis hardness he wants.'

'That Kierley business was a rotten business?'

'It was all that,' agreed Paddy Bawn.

'Martin Kierley – what was he – a bad 'un?'

'I couldn't tell you that. I wasn't in the know, but I'm thinking
where the rottenness was, the rottenness was paid for.'

'And this Nuala Kierley – was she a bad 'un too?'

'I couldn't tell you that either. 'Tisn't badness you'd be thinking
of with her before you – and I dunno about that either.'

'I saw her only once.'

'You won't forget her then – she stays in a man's mind.'

'That's true,' I agreed. 'Queer, too, but I feel that I shall see her
again – some day.'

'God and the Mother o' God protect you!' said Paddy Bawn
fervently. 'Look now! That woman brings trouble with her always.
There's something in her, I tell you. She'd be bad for you.'

'She was bad for Sean Glynn?'

'Maybe Sean Glynn was bad for her,' said Paddy Bawn.
'I'll be hard on him,' said I.

III

Hugh Forbes and Mickeen Oge Flynn were at the house before us.
They were glad to see me. And a third hard night was spent in the
house of Leaccabuie.

Hugh Forbes, the Small Dark Man of Glounagrianaan, was a
remarkable man, full of vital force; not tall, but powerfully built,
and his broad-jawed, aquiline face the face of a warrior – except
for the lustrous, kindly eyes that, time and again during the night,
were turned anxiously on Sean Glynn getting drunk. He was worried
about Sean, I saw, but he himself took his due share of the punch with
no other effect than the enriching of his astonishing expletives.

Michael Flynn – Mickeen Oge Flynn, as he was known in all
Ireland – was quite as remarkable a man as Hugh Forbes. Tall, lean,
virile, with a lined, austere face, he held to his beliefs in all winds. He
had spent three years reading divinity in Maynooth until the woman
Erin possessed him; was an unconditional republican; had refused
to accept the Treaty; was captured in the civil war; did forty days'
hunger-strike; escaped daringly from an internment camp; and took
to the hills until peace came. Even now it was known that he kept
his IRA organisation alive underground and was reputed to control
several secret dumps of arms.

That was a night of talk in Leaccabuie, before, during and after
dinner; and good talk too, remarkable and not unoriginal talk for
that mountain land on the ultimate edge of Europe. Midnight came
all too soon, and the clock in the hall chapped its twelve slow strokes.
And there was Paddy Bawn in the doorway. A single glance at his
white face and shining eyes showed that his year's ration of whiskey
had done its little worst.

'Hugh Forbes,' said he, 'your flivver is stone cold out in the
yard; it smells like snow, and maybe your wife will be waiting up
for you.'

'Go to hell, you broken-down pug!' Hugh said amicably. 'I'll go
home when I like.'

'This is no place for a respectable married man on St Stephen's
morning.'

'Blazes! but you're right there, Bawn.' He looked round at us. 'One

– two – four hardshell old bachelors, the Lord forgive them! 'Tis a wonder Frances Mary let me out.'

'Any woman would,' remarked Mickeen Oge, 'and call her soul her own for an hour or two.'

Hugh thrust forward his head in a way he had, and there was a wise, mocking, kindly light in his eye.

'You are a hardshell old bachelor, aren't you, Mickeen Oge, boy?'

'So you say,' said Mickeen Oge equably. 'You've been drinking, Paddy Bawn.'

'I will,' said Paddy Bawn.

'My brave fellow! Give him a drink, Sean.'

Sean turned a slow head. 'White Patrick Enright,' he enunciated deliberately, 'thirsty you will be tomorrow, and thirsty you will remain.'

'God's will be done – blast it! 'Twas the bargain we made – but I'll absolve you tomorrow. No, begor! I won't aither.'

'I know, brother. Not while you have Sean Glynn to put to bed. Very well so! We will have our last drink together for another year – another long year, Paddy Bawn. Hugh, take hold of that kettle, and leave Mickeen Oge Flynn alone; what does he know about women?'

'You'd wonder,' said Hugh, and poised the kettle.

Our visitors left after that sturdy final punch. I saw them out, while Paddy Bawn stayed behind to get Sean Glynn to bed.

We stood at the bonnet of the old flivver, and they were in no hurry to go. We talked in low tones.

'We hope you'll be good for him, Archie.' There was anxiety in Hugh's voice. 'What do you think?'

'Was it this – this lover's quarrel that set him off?'

'There was that in it.'

'No – no!' protested Mickeen Oge firmly. 'That was only the final straw. As you may have guessed, Major, he had to do something terrible during the war here, something that touched the very roots of his reason, and, as I see it, he is only taking his own way of holding himself in time and place.'

'Where is Nuala Kierley now?' I asked suddenly, and he nodded understandingly.

'We don't know. She went abroad and left no trace.'

'We are searching for her high and low,' said Hugh. 'Mickeen Oge has a theory about her and Sean.'

'With a risk in it. You see,' explained Mickeen Oge, 'Sean's obsession is that Nuala Kierley has gone wrong and himself to blame. My theory is that if we could show him that she has not –'

'But if she has?'

'Ah, then!' said Mickeen Oge gloomily. 'That's the risk.'

'I have a theory myself,' said Hugh, 'and it is that the hurt caused by one woman can be cured by another.'

'Well?'

'He won't see her. He builds up this damn border of his. We hoped you'd break it down. You haven't?'

'No.'

'Hang on, Highlandman.'

And with that they left me.

Sean Glynn was not yet to bed when I got back to the dining-room. He lay back in his chair, Paddy Bawn standing by his side, and his brilliant, dazed eyes met mine out of a sardonic face.

'What did my two guardians tell you, Archie?'

I made no reply, and he chuckled at me.

'They are my guardians, you know. They come over once a month to see how their keeper is doing his work.'

'Keeper be damned!' swore Paddy Bawn.

'Why stay here, then, and your quiet place waiting for you?'

'This place is quiet enough for me.'

'Sorry I haven't enough grit to kick you out, but – but I can't do without you, Bawn.' He turned to me. 'Didn't know I was a bit touched, Archie?'

'Bosh!'

'Well, I am. But I am keeping it to myself within my own border.'

So that was it. I could not meet his eye.

'This is a bad house, my brother,' he said sadly, 'and you should leave it to this man and me. I'm sorry you came, and I'll be sorry when you go.'

'It is not a bad house,' I said firmly. 'It is a fine old house, but a lonely house for you alone, and not having what it wants, it must have something. Night after night – how long is it to go on, Sean?'

'Only God knows.'

'I know what this house wants.'

'So do I, Archie – and it will not get it by me. Go to your bed, son! Come, Bawn!'

'Wait, Paddy Bawn,' I commanded, the last punch alive in me. 'Did I come to this house to drink malt whiskey or –?'

'You drink malt whiskey damn well, anyway,' said Paddy Bawn, and then his voice changed. 'But if God sent you to us, Major MacDonald, maybe God will show it. Come, *achara*!'

Chapter Five

I

It was Paddy Bawn's fault that I shot that hare. He forgot to warn me.

Sean, he and I had left the house about noon on Boxing Day – or St Stephen's Day as it is called in the South – after a visit from the 'Wren Boys,' masked youths in fancy costumes, carrying a wren in a ribboned bush and dancing intricately dexterous step-dances. After a long and not very successful drive through the sallys of Killersheragh, Paddy Bawn proposed a beat over the dry rolling moors behind on the chance of picking up an old grouse.

'You two nefarious scoundrels try it,' suggested Sean. 'I'll trot back to the house and do some accounts.'

I had a sarcastic comment on the tip of my tongue, but succeeded in swallowing it.

When he had left us I put one or two questions to Paddy Bawn.

'How far are we from the Leaccabuie border?'

'Over there – a mile and a half – good.'

'Whose ground is beyond?'

'The Hylands of Janemount.' He looked sideways at me.

'Exactly! Well, let us get on with this illegal slaughter of ours.'

But the old cock grouse were wary and wild as hawks, and we were lucky to wing a brace at long range.

In the night there had been a sprinkling of snow on these higher grounds, and, while the winter sun had already licked most of it up, a drift or two still snuggled in the northern folds of the moor. It was close to one of these wreaths, some time late in the afternoon, that Boroimhe, the big setter, pointed and put up a hare so light in colour that I took it for one of our own white mountain breed. As a matter of course I brought gun to shoulder, for in the Highlands we blaze away at hares if we happen to beat them up.

And at that an amazingly anguished yell from Paddy Bawn startled me. 'No-o! Oh! Lord Almighty!'

But brain had already given the signal to finger, and the shot went on its errand. The hare pitched over, was on its feet again, stumbled, and was off on three legs amongst the tall heather tussocks.

'Down, Bor'u – down! Black Vilette, you bastard!' And the well-trained dogs stopped dead, crouching.

'What the devil do you mean, Bawn?' I was angry.

Paddy Bawn was not looking at me. His old cap was in one hand, his gun in the other, and both were held away from his body; his head was craned forward and his eyes searching the landscape, while his expression was compounded of fear, dismay and a little hope. He swung full circle and then, his face clearing, drew in a long breath.

'We'd be ruinated all to hell if anyone saw that.'

'Darn it, man! It was only a hare.'

At that he threw his cap on the ground and kicked it. 'Oh! the thunderin' fool I am! I ought to have warned you.'

'Of what?'

He cooled down to explain. 'All my own fault, Major. Look now, would they be shooting foxes in England beyond?'

'Phew!' I whistled. 'Beagles?'

'Greyhounds – coursing. All the tenants of the four glens are in an association, and, dedamned! if I am not their keeper. Any lad caught coursing out o' season or shooting a hare pays his five pounds fine – and glad to get off with it.'

'I am very sorry, old chap,' I apologised. 'We think nothing of shooting hares in the North. You'll fine me that fiver, of course?'

His face relaxed in a grin. 'Faith! an' I did that same the minute you pulled the trigger. We need the money.' But again gloom came over him. 'But 'tis worse than killing a hare, Major. Between us we have ruined the famousest hare in Munster. You saw that fellow?'

'An ordinary mountain hare – smallish.'

'No – he's a sport. That's the *Lua-Bawn-Shee* – the Fairy Hare, as he's called. He was coursed five times last season with picked dogs – Master Ross himself was one – and ne'er a dog took more than two turns out of him. An' now he's off with a leg hangin', and if anyone saw us I'll never lift head again.'

Once more he scrutinised the slopes all round us, and I looked as keenly as he did.

'You could never be telling,' he said glumly. 'Some *bocagh* might be watching us over a boss of heather, and if he's seen going round on three legs.' He looked at me hopefully. 'A lie would come hard on you, maybe?'

'It would. I never heard of any hare called the Fairy Hare. I never fired a shot at a hare in all my life – and I despise any man that would. But did you see that fine buck rabbit I bowled over?'

'I did so. A tame lad gone wild – I lost him myself in harvest-time.'

'And forby, I'll not have him going round on three legs. You scout round with Vilette, and I'll take Bor'u. He can't have gone far.'

'You might be seen.'

'My lookout – and five pounds' worth.'

'Well, maybe it's the best way. Make sure of him this time with both barrels. Oh, our bloody luck!'

II

That stalk led me on a longer trail than I had bargained for.

Sometimes I wonder if the Fairy Hare was not really that, and ordained to lead me where it led me that evening. For it led me as no wounded hare should. A wounded hare invariably circles in its own territory, but this one went straight and true a full mile and more. The big setter never once faltered on the scent but pressed steadily forward between the heath and blaeberry clumps, and, putting my best foot foremost, I kept within striking distance without slowing him down.

In half a mile or so we came to a sagging wire fence, and I threw a leg over and followed on. I guessed I was now trespassing on Janemount ground, but I had made up my mind to get that hare or break a bone.

We had no time to waste. The sun was a red ball down on the crown of the moors, and Leaccabuie was, even now, an hour's tramp away. Concentrated on the dog, I was not too careful of where I set foot and gave myself one good tumble over a short peat bank and a head-over roll into a drift of snow. The dog was going so well at the time that I did not take time to curse but scrambled out and hurried on.

And then we came round the flank of a slope, and over there, not a hundred yards away, was a thatched bothy. I whistled Boroimhe his down-signal, and the wise dog crouched on the scent and waited. I ran an eye over the place. Its back was to me; it was old and the lime-wash peeling off its clay walls; its thatch was ridged and pitted; the red glow of sunset showed where broken panes had been replaced with match-boarding, and no plume of smoke came from its ruined chimney. A vacant and forlorn cottage – probably a disused shooting-bothy.

I clicked tongue to the setter and went on, curving towards the front of the house; and I had a queer fancy that the *Lua-Bawn-Shee* might use this hut for its form, and within it resume its fairy shape. I got a more startling surprise. For, coming into a side-view of the front of the house, I saw a chestnut saddle-horse tied at the door. And at that very moment Boroimhe stiffened at point, a foreleg lifted and feathered tail out behind. Not ten yards from his muzzle the white hare was crouched into a ball, its ears flat and its great eyes fixed. I suppose the dour spirit in which I had pursued the little wounded beast and my desire to end its pain were uppermost, for, without hesitation, I threw up the fowling-piece, looked along the barrels and touched trigger.

The terrific bang, the flaming flash within my head and a clanging darkness shot with stars were all mixed together.

III

I opened my eyes in a half-darkness, and the dimly yellow light of a tallow candle wavered on the edge of a black hob.

I had the strange impression that I was again looking along the path of light from my window at Leaccabuie, and that the woman in the hooded cloak was looking at me. There were the same black pools of the eyes and the same lift of chin. And then the face came close and the light shone on it. It was the face of Joan Hyland.

I was lying on my back on a dry clay floor, and Joan Hyland's riding-habit was folded under my head.

'What is it?'

'Take your time – you are doing nicely. You'll be all right in a minute.' There was soothing in her low-pitched voice.

I turned on my side, got an elbow under, and a wave of dizziness tremored over me. At once her hand was steadying me.

'Easy now – easy!'

But I persisted and sat up. The wall was behind me, and, very expertly, she whipped her riding-habit behind my head and pressed me gently back.

'So! Don't rush it now. You very nearly did for yourself.'

'When – how?'

'Your gun burst – out there – twenty minutes – half an hour ago.'

'Oh!' I remembered then. When I had fallen in that snowdrift I must have choked the barrels and had been in too big a hurry to look.

I lifted a hand to an ache above my right temple and flinched; and she caught my hand in hers and drew it away; and I noticed that her hands were big and finely made – strong hands.

'Leave it be,' she chided soothingly. 'The skin is not broken, and it's a nice little duck egg.'

She straightened up and stood looking down at me for a moment; and then she went across the narrow floor and sat on a rough plank supported on two big stones.

'No hurry,' she said.

My brain was slowly clearing, and I gradually came alive to a stouning head. I moved my eyes around. Except for that plank seat there were no furnishings in the place, and there was that cold odour of long-quenched peat fires. The black-coupled roof swallowed the dim light from the inch of tallow candle. The door opposite me, near her shoulder, was wide open, and outside it was the winter twilight fast falling into darkness. Half an hour would be about right! And where the devil was Paddy Bawn?

'How did I get here – Paddy Bawn?'

'No. I brought you. At first I thought you were dead. You know, the gun barrels were gone at the stock. And then I could not bring you round. So, before going for help, I brought you in here.'

'You brought me in by yourself?'

'You are no light weight either; but I am strong.'

She had the fine shoulders and supple lines of vigour. I contemplated myself clasped in those long arms. She now wore a short white blouse, light riding-breeches and long boots; and she might be taken for a long-legged youth till one looked at her face; and her face was the face of a woman – that wide, strangely Eastern face, deep of eye, with the curved-in, finely cut nose and the saturnine mouth – a mouth too serious for youth.

And, again, looking at her in that dim light, I had that strange feeling of looking on the hooded woman in the gateway of Leaccabuie House that night when Sean Glynn knocked over the Christmas candles that were lit to light woman, and she in her need.

I suppose when a man has been completely knocked out and is

coming round, his mind, not yet normal, fixes on the problem that had most strongly possessed him and treats that problem in some abnormal fashion. That is what my mind did.

Here now was Joan Hyland alone with me in this bothy, and my mind at once gathered in Sean Glynn. He had been in love with this girl and had lost her. Was he in love with her now? With a complete sureness I decided that he was. She was a woman made to be loved, and, losing her, a man would have a torment added to his already heavy burden. I had been unfair to my friend. He was stronger than I knew: grimly fighting his trouble, not yielding to it, retaining his own secret dignity, keeping some unquenchable spark alive above the lifting tide.

And there I was sorry for Sean Glynn. And with that sorrow came an intense desire to rid him of his trouble that, only now, I fully understood. I felt my stouning head moving on my shoulders with the force of perplexity and desire.

Joan Hyland moved restlessly, drew her feet in and swayed her body forward. She was feeling the disturbance in my mind.

'What were you shooting at?' she asked suddenly, as if to avoid her own thoughts.

'A rabbit.' I could not fail Paddy Bawn. 'A white buck rabbit.'

'Not the *Lua-Bawn-Shee*, I hope?'

'If that was the name of Paddy Bawn's tame rabbit that went wild on him in harvest-time.' Unconsciously I used his very brogue.

'We Irish are famous liars,' she remarked shrewdly. 'I hope you didn't kill it.'

'Nearly did that for myself. It was very lucky for me, Miss Hyland, that you were riding in this wilderness.'

'Oh, I often ride this way. This is our land, you know – the boundary is back there – and I was taking a look at the fences.'

'Do you ever ride over the border?'

She did not answer. She was leaning forward, her hands on the plank, and her eyes on the clay floor – in a web of thought that I could not break. But I had the talk in the airt I wanted and would not be baulked.

'I know a man,' I told her, 'who will not cross his own border for god, dog or devil – or for woman either.'

She jerked her head quickly, just as if I had clipped her sharply under the chin.

'Do you ever see that man as you ride your own borders?'

'No. I never see him,' she replied simply.

There was a line or two I remembered from somewhere, and I said them slowly. 'She rides alone in the wilderness, her eyes on the horizon of the moors, empty like the heart that waits him.'

'That is a hard thing to say,' she murmured.

She did not resent my boldness, nor was she surprised. I was only voicing her own thoughts, long dwelt on. This girl was in the narrows too, and I would go on testing her nearer the core.

'Paddy Bawn Enright tells me,' I said, 'that tall candles are lit on Christmas Eve to light the Mother o' God and she in her need. We had two wax candles at Leaccabuie, and a hooded woman looked in at them – and she had crossed her own borders.'

Her face flamed at me, but she had courage. 'The candles were quenched as she looked.'

'What need was on her, Joan Hyland?'

'You think you know,' she said bitterly, 'but you do not understand.'

'I might surprise you,' I gave back grimly.

She was roused now to something of my own abnormality and would take a hand in the game, and in her own direct way.

'Is it true that Sean Glynn is drinking himself to death?'

'No. He is only drinking to keep himself alive. But you did not answer my question?'

She could not, and I knew that. She swerved away from it.

'Look here, Major MacDonald! We have nearly four miles to walk to Janemount'

'Janemount? Haven't you your horse?'

She laughed without much mirth. 'You frightened Laddo thoroughly this time – he'll be in Janemount by now, and my mother wondering. He broke his bridle when your gun exploded.'

'I am very sorry,' I said.

But I was not sorry. That clouted headpiece of mine was working admirably and went on doing its duty.

'Is not Leaccabuie quite as near as Janemount?'

'Nearer – a mile or two – but,' she looked at me hesitatingly, 'could you make it by yourself?'

'I wouldn't care to try just yet.' And then I tempted her. 'Paddy Bawn would drive you home in twenty minutes behind the stepper.'

'No! No-o!' But she was tempted.

I had this girl here like a salmon in a pool, my line fast to her; and even my enemies will admit that I can play a salmon. I gave her a little more line.

'To walk to Janemount would be foolish, and, moreover, Paddy Bawn cannot be far away. We were on the moor together, and Bor'u, the setter, will bring him this way looking for me.'

'In that case we will wait a little,' she said, and eased herself on the plank. 'Are you quite comfortable?'

'Quite.'

I turned my eyes to the open door, and there was Paddy Bawn himself. He stood, still as a stock, just outside the threshold, within the slanting ray of the candle-light, and the setters crouched, one behind each knee. I looked at Joan Hyland. Her gaze was again downwards, and her heel was tapping restlessly on the clay floor, wondering where my next thrust would come from. My eyes still on her, I lifted my hand slowly, placed finger to lip, and gave thumb a sideward twist. When I looked back at the doorway Paddy Bawn was gone, and his nailed brogues had made no smallest click on the cobbles. A sound scout, this Paddy Bawn.

'Your mother will be anxious, Miss Hyland,' I said.

'It will do no harm,' she answered with a touch of unfilial hardness. A damn foolish ould blether of a mother, Paddy Bawn had said.

'If Paddy Bawn would only come,' I went on, 'we could send him on ahead to Leaccabuie, to meet us at the hill-road with the pony.'

I looked at her suggestively, and she nodded her head in agreement.

'And it might save time,' I went on, 'if we set out on the road I came; the dogs will easily find us.'

'Do you think you could manage?'

'Fine that! with a hand occasionally.'

She came quickly to my assistance as I reached my feet and swayed, one hand on the wall. There was really no need for me to sway, for I possess a hard Scots head, and, at a pinch, could have made Leaccabuie under my own steam. And the abnormal excitement or incitement that I was holding down deadened for a time the shock to my head-piece.

She slipped into her riding-habit. I took a firm grip of her arm, and we went out into the deepening night, leaving the candle-end to gutter itself out on the hob.

IV

I grasped her arm firmly, her shoulder against mine, and occasionally
I let my weight lean on that sound prop – and I kept from wishing
that I was Sean Glynn.

'You know the way?' I queried.

'Of course. There is a right-of-way and a good path down by the
boundary fence.'

'And a good path down to Janemount, too?'

'There is.'

'I thought so.'

She felt my inward chuckle. 'What is it?'

'I was just wondering.'

'Yes,' she said simply, 'Sean and I used often to meet at the *bothan*.'

'That plank seat puzzled me for a bit,' I said. 'Would it take much
to make you meet there again?'

'Nothing the world holds,' she said mournfully. 'You don't know
Sean.'

'I'll make a guess,' said I, 'and put my shirt on it.'

We held on our way steadily. The rolling, black-silhouetted breasts
of the moor lifted against the green-lit western sky, and, now and
then, a small fresh cold air blew about us. There was no sign or
sound of the dogs or of Paddy Bawn. Once I thought I saw a clump
of heath on the skyline shift and fade, and once I thought I heard
the swish of dogs' feet across shallow water.

That was all. Paddy Bawn had not been a guerilla fighter for
nothing.

I held her arm with a holding grip and put my next question to
her suddenly.

'Did you know Nuala – Mrs Kierley, Miss Hyland?'

I felt her arm quiver, so I knew I was near her trouble.

'No. I saw her once or twice.'

'She was good-looking?'

'She was very beautiful.' And, if one might judge by her tone,
beauty was Nuala Kierley's worst fault.

'From what appeared in the press at the time, I gathered that she
was a distant relative of Sean's.'

'A second cousin, once removed – her own name was O'Carroll.'
Like all the Gaels, this girl was versed in kinship.

'Was she – I mean – her reputation was all right?'

'I – oh! how do I know? How could I know?'

'Of course not. Apparently she left or ran away from her husband – a queer one, I believe – with Sean, and stayed some time at Leaccabuie.'

'And they went away together.'

'That was all?'

'Was it not enough?'

'Did you make sure that it was enough?'

It was a hard question, and she did not answer it.

'Ah well! if you did not.'

'I was foolish, I know, and Sean – Sean was rotten about it. Oh! I don't know! My mother –'

Her voice hardened at that name.

'Yes? Your mother?'

'She said that Sean – I was very young – that he was a bad Catholic – neglecting his duty – losing his faith – his soul lost.'

'And his friends would follow him to hell tomorrow.'

'You are very hard on me, Major MacDonald,' she said almost humbly. 'I know you despise and hate me, like all his friends, Hugh Forbes, Mickeen Oge Flynn and Paddy Bawn. You are very loyal.' Her voice was wistful. 'You men can be so unfailingly loyal to each other. And we – I could do so little – after the trouble – after we – Sean has such a temper, and mine was worse. I was young – what could I do?'

'Nothing then – nothing at all,' I agreed.

I felt her shoulder shaking, and, for a time, I took no supporting.

'A man,' I mused sententiously, 'is often at the mercy of a woman, and that is contrary to the accepted belief. A woman never loses her soul, and a man does; and a woman sometimes – very rarely – saves a man's soul, and always helps him to lose it.'

'I did not help –'

'No!' I stopped her sharply. 'Would you help him to save it?'

'Oh!'

We went on silently, the quiet moors about us.

'Sean never explained anything to you?' I put to her at last.

'No. I never asked him.'

'Fine – and very right!' I commended her. 'You were not as young as you thought. You are very old now, of course.'

I heard her sad little chuckle. 'I suppose I am still young.'

'But wiser – ever so much wiser – and a wise woman knows a thing or two. Men are queer brutes, and the wise woman knows that if they are worth anything – and generally they are not – they must be fought for all the time. Not once – all the time. We don't know what Sean Glynn did, we don't know what he was driven to do, but –'

'Please!' she whispered. 'Don't say anything more now – I cannot bear it.'

'Not another word except this,' I said. 'Sean Glynn is worth saving if he is worth loving – and you'll know that.'

Again I felt her arm quiver. I decided then that I had said enough.

I, at any rate, did not find that walk too long. Before I was well aware of it we were out on the high-road, and there were the gates of Leaccabuie in front. They were wide open for us, and I thought I heard a shod foot move and fade out up the rough avenue.

Joan Hyland stopped in the middle of the road. 'But where is Paddy Bawn?'

'Must have missed us. Down at the house probably.'

'I couldn't,' she whispered in reply to my unspoken thought. 'I dare not go there – the candles were quenched.'

I still held her arm. 'I assure you, Miss Hyland, that no one – no one – will know. I could quietly get Paddy Bawn out to tackle the pony, and – I can't leave you here alone, can I?'

'Very well,' she agreed resignedly, giving in because she had to.

We went up the lifting road, dark between its bushes, and I felt her arm – a warm and strong arm – tremble. Almost, I thought, I felt her heart beat against my sleeve. We flanked the walnut tree, went through the big gate, round the blank gable end, and there was the door of the house facing us. We halted then. The door was closed, but, farther along the wall, the unblinded dining-room window sent out a broad ray of light across the cobbles. This was unusual, for that window used to be carefully blinded with the lighting of the lamp.

'Just a moment,' I whispered; and, slipping along the front of the house, I looked in through the lighted window. The lower sash was lifted six inches, and the curtains inside swayed gently apart in a light draught of air. I looked, and then I went back to where Joan Hyland waited for me.

'Let me show you something!' I whispered. 'There is no fear.' I had hold of her arm. 'Come!'

My will dominated hers; rather, was in tune with hers. She allowed herself to be led to that lighted window.

'Look!' said I. 'That is what you have done to Sean Glynn.'

v

Sean, as was his custom, sat at the end of his own table. But, as was not usual, he was now fallen forward, his head resting on one arm on the white cloth, and the other hand, at full stretch, holding the stem of a tall glass. The decanter was in front of him.

'Oh, Sean – Sean!' Joan Hyland whispered desperately.

'Can you save him now,' I said bitterly, 'or are you still young enough to be a damn fool?'

And then she surprised me. She threw my arm from her with a gesture almost angry, stepped forward, ran up the heavy sash with the full vigour of her young strength, and was through the window with one swift movement. She took one stride into the room and stopped.

'Sean!'

The noise, the voice – in ear or heart – roused Sean. His hand jerked and the tall glass fell over on the cloth. He lifted his head, and his gaze widened, narrowed, widened on Joan Hyland; then he ran a hand across his eyes and again looked, and slowly came to his feet, no longer drunk.

'Good evening, ghost,' he saluted her sadly. 'Has it come to this at last? I was always afraid that it would.'

He turned to the table with a steady slowness and lifted the decanter with a steady hand; and I very nearly leapt into the room. But his voice held me, and it held Joan Hyland.

He looked through the amber liquor. 'So you have failed me at the bitter end, and I have nothing now to hold me in time or place. Very well.'

He laid the decanter gently down and pushed it away across the cloth. It was an act of final abnegation.

He turned to Joan and smiled sadly, his dark eyes gleaming, and his voice a slow monotone.

'You are still there? I used to see you in dreams, but this is more beautiful than any dream.' He sat down. 'You are stronger than wine. You know, my friends knew better than I did. They thought I was a little touched, because of a small, small shadow that was at the back

of my mind, but I knew – I knew I was sound enough – except –
sometimes – in the lamplight, out of the corner of an eye, over there
in the shadow – I used to see the face of a woman accusing me. Not
you, girl. A woman I broke in my two hands, for the cause, my eyes
open. But I will not see her any more now: I will see you – and keep
the secret to myself – till we are alone.' He went on muttering, and
then suddenly he heaved to his feet and shouted:

'Archie – Archie! Where are you?'

'Sean! look at me!' Her low voice was firm, and she walked slowly,
very slowly, across the room.

Sean's shoulders flinched, and he swayed on his feet.

'Oh God!'

Her hand touched his breast. 'Sit down, Sean!' And he sank into
his chair, his eyes staring up at her.

'It is all right, Sean,' her voice crooned over him. 'It is all right,
Seaneen. I will not leave you any more.' She drew his head against
her breast, and her strong hand went through his hair soothingly.
'There! We were very foolish and unhappy, but we will never hurt
each other again.'

His voice was muffled deep against her breast. I did not hear what
he said.

VI

Paddy Bawn's arm was behind my shoulder, and was needed
there.

'We'll be going now, Highlandman. I knew always you were sent.'
He drew me away by the wall.

'I have the devil's own head, Paddy Bawn,' I told him. 'The gun
burst and nearly killed me.'

'Was that it? Sure, nothing could kill you in the four glens – and
we'll give you your own choice of heads. Man alive! didn't things
work out like – like day after dark – an' me opening the window
when I found him asleep. Everything will be all right now – and
my own little quiet place waiting for me up on Knockanore Hill.'

But a strange thought still obsessed me. Suddenly I felt extraordi-
narily bitter.

'They are all right in there,' I said, 'and you are all right too, Paddy
Bawn, but what about Nuala Kierley? The broken one! Who thinks
of her?'

'You do,' said Paddy Bawn.

'Because I am sorry for her.'

'God help her – and you too!' He pressed my arm. He was not worrying about any woman yet. 'Whisper!' he said. 'I got the fright of my life this night. You saw the *Lua-Bawn-Shee* going off on three legs, and him full of shot?'

'On three legs – yes!'

'Listen! I put him up again before the door of the *bothan* back there, and he went off – whisper! he went off on four sound legs. Four sound legs, I'm sayin', and the dogs never looked at him under their noses.'

'Could you see in the dark?'

'Right forninst the door and the light on him. It was God sent him – and you too – and tomorrow I'll prove it to you!'

But tomorrow is another day.

The Quiet Man

The Quiet Man he sate him down, and to himself did say,
'I'll sit and look at Shannon's Mouth until my dying day:
For Shannon Mouth and Ocean-blue are pleasant things to see,
But Woman's mouth and sky-blue eye! – to hell with them!' said he.

————

I

Paddy Bawn Enright, a blithe young lad of seventeen, went to the States to seek his fortune – like so many of his race. And fifteen years thereafter he returned to his native Kerry, his blitheness sobered and his youth dried to the core; and whether he had found his fortune, or whether he had not, no one could be knowing. For he was a quiet man, not given much to talking about himself and the things he had done.

A quiet man, slightly under middle height with good shoulders and deep-set steadfast blue eyes below brows darker than his dark hair – that was Paddy Bawn Enright. Paddy Bawn means White Patrick, and he got that ironic nickname because there was not a white hair on him. One shoulder had a trick of hunching slightly higher than the other, and some folks said that that came from a habit acquired in shielding his eyes in the glare of an open-hearth steel furnace in a place called Pittsburgh, while others said it was a way he had learned of guarding his chin that time he was some sort of sparring partner punch-bag at a boxing-camp in New York State.

He came home at the age of thirty-two – young enough still for romance or for war – and found that he was the last of his line of Enrights, and that the farm of his forefathers had added its few acres to the ranch of Red Will O'Danaher of Moyvalla. Red Will – there was a tradition of redness in the Danaher men, hair and disposition – had got hold of the Enright holding meanly; and the neighbours waited with a lively curiosity to see what Paddy Bawn would do about it; for no one, in living memory, remembered an Irishman who had taken the loss of his land quietly – not since the Fenian times, at any rate. But that is exactly what Paddy Bawn did. He took no action whatever. Whereupon folks nodded their heads and said contemptuous things, often enough, where they might be relayed back to Paddy Bawn.

'Maybe the little fellow is right, too! For all the boxing tricks he is supposed to have picked up in New York, what chance would he have against Red Will?'

'That tarnation fellow would break him in three halves with his bare hands.'

But Paddy Bawn only smiled in his own quiet way. The truth was that he had had enough of fighting. All he wanted now was peace –

'a quiet, small little place on a hillside,' as he said to himself; and he quietly went out amongst the old and kindly friends and looked about him for the place and the peace he wanted. And, when the place was offered, the wherewithal to acquire it was not wanting.

It was a neat, handy small croft on the first warm shelf of Knockanore Hill below the rolling curves of heather. Not a big place at all, but in sound heart, and it got all the sun that was going; and, best of all, it suited Paddy Bawn to the tip-top notch of contentment, for it held the peace that tuned to his quietness and it commanded the widest view in all Kerry – vale and running water, and the tall ramparts of distant mountains, and the lifting green plain of the Atlantic Sea out between the black portals of Shannon Mouth.

And yet, for the best part of five years Paddy Bawn Enright did not enjoy one quiet day in that quiet place.

The horror and the dool of the Black-and-Tan war settled down on Ireland, and Paddy Bawn, driven by an ideal bred closer in the bone of an Irishman than all desire, went out to fight against the terrible thing that England stood for in Ireland – the subjugation of the soul. He joined an IRA Flying Column, a column great amongst all the fighting columns of the South, commanded by Hugh Forbes, with Mickeen Oge Flynn second in command; and with that column he fought and marched until the truce came. And even thereafter the peace of Knockanore Hill was denied him.

For he was a loyal man, and his leaders, Hugh Forbes and Mickeen Oge Flynn, placed a fresh burden on him. They took him aside and talked to him at Sean Glynn's farmhouse of Leaccabuie above the Ullachowen valley.

'Paddy Bawn, *achara*,' said Hugh in that booming voice that no man could resist, 'our friend Sean is in a bad way – with a shadow on him.'

'I know it,' said Paddy Bawn.

'And you know that he is a man that we cannot forsake, as he has not forsaken us to the brink of darkness?'

'What do ye want me to do?'

'You will take a job as his land-steward and you will stand by him till the shadow lifts.'

'It will not be long, with God's help,' said Mickeen Oge.

'Long or short,' said Paddy Bawn, 'I will stand by him, for, sure, my own little place will not run away, with Matt Tobin to keep an eye on it – and it will be all the better at the end.'

And, as has been told, he stood by Sean Glynn till the shadow lifted and Sean became a douce married man.

Then at last, and for all time – as he told himself – he turned his steadfast face to Knockanore Hill.

II

There, in a four-roomed, lime-white thatched cottage, Paddy Bawn settled smoothly into the life that he meant to live till days were done and eternal night quiet about him. Not once did he think of bringing a wife into the place, though, often enough, his friends, half in fun, half in earnest, hinted his needs and obligations. But though the thought had neither web nor woof, Fate had the loom set for the weaving of it.

Paddy Bawn was no drudge toiler. He knew all about drudgery and the way it wears out a man's soul. He hired a man when he wanted one; he ploughed a little and sowed what was needed; and at the end of a furrow he would lean on the handles of the cultivator, wipe his brow, if it needed wiping, and lose himself for whole minutes in the great green curve of the sea out there beyond the high black portals of Shannon Mouth. And sometimes, of an evening, he would see, under the orange glory of the sky, the faint smoke smudge of an American liner. Then he would smile to himself – a pitying smile – thinking of all the poor young lads, with dreams of fortune luring them, going out to sweat in Ironville, or to bootleg bad whiskey down the hidden way, or to stand in a bread line in the gut of sky-scrapers. All these things were behind Paddy Bawn forever.

He was fond of horses and he bought an old brood mare of hunter blood, hoping to breed a good-class jumper; he had a black hound dog – out of Master Ross – with a turn of speed, and there were mountain hares to test it; and he had a double-barrel shot-gun presented to him by Sean Glynn, and Knockanore heather reared two or three brood of grouse every season; and on summer Sundays he used to go across to Galey River and catch a mess of trout. What more in all the world could a man want?

Market days he would go down and across to Listowel town, seven miles, to do his bartering, and if he met a friend he would have two drinks and no more. And sometimes, in the long evenings slipping slowly into the endless summer gloaming, or on Sundays after Mass, his friends would come across the vale and up the long winding path to see him. Only the real friends came that long road, and they were welcome. Mostly fighting men who had been out in the Tan war: Matt Tobin, the thresher, who had worked a Thompson gun with him in many an ambush; Sean Glynn of Leaccabuie, boasting of his first son; Mickeen Oge Flynn, all the way from Lough Aonach; Hugh Forbes, the Small Dark Man, making the rafters ring: men like that. And once Mickeen Oge Flynn brought Major Archibald MacDonald across from Lough Aonach where he was fishing, and that sound man was satisfied that Paddy Bawn had found his quiet place at last.

Then a stone jar of malt whiskey would appear on the table for those who wanted a drink, and there would be a haze of smoke and a maze of friendly, warm disagreements.

'Paddy Bawn, old son,' one of them might hint, 'aren't you sometimes terrible lonesome?'

'Like hell I am! Why?'

'Nothing but the daylight and the wind, and the sun setting like the wrath o' God!'

'Just that! Well?'

'But after the stirring times out about – and beyond in the States.'

'The stirring times wore us to the bone, and tell me, fine man, did you ever see a furnace in full blast?'

'Worth seeing, I'm told.'

'Worth seeing, surely. But if I could jump you into an iron foundry this minute you would think that God had judged you faithfully into the hot hob of hell. Have sense, man!'

And then they would laugh and, maybe, have another small one from the stone jar.

On Sundays Paddy Bawn used to go to church, three miles down to the grey chapel above the black cliffs of Doon Bay. There Fate, with a cunning leisureliness, laid her lure and drew her web about him. Listen now!

Sitting quietly on his wooden bench, or kneeling on the dusty footboard, he would fix his steadfast deep-set eyes on the vestmented celebrant and say over his beads slowly, or go into that strange trance, beyond dreams or visions, where the soul is almost at one with the unknowable.

And then, after a time, Paddy Bawn's eyes no longer fixed themselves on the celebrant. They went no farther than two seats

ahead. A girl sat there, her back to him. Sunday after Sunday she sat
there. Paddy Bawn did not know how her presence grew about him.
He just liked to see her sit there. At first his eyes hardly noted her,
and then noted her with a casual admiration; and slowly, slowly that
first casual admiration took on body and warmth. She was a bit of the
surroundings, she was part of the ceremony, she was secret partner to
himself. And she never even looked his way.

On the first Sunday of the month, when she went to early Mass
and Communion, Paddy Bawn used to miss her strangely, and his
prayers suffered. And gradually he got into the habit of being a
monthly communicant himself. Holiness is induced by many roads,
but seldom by an inclination that way.

She had a white nape to her neck and short red hair above it, and
Paddy Bawn liked the colour and wave of that flame; and he liked
the set of her shoulders, and the way the white neck had of leaning a
little forward, and she at her prayers – or her dreams. And after the
Benediction he used to stay in his seat so that he might get one quick
but sure glance at her face as she passed out. And he liked her face
too – the wide-set eyes like the sky of a quiet night, the cheek-bones
firmly curved, the lips austere and sensitive.

And he smiled pityingly at himself that one of her name should
make his pulse stir. For she was a Danaher of Moyvalla, and Paddy
Bawn was enough Irish to dislike every bone of Red Will O'Danaher
of that place who had snitched the Enright acres.

'I'll keep it to myself,' said Paddy Bawn. ''Tis only to pass the time.'
And he did nothing.

One person, only, in the crowded little chapel noted Paddy Bawn's
look and the thought behind the look. Not the girl – she barely knew
who Paddy Bawn was, but her brother, Red Will himself. And that
man smiled secretly – the ugly, contemptuous smile that was his by
nature – and, after another habit of his, tucked away his bit of
knowledge in a mind corner against a day when it might come in
useful for his own purposes.

III

The girl's name was Ellen – Ellen Roe O'Danaher. But, in truth,
she was no longer a girl. She was past her first youth into that
second one that has no definite ending. She might be twenty-eight
– she was no less – but there was not a lad in the countryside

who would say she was past her prime. The poise of her and the firm set of her bones below clean flesh saved her from the fading of mere prettiness. Though she had been sought in marriage more than once, she had accepted no one, or rather, had not been allowed to encourage anyone. Her brother saw to that.

Red Will O'Danaher was a huge, raw-boned, sandy-haired man with the strength of an ox, and a heart no bigger than a sour apple – an overbearing man given to berserk rages. Though he was a church-goer by habit, the true god of that man was Money – red gold, shining silver, dull copper, these the trinity he worshipped in degree. He and his sister, Ellen Roe, lived in the big ranch farm of Moyvalla, and Ellen was his housekeeper and maid of all work. She was a careful housekeeper, a good cook, a notable baker, and she demanded no wage. Her mean brother saw that she remained without a sweetheart and hinted at his inability to set her out with a dowry. A wasted woman.

Red Will himself was not a marrying man. There were not many spinsters with a dowry big enough to tempt him, and the few there were had acquired expensive tastes – a convent education, the deplorable art of hitting jazz out of a piano, the damnable vice of cigarette-smoking, the purse-emptying craze for motorcars – such things.

But in due time the tocher and the place – with a woman tied to them – came under his nose, and Red Will was no longer tardy.

His neighbour, James Carey, died of pneumonia in November weather and left his fine farm and all on it to his widow, a youngish woman without children, and a woman with a hard name for saving pennies. Red Will looked once at Kathy Carey, and she did not displease him; he looked many times at her sound acres and they pleased him better, for he had in him the terrible Irish land hunger. He took the steps required by tradition. In the very first week of the following Shrove-tide he sent an accredited emissary to open formal negotiations.

The emissary was back within the hour.

'My soul!' said he to Red Will, 'but she is the quick one. I hadn't ten words out of me when she up and jumped down my throat. "I am in no hurry," says she, "to come wife to a house with another woman at the fire corner." "You mean Ellen Roe," says I. "I mean Ellen Roe," says she. "Maybe it could be managed –" "Listen!" says she. "When Ellen Roe is in a place of her own – and not till then – I will be considering what Red Will O'Danaher has to say. Take that back to him." And never asked me had I a mouth on me.'

'She will, by Jacus!' Red Will mused. 'She will so.'

There, now, was the right time to recall Paddy Bawn Enright and the look in his eyes; and Red Will's mind corner promptly delivered up its memory. He smiled that knowing, contemptuous smile. Patcheen Bawn daring to cast a sheep's eye at an O'Danaher! The little Yankee runt hidden away on the shelf of hungry Knockanore! Fighting man, *moryah!* Looter more like, and him taking the loss of the Enright acres lying down! But what of it? The required dowry would be conveniently small, and Ellen Roe would never go hungry anyway. And that was Red Will far descended from many chieftains.

He acted promptly. The very next market day at Listowel he sought out Paddy Bawn and placed a great sandy-haired hand on the shoulder that hunched to meet it.

'Paddy Bawn, a word with you! Come and have a drink.'

Paddy Bawn hesitated. 'Very well,' he said then. He disliked O'Danaher, but he would hurt no man's feelings.

They went across to Tade Sullivan's bar and had a drink – and Paddy Bawn paid for it. Red Will came directly to his subject, almost patronisingly, as if he were conferring a favour.

'I am wanting to see Ellen Roe settled in a place of her own,' said he.

Paddy Bawn's heart lifted into his throat and beat there. But that steadfast face, strong-browed, gave no sign; and, moreover, even if he wanted to say a word he could not, with his heart where it was.

'You haven't much of a place up there,' went on the big man, 'but it is handy, and no load of debt on it – so I hear?'

Paddy Bawn nodded affirmatively, and Red Will went on, 'I never heard of a big fortune going to hungry Knockanore, and 'tisn't a big fortune I can be giving Ellen Roe. Say a hundred pounds – one hundred pounds at the end of harvest – if prices improve. What would you say to that, Paddy Bawn?'

Paddy Bawn swallowed his heart. Slow he was, and cool he seemed.

'What does Ellen say?'

'I haven't asked her. But what the hell would she say, blast it?'

Paddy Bawn did not say anything for a long time.

'Whatever Ellen Roe says, she will say it herself, not you, Red Will,' he said at last.

But what could Ellen Roe say? She looked within her own heart and found it empty, she looked at the granite crag of her brother's face and contemplated herself a slowly withering spinster at his fire corner; she looked up at the swell of Knockanore Hill and saw the white cottage among the green small fields below the warm brown of the heather – oh! but the sun would shine up there in the lengthening spring day, and pleasant breezes blow in sultry summer. And finally she looked at Paddy Bawn, that firmly built, not-too-big man, with the cleancut face and the deep-lit eyes below steadfast brow. She said a prayer to her God and sank head and shoulders in a resigned acceptance more pitiful than tears, more proud than the pride of chieftains. Romance? Well-a-day!

Paddy Bawn was far from satisfied with that resigned acceptance, but he was well aware that he should have looked for no warmer one. He saw into the brother's mean soul and guessed what was in the sister's mind; and knew, beyond all doubt, that, whatever he decided, she was doomed to a fireside sordidly bought for her. That was the Irish way. Let it be his own fireside then. There were many worse ones – and God was good. So in the end his resignation to Fate was equal to hers, whatever his hopes might be.

Paddy Bawn and Ellen Roe were married. One small statement – and it holds the risk of tragedy, the probability of resigned acceptance, the chance of happiness: choices wide as the world. It was a hole-and-corner marriage at that. Red Will demurred at all foolish expense, and Paddy Bawn agreed, for he knew that his friends were more than a shade doubtful of the astounding and unexpected step he had taken. Except for Matt Tobin, his side-man, there wasn't a friend of his own at the wedding breakfast.

But Red Will O'Danaher, for all his promptness, did not win Kathy Carey to wife. She did not wait for him. Foolishly enough, she took to husband her own cattleman, a gay night-rambler from Clare who proceeded to give her the devil's own time and a share of happiness in the bygoing. For the first time Red Will discovered how mordant the wit of his neighbours could be: and, for some reason, to contempt for Paddy Bawn Enright he now added a live dislike.

IV

Paddy Bawn had got his precious red-haired wife under his own roof now; but he had no illusions about her regard for him. On himself, and on himself only, lay the task of moulding her into wife and lover. Darkly, deeply, subtly, with gentleness, with understanding, with restraint beyond all kenning, that moulding must be done; and she that was being moulded must never know. He must hardly know himself.

First, he turned his attentions to material things. He hired a small servant-maid to help her with the rough work, gave her her own housekeeping money, let her run the indoors as she thought best. She ran it well and liked doing it. Then he bought a rubber-tyred tub-cart and a half-bred gelding with a reaching action. And on market days husband and wife used to bowl down to Listowel, do their selling and their buying, and bowl smoothly home again, their groceries in the well of the cart, and a bundle of second-hand American magazines on the seat at Ellen's side.

And in the nights, before the year turned, with the wind from the plains of the sea keening about the chimney, they would sit at either side of the fine-flaming peat fire, and he would read aloud strange and almost unbelievable things out of the high-coloured magazines. Stories, sometimes, wholly unbelievable.

Ellen Roe would sit and listen and smile and keep on with her knitting or her sewing; and after a time it was sewing she was at mostly – small things. And when the reading was done, and the small servant-maid to bed, they would sit on and talk in their own quiet way. For they were both quiet. Woman though she was, or that she was, she got Paddy Bawn to do most of the talking. It could be that she, too, was probing and seeking, unwrapping the man's soul to feel the texture of it, surveying the marvel of his life as he spread it diffidently before her.

He had a patient, slow, vivid way of picturing for her the things he had seen and felt. He made her see the glare of molten metal, lambent yet searing, made her feel the sucking heat, made her hear the clang; she could picture the roped square under the dazzle of the hooded arcs, with the up-drifting smoke layer above and the gleam of black and white going away up and back into the dimness; she came to understand the explosive restraint of the game, admire the indomitable resolution that in a reeling world held on and waited for the opportunity that was being led up to, and she thrilled when he showed her, the opportunity come, how to stiffen wrist for the final devastating right hook. And often as not, being Irish, the things he told her were humorous or funnily outrageous; and Ellen Roe would chuckle or stare or throw back her lovely red curls in laughter. It was grand to make her laugh.

But they did not speak at all of the Black-and-Tan war. That was too near them. That made men frown and women shiver.

And, in due course, Paddy Bawn's friends, in some trepidation at first, came in ones and twos up the slope to see them – Matt Tobin, the thresher, from the beginning, and then Sean Glynn, Mickeen Oge Flynn, Hugh Forbes and others. Their trepidation did not last long. Ellen Roe put them at their ease with her smile that was shy and, at the same time, frank and welcoming; and her table was loaded for them with cream scones and crumpets and cheese-cakes and heather honey; and, at the right time, it was she herself brought forth the decanter of whiskey – no longer the half-empty stone jar – and the polished glasses. Paddy Bawn was proud as sin of her.

She would go out and about then at her own work and leave the men to their talk, but not for so long as to make them feel that they were neglecting her. After a while she would sit down amongst them and listen to their discussions, and, sometimes, she would put in a word or two and be listened to; and they would look to see if her smile commended them and be a little chastened by the tolerant wisdom of that smile – the age-old smile of the matriarch from whom they were all descended. And she would be forever surprised at the knowledgeable man her husband was: the turn of speech that summed up a man or a situation, the way he could discuss politics and war, the making of songs, the training of a racing dog, the breaking of colt and filly – anything worth talking about.

Thus it was that, in no time at all, Hugh Forbes, who used to think, 'Poor Paddy Bawn! Lucky she was to get him,' would whisper to Sean Glynn, 'Flagstones o' Hell! That fellow's luck would astonish nations.' And the next time the two came up they brought their wives with them, to show them what a wife should be to a man; and Hugh threatened his Frances Mary: 'The next one will be a red-head, if God spares me.'

Wait now!

Woman, in the decadent world around us, captures a man by loving him and, having got him, sometimes comes to admire him, which is all to the good; and, if Fate is not unkind, may descend no lower than liking and enduring. And there is the end of lawful romance. Look then at Ellen Roe! She came up to the shelf of Knockanore, and in her heart was only a nucleus of fear in a great emptiness; and that nucleus might grow and grow. Oh, horror! Oh, disgust!

But Glory of God! She, for reason piled on reason, found herself admiring this man Paddy Bawn; and, with or without reason, presently came a quiet liking for this man who was so gentle and considerate – and strong too. And then, one heart-stirring dark o' night she found herself fallen head over heels, holus-bolus, in love with her own husband. There is the sort of love that endures, but the road to it is a mighty chancy one.

v

Pity things did not stay like that! If they did, Paddy Bawn's story would finish here. It was Ellen Roe's fault that they did not, and the story goes on.

A woman, loving her husband, may or may not be proud of him, but she will play tiger if anyone, barring herself, belittles him. And there was one man who belittled Paddy Bawn. Her own brother, Red Will O'Danaher. At fair or market or chapel that dour giant deigned not to hide his contempt and dislike. Ellen Roe knew why. Well she knew. He had lost a wife and farm; he had lost in herself a frugally cheap housekeeper; he had been made the butt of a biting humour, and that he liked least of all. In some twisted way he blamed Paddy Bawn. But – and here came in the contempt – the little Yankee runt, the IRA ex-looter who dared do nothing about the lost Enright acres, would not now have the gall or the guts to insist on the dowry that was due to him. Lucky the hound to steal a Danaher to hungry Knockanore! Let him be satisfied with that luck, or, by God! he'd have his teeth down his throat. Thus, the big brute.

So, one evening before market day, Ellen Roe spoke to her husband.

''Tis the end of harvest, Paddy Bawn. Has Red Will paid you my fortune?'

'Sure, there's no hurry, girl,' deprecated Paddy Bawn.

'Have you asked him?'

'I have not, then. I am not looking for your fortune, Ellen.'

'And that is a thing Red Will could never understand.' Her voice firmed. 'You will ask him tomorrow.'

'Very well, so, *agrah*,' he agreed carelessly. He did not foresee any trouble about a few pounds back or fore, for the bad money lust had never touched him.

And next day, in Listowel Square, Paddy Bawn, in that quiet, half-diffident way of his, asked Red Will.

But Red Will was neither quiet nor diffident; he was brusque and blunt. He had no loose money, and Enright would have to wait till he had. 'Ask me again, Patcheen – don't be a bit shy,' he said, his face in a mocking grin, and, turning on his heel, ploughed his great shoulders through the crowded square.

His voice had been carelessly loud and people had heard. They laughed and talked amongst themselves, knowing their Red Will. 'Begobs! did ye hear him?' 'The divil's own boy, Red Will!' 'And money tight, *moryah*! 'Tisn't one but ten hundred he could put finger on – and not miss it.' 'What a pup to sell! Stealing the land and denying the fortune.' 'Ay! and a dangerous man, mind you, that same Red Will! He would smash little Bawn at the wind of the word – and divil the care for his Yankee sparrin' tricks!'

Paddy Bawn's friend, Matt Tobin, the thresher, heard that last and lifted his voice, 'I would like to be there the day Paddy Bawn Enright loses his temper.'

'A bad day for him!'

'It might, then,' said Matt agreeably, 'but I would come from the other end of Kerry to see the badness that would be in it for someone.'

Paddy Bawn had moved away with his wife, not hearing or not heeding.

'You see, Ellen?' he said in some discomfort. 'The times are hard on the big ranchers – and we don't need the money anyway.'

'Do you think Red Will does?' Her voice had a cut in it. 'He could buy you and all Knockanore and not be on the fringe of his hoard.'

'But, girl dear, I never wanted a fortune with you.'

She liked him to say that, but far better would she like to win for him the respect and admiration that was his due. She must do that now, once the gage was down, or her husband would become the butt of a countryside never lenient to a backward man.

'You foolish lad! Red Will would never understand your feelings with money at stake. You will ask him again?'

She smiled, and a pang went through him. For her smile held a trace of the contempt that was in the Danaher smile, and he did not know whether the contempt was for himself or for her brother.

He asked Red Will again. He was unhappy enough in the asking, but, also, he had some inner inkling of his wife's object; and it is possible that the fighting devil in him was not altogether subdued to his ideal of quietness – the fighting devil that lifted hackle despite him every time he approached Red Will.

And he asked again a third time. Though Paddy Bawn tried to avoid publicity, Red Will called for it with his loud voice and guffawing attempts at humour. The big man was getting his own back on the little runt, and he seemed quite unaware that decent men thought less of him than ever.

Very soon the issue between the brothers-in-law became a notorious one in all that countryside. Men talked about it, and women too. Bets were made on it. At fair or market, if Paddy Bawn was seen approaching Red Will, men edged closer and women, pulling shawls over head, moved away. Some day, men said, the big fellow would grow tired of being asked, and, in one of his terrible rages, half-kill the little lad as he had half-killed stronger men. A great shame to the world! Here and there a man advised Paddy Bawn to give up asking and put the affair in a lawyer's hands. 'I wouldn't care to do that,' said Paddy Bawn. Our Quiet Man was getting dour. None of his prudent advisers were among his close friends. His friends frowned and said little, and were never far away.

Right enough, the day at last came when Red Will O'Danaher grew tired of being asked. That was the big October cattle fair at Listowel. All Kerry was there that day. Sean Glynn of Leaccabuie was there to buy some winter stores, and Mickeen Oge Flynn to sell some, and Matt Tobin to hire out his threshing-machine among the farmers. Red Will had sold twenty head of polled-Angus cross-breds at a good price, and he had a thick wad of bank-notes in an inner pocket when he saw Paddy Bawn and Ellen Roe coming across to where he was bargaining with Matt Tobin for a week's threshing. Besides, the day being dank, he had inside him a drink or two more than was good for him, and the whiskey loosened his tongue and whatever he had of discretion.

The first flare in the big man's mind urged him to throw the money in Paddy Bawn's face and then kick him out of the market. No! be the powers! That would be foolish; but, all the same, it was time and past time to deal with the little gadfly and show him up before the crowd. He strode to meet Paddy Bawn, and people parted out of his savage way and closed in behind so as not to lose any of this dangerous game.

Red Will caught the small man by a hunched shoulder – a rending grip – and bent down to grin in his face.

'What is it, Patcheen? Don't be ashamed to ask.'

Mickeen Oge Flynn was, perhaps, the only man there to notice the ease with which Paddy Bawn shook his shoulder free – that little explosive jerk with the snap of steel – and Mickeen Oge smiled grimly. But Paddy Bawn did nothing further and said no word; and his eyes were steadfast as ever.

Red Will showed his teeth mockingly.

'Go on, you little cleg! What do you want?'

'You know, O'Danaher.'

'I do. Listen, Patcheen!' Again he brought his hand clap on the hunched shoulder. 'Listen, Patcheen, and let it be heard! If I had a fortune to give Ellen Roe, 'tisn't a throw-out like Paddy Bawn Enright of hungry Knockanore would get her. Go to hell out o' that!'

His great hand gripped, and he flung Paddy Bawn backwards as if he were no more than the shape of a man filled with chaff.

Paddy Bawn went backwards but he did not fall. He gathered himself like a spring, feet under him, arms half-raised, head forward with chin behind hunched shoulder. But, quickly as the spring coiled, as quickly it slackened, and he turned away to his wife. She was there facing him, tense and keen, her face gone pallid, and a gleam of the race in her eye.

'Woman, woman!' he said in his deep voice. 'Why would you and I shame ourselves like this?'

'Shame!' she cried. 'Will you let him shame you now?'

'But your own brother, Ellen – before them all?'

'And he cheating you.'

'God's glory, woman!' His voice was distressed and angry too. 'What is his dirty money to me? Are you a Danaher after all?'

That stung her, and she stung him back in one final hurting effort. She placed a hand below her breast, and looked close into his face. Her voice was low and bitter.

'I am a Danaher. It is a great pity that the father of this, my son, is an Enright coward.'

The bosses of Paddy Bawn's cheek-bones were hard as marble, but his voice was soft as a dove's.

'Is that the way of it? Let us be going home then, in the name of God.'

He placed a hand on her arm, but she shook it off. Nevertheless, she walked at his side, head up, through the jostle of men that broke apart for them. Her brother mocked her with his great bellowing laugh.

'That fixes the pair of ye,' he cried, brushed a man who laughed with him out of his way and strode off through the market place.

There was talk then – plenty of it. 'Murdher! but that was a narrow squeak!' 'Did you see the way he flung him?' 'I'll wager he'll give Red Will a wide road after this day – and he by way of being a boxer!' 'That's a pound you owe me, Matt Tobin.'

'I'll pay it,' said Matt Tobin. He stood wide-legged, looking at the ground, his hand ruefully rubbing the back of his head under his tilted bowler hat, blank dismay on his face. His friend had failed him in the face of the people.

Then Mickeen Oge Flynn spoke.

'I'll take over that bet, friend, and double it.'

The man looked at him doubtfully. He knew Mickeen Oge. Everyone did.

'Is the IRA in it?' he enquired.

'No. Paddy Bawn, himself only.'

'Right, begod! You're on.' The man was a sportsman. 'An' I won't care a if I lose, aither.'

'You'll lose all right, honest man,' said Mickeen Oge, 'and we'll spend the money decently.'

Sean Glynn of Leaccabuie touched him on the shoulder and the two friends went away together.

'Paddy Bawn is in the narrows at last,' said Sean sadly. 'Maybe we were right to be against it in the beginning.'

'We were not,' said Mickeen Oge.

'He will have to do something now?'

'He will.'

'Whatever it is, I'll stand by him as he stood by me. I'm not going home tonight, Mickeen Oge.'

'No?'

'No. I'll go out to see him tomorrow.'

'Very good!' said Mickeen Oge. 'I'll go with you. I have the old car here.'

VI

Paddy Bawn and Ellen Roe went home in their tub-cart and had not a single word or a glance for each other on the road. And all that evening, at table or at fireside, a heart-sickening silence held them in its unloosening grip. And all that night they lay side by side still and mute. There was but one disastrous thing in both their minds, and on that neither would speak. He was an Enright and she was a Danaher, and the feud was on. They slept little.

Ellen Roe, her heart desolate, lay on her side, her dry eyes closed, repentant for the grievous thing she had said, yet knowing that she could not unsay it. Disproof had to come first – but how – how?

Paddy Bawn lay on his back, his open eyes staring into the dark, and his inner vision seeing things with a cold clarity. He realised that he was at the fork of life, and that a finger pointed unmistakably. There was only one thing to do. He must shame man and woman in the face of the world. He must shatter his own happiness in this world and the next. He must do a thing so final and decisive that never again could it be questioned. And there was just one small hope that a miracle would take place. He cursed himself. 'Damn you, you fool! You might have known that you should never have taken a Danaher without first breaking O'Danaher.'

He rose early in the morning at his usual hour and went out as usual to his morning chores – rebedding and foddering his few cattle, rubbing down the half-bred, helping the servant-maid with the creaming-pans – and at the usual hour he came in to breakfast and ate it unhungrily and silently, which was not usual. Thereafter, he again went out to the stable, harnessed the gelding and hitched him to the tub-cart. Then he returned to the kitchen and spoke to his wife for the first time that morning.

'Ellen Roe, will you come down to Moyvalla with me to see your brother?'

She threw her hands wide in a hopeless, helpless gesture as much as to say, 'What's the use?'

'I must go,' said he. 'Will you come, please?'

She hesitated. 'Very well,' she said then, tonelessly. 'But, if I set foot inside Moyvalla, there I may stay, Paddy Bawn.'

'That is on me,' he said bleakly, 'and I will take the blame now or later. 'Tis Enright or Danaher this day – and Enright it is before the face of God!'

'I will be ready in a minute,' said Ellen, and her heart stirred in her.

And they went the four miles down into the vale towards the farm of Moyvalla. It was a fine, clear mid-October morning, and a perfect day for harvesting the potato crop or threshing corn. As they turned out of the cross-roads at Lisselton they met Sean

Glynn and Mickeen Oge Flynn chugging along in an ancient touring-car.

'A slack season of the year,' lied Sean, 'and being as far as Listowel we thought we would come out and see ye.'

'Ye are welcome,' said Ellen Roe, and looked at her husband.

Paddy Bawn's heart had lifted in his breast at the sight of his two friends. Whatever befell, these men would stand by him – and God was good after all.

'I am glad to see ye,' he said. 'Will ye come with me now and be my witnesses and –' he fixed them with his eye – 'leave it in my hands?'

'Anywhere – anyhow,' said Mickeen Oge.

The gelding went off at its reaching trot, and the car couldn't do much better than hold its place. So they drove into the big square of cobbled yard of Moyvalla and found it empty.

On one side of the square was the long, low, lime-washed farm-house; on the opposite side, fifty yards distant, the two-storied line of steadings with a wide arch in the middle; and through the arch came the purr and zoom of a threshing-machine.

As Paddy Bawn tethered the half-bred to the wheel of a farm-cart, a slattern servant-girl leaned over the kitchen half-door and pointed through the arch. The master was beyont in the haggard – an' would she run for him?

'Never mind, colleen,' called Paddy Bawn. 'I'll get him. Ellen, will you go in and wait?'

'I'll come with you,' said Ellen quietly, and, when her husband was not looking, she beckoned with her head to his two friends – and hers, she hoped. She knew the man her brother was.

As they went through the arch the purr and zoom grew louder, and, turning a corner, they walked into the midst of activity. A long double-row of cone-pointed corn-stacks stretched across the haggard, and, between, Matt Tobin's portable threshing-machine was working full steam. The smooth-flying eight-foot driving-wheel made a sleepy purr, and the black driving-belt ran with a sag and sway to the red-painted thresher. Up there on the platform, bare-armed men were feeding the drum with unbound corn-sheaves, their hands moving in a rhythmic swing; and as the toothed drum bit at the ears it made a gulping snarl that changed and slowed to a satisfied zoom. The wide conveying-belt was carrying the straw up a steep incline to where many men were building a long rick; other men were perched forking on the truncated cones of the stacks; still more men were attending to the corn-shoots and shoulder-bending under the weight of full sacks as they ambled across to the granary. Matt Tobin himself bent at the face of his engine, his bowler hat on his back hairs, feeding the firebox with divots of black hard peat. In all there were not less than two-score men about the place, for, as was the custom, Red Will's friends and neighbours were choring him at the threshing – the 'day in harvest' that is half work, half play, full of wit, devilment and horseplay, with a dance in the evening and a little courting on the side.

Red Will O'Danaher came round the flank of the engine and swore. He was open-necked, in his shirt-sleeves, and his broad chest and great forearms were covered with sandy hair.

'Hell and blazes! Look who's here!'

He was in the worst of tempers this fine morning that was made for pleasant labour and the shuttle-play of Kerry wit. The stale dregs of yesterday's whiskey had put him in a humour that, as they say, would make a dog bite its father. He took two slow strides and halted, feet apart and head truculently forward.

'What is it this time?' he shouted – an un-Irish welcome, indeed.

Paddy Bawn and Ellen Roe came forward steadily, Sean and Mickeen Oge pacing behind; and, as they came, Matt Tobin slowly throttled down his engine. Red Will heard the change of pitch and looked angrily over his shoulder.

'What the devil do you mean, Tobin? Get on with the work!'

'To the devil with yourself, Red Will! This is my engine.' And Matt drove the throttle shut, and the purr of the flywheel slowly sank.

'We'll see in a minute,' threatened the big man and turned to the two near at hand.

'What is it?' he growled.

'A private word with you,' said Paddy Bawn. 'I won't keep you long.'

'You will not – on a busy morning,' sneered Red Will. 'You ought to know by now that there is no need for private words between me and you.'

'There is need,' urged Paddy Bawn. 'It will be best for you to hear what I have to say in your own house.'

'Or here on my own land. Out with it! I don't care who hears.'

He looked over Paddy Bawn's head at Mickeen Oge and Sean Glynn, his eyes fearless.

'Is the IRA in this too?' he enquired contemptuously.

'We are here as Paddy Bawn's friends,' said Sean mildly.

'The IRA is not in this, O'Danaher,' said Mickeen Oge, and he threw up his lean head and looked slowly round the haggard. There was something in that bleak look that chilled even Red Will. 'If the IRA were in this, not even the desolation of desolation would be as desolate as Moyvalla,' that look seemed to say.

Paddy Bawn looked round him too. Upon the thresher, up on the stacks, over there on the rick, men leaned on fork handles and looked at him; here and there about the stack yard men moved in to see, as it might be, what had caused the stoppage, but only really interested in the two brothers-in-law. He saw that he was in the midst of the Clan Danaher, for they were mostly of the Danaher kin: big, strong, blond men, rough, confident, proud of their breed. Mickeen Oge, Sean Glynn, Matt Tobin were the only men he could call friends. Many of the others were not unfriendly, but all had contempt in their eyes, and, what was worse, pity.

Very well so! The stage was set, and Red Will wanted it so. And it was not unfitting that it be set here amongst the Danaher men. Deep down in Paddy Bawn a hackle lifted.

He brought his eyes back to Red Will – deep-set eyes that did not waver.

'O'Danaher,' said he, and he no longer hid his contempt, 'you set great store by money?'

'No harm in that? You do yourself, Patcheen.'

'Take it so. It is the game I am forced to play with you till hell freezes.' In stress he used strange little Americanisms. 'You bargained away your sister and played cheat, but I will not be cheated by any Danaher that ever sucked miser's milk. Listen, you big brute! You owe me a hundred pounds. Will you pay it?'

There was some harsh quality in his voice that was actually awesome. Red Will, ready to start forward overbearingly, took a fresh thought, and restrained himself to a brutal playfulness.

'Oho! Yankee fighting cock! I will pay what I like when I like.'

'One hundred pounds – today.'

'No. Nor tomorrow.'

'Right! That breaks all bargains.'

'What's that?'

'If you keep your hundred pounds, you keep your sister.'

'What is it?' shouted Red Will. 'What's that you say?'

'You heard me. Here is your sister Ellen. Keep her!'

'Fires o' hell!' He was astounded out of his truculence. 'You can't do that.'

'It is done,' said Paddy Bawn Enright.

VII

Ellen Roe had been quiet as a mouse at Paddy Bawn's shoulder. But now, slow like doom, she faced him, and he was compelled to look at her. Eye to eye, and behind the iron of his, she saw the pain.

'To the mother of your son, Paddy Bawn Enright?' Only he heard that whisper.

'To my treasure of the world – before the face of God. Let Him judge me.'

'I know – I know. Let Him direct you.'

That is all she said, and walked quietly across to where Matt Tobin stood at the face of the engine. Her two friends went with her, and Sean Glynn placed a firm hand on her arm.

'Give him time, Ellen Roe,' he whispered. 'This had to be, and all he needs is time. He's slow to start, maybe, but he's death's tiger when he moves.'

'Praises be to all the saints and devils that brought me here this day!' said Matt Tobin.

Mickeen Oge Flynn said nothing.

Big Will O'Danaher was no fool. Except when in a berserk rage, he knew as well as any man how far he could go; and, somehow, the berserk rage was chilled in him at birth this morning. Some indomitable quality in the small man warned him that brute force would not serve any purpose. He used his head. Whatever disgrace might come to Paddy Bawn, public opinion would flay himself alive. He could never lift head again – and all over one hundred pounds. His inner vision saw mouths twisted in sly laughter, eyes leering in derision. The scandal on his name! Even now, that would come, but there might be time yet to lay the foundation of his future attitude – just a bit of fun at a Yankee upstart. That was it.

Thus the thoughts shuttled in his mind, while he thudded the ground with iron-shod heel. Suddenly, then, he threw up his head and bellowed his laugh.

'You damn little fool! Don't be taking things so seriously. I was only having my fun with you. What the hell are your dirty few pounds to the likes of me? Stay where you are, blast you!'

He ground round on his heel, strode off with a furious swing of shoulder and disappeared through the arch.

Paddy Bawn stood alone in that wide ring of men. The workers had come down off the rick and stack to see closer; and with the instinct of the breed they knew that no man dared interfere now. They moved back and aside, looked at one another, looked at Paddy Bawn and Ellen Roe, at her friends, frowned and shook their heads. This smallish man from Knockanore was at last displaying the force that was in him. They looked at him again and wondered. Could he fight? Oh, bah! They knew their Red Will, and they knew that, yielding up the money, his savagery might break out into an explosion in which this little man's boxing tricks would be no more use than a rotten kippen. They waited, most of them, to prevent that savagery going too far.

Paddy Bawn Enright did not look at anyone. He stood easily in their midst, his hands deep in his pockets, one shoulder hunched forward, his eyes on the ground, and his face strangely unconcerned. He seemed the least perturbed man there. Perhaps he was remembering the many times he had sat in his corner and waited for the bell. Matt Tobin whispered in Ellen's ear, 'God is good, I tell you.' But Ellen's eyes, looking and looking at her husband, saw their own god.

Red Will was back in two minutes and strode straight down on Paddy Bawn.

'Look, Patcheen!' In his raised hand was a crumpled bundle of greasy bank-notes. 'Here is your money! Take it – and what's coming to you! Take it!' He thrust it into Paddy Bawn's hand. 'Count it. Make sure you have it all – and then get kicked out of my haggard. And look!' He thrust forward that great hairy right hand. 'If ever I see your face again I will drive that through it. Count it, you spawn!'

Paddy Bawn did not count it. Instead, he crumpled it into a ball in his strong fingers. Then he turned on his heel and walked with cool slowness to the face of the engine. He gestured with one hand to Matt Tobin, but it was Ellen Roe, quick as a flash, who obeyed the gesture. Though the hot bar scorched her hand, she jerked open the door of the firebox, and the leaping peat flames whispered out at her. And, forthwith, Paddy Bawn, with one easy sweep of the arm, threw the crumpled ball of bank-notes into the heart of the flames. The whisper lifted one tone, and a scrap of charred paper floated out of the funnel top. That was all the fuss the fire made of its work.

There was fuss enough outside.

Red Will gave one mighty shout. 'No!' It was more an anguished yell than an honest shout.

'My money – my good money!'

He sprang into the air, came down in his tracks, made two furious bounds forward, and his great arms came flinging to crush and kill. Berserk at last!

But those flinging fists never touched the small man.

'You dumb ox!' said Paddy Bawn between his teeth, and seemed to glide below the flinging arms.

That strong hunched shoulder moved a little, but no one there could follow the terrific drive of that hooked right arm. The smash of bone on bone was sharp as whip-crack, and Red Will, two hundred pounds of him, stopped dead, went back on his heels, swayed a moment and staggered three paces.

'Now and forever, man of the Enrights!' roared Matt Tobin, ramming his bowler hat over his head and levering it loose again.

But Red Will O'Danaher was a mighty man. That blow should have laid him on his back – blows like it had tied men to the floor for the full count. Red Will only shook his head, grunted like a boar and threw all his weight at the smaller man. Now would the Danaher men see an Enright torn apart!

But the little man, instead of circling away, drove in at the big fellow, compact of power, every hackle lifted, explosive as dynamite. Tiger Enright was in action.

The men of the Danahers saw then an exhibition that they had not knowledge enough to appreciate fully, but that they would not forget all their days. Multitudes had paid as much as ten dollars a head to see Tiger Enright in action: his footwork, his timing, his hitting from all angles, the sheer explosive ferocity of the man. But never was his action more devastating than now. He was a thunderbolt on two feet. All the stored dislike of years was in his two terrible hands.

And the big man was a glutton. He took all that was coming and came for more. He never once touched his opponent with clenched fist. He did not know how. The small man was not there when the great fist came hurtling, yet the small man was the aggressor from first to last. His very speed made him that. Actually forty pounds lighter, he drove Red Will by sheer hitting back and fore across the yard. Men, for the first time, saw a two-hundred-pound man knocked clean off his feet by a body blow.

Five minutes. In five packed minutes Paddy Bawn Enright demolished his enemy. Four – six – eight times he sent the big man neck-and-crop to the ground, and each time the big man scrambled furiously to his feet, staggering, bleeding, slavering, raving, vainly trying to rend and kill. But at last he stood swaying, mouth open, and hands clawing futilely: and Paddy Bawn finished the fight with his dreaded double hit, left below the breast-bone and right under the jaw.

Red Will lifted on his toes, swayed and fell flat on his back. He did not even kick as he lay.

Paddy Bawn did not waste a glance on the fallen giant. He swung full circle on the Danaher men; he touched his breast with middle finger, his voice of iron challenged them.

'I am Patrick Enright of Knockanore Hill. Is there a Danaher amongst you thinks himself a better man? Come, then.'

His face was like a hard stone, his great chest lifted, the air whistled in his nostrils; his deep-set flashing eyes dared and daunted them.

'Come, Danaher men!'

No man came.

'*Mo yerm thu, a Phadraig Ban!* My choice thou, white Patrick!' That was Matt Tobin's exultant bugle.

Paddy Bawn walked straight across to his wife and halted before her. His face was still cold as stone, but his voice, quiet as it was, had in it some dramatic quality full of life and the eagerness of life.

'Mother of my son, will you come home with me?'

She lifted to the appeal voice and eye.

'Is it so you ask me?'

'As my wife only, Ellen Roe Enright?'

'Very well, heart's treasure.' She caught his arm in both her hands. 'Let us be going. Come, friends!'

'God is good, surely,' said Paddy Bawn.

And she went with him, proud as the morning, out of that place. But, a woman, she would have the last word.

'Mother o' God!' she cried. 'The trouble I had to make a man of him!'

'God Almighty did that for him before you were born,' said Mickeen Oge sternly.

The Red Girl

The Red Girl, who now sings her,
Dead two hundred years?
The lost one! No word of praise,
No prayer, not even tears
Shall call to mind the Faith she held and died for:
Thou shalt not love a traitor,
Yield mercy to a spy,
Who sell what men will fight for,
Strive for, dream for, die:
The Love of Land, the Faith of Men, and Honour.

———————

Chapter One

The hotel lounge was Big Michael Flynn's best room: wide and low, with a beamed ceiling, open hearth, comfortable chairs, and many windows looking down on Lough Aonach a quarter-mile below. And it was strictly reserved for the anglers – and the ladies who owned the anglers. There were five people in it now: Major-General Kelly Cuthbert and his niece Kate O'Brien; Marcus Caverley and his daughter Betty; and Major Archibald MacDonald. And, curiously enough, they were talking of the tragic legend of the Red Girl.

The Major-General, softly drawing on his after-dinner cigar, stood looking down on the four grouped round a card-table near the French window; and Archibald MacDonald, lean and serious, leisurely dealt the cards and murmured, as if to himself, speculatively but not sceptically:

'I wonder! Was there ever a Red Girl – in fact?'

'In fact – beyond doubt,' said Kate O'Brien and added, 'her name was my name.'

'Of your blood?'

'Of my race – and yours perhaps.'

She picked up her cards and slowly sorted four high spades in a strong hand. The spades were no darker than her hair, and the white ground of the cards was lifeless compared with the clean pallor of her face. A fine, sorrowful timbre came into her voice:

'More than two hundred years ago, in Stuart times, when the fate of Europe was played out on Irish ground, and Irish ground was wet with Irish blood, she lived and loved – and died – oh! so young. A renegade Irishman betrayed her lover to the Sassenach, and her lover died – and the traitor died – and the Red Girl died too. But, it is said, her unquiet spirit moves still about Castle Aonach; and it is said, too, that she is only seen when a renegade Irishman has to die.'

'Do you believe that nonsense, Miss O'Brien?' enquired the hard-headed Marcus Caverley. 'You sound like it.'

'Perhaps I only believe that an Irish renegade should not be in life.'

'When was she last seen?' Major MacDonald looked interrogatively at the dark girl, his brows down, and she nodded.

'Yes, you might remember – you were a prisoner here about that time. The Black-and-Tan war. She was seen, and a man was found drowned in *Poul Cailin Rua*, the Red Girl's pool.' Her voice was lowered. 'He was an Irishman, but those who know will not say that he was a traitor.'

'Martin Kierley?'

She nodded.

'Probably executed by Mickeen Oge Flynn and his IRA gunmen!' put in the soldier warmly.

'Not by guns, uncle – drowned.'

MacDonald was looking at his cards, his face queerly saturnine.

'He had a wife – this Kierley?' he half queried.

'Nuala Kierley – and no traitor. She did not fail.'

'What happened her?'

'I wish we knew. She disappeared – absolutely.'

'Better she suffered the fate of the Red Girl,' and then he murmured to himself an old and remembered scrap of talk. 'Where is she now, how does she live, what does she sell?'

Betty Caverley stirred restlessly in her chair. She was a slender girl – flaxen-haired, with soft grey eyes and delicate colouring, but any discerning eye must see that she was of the blood and bone of the hale and ruddy Englishman, her father. Now she spoke gently but definitely.

'Young Michael Flynn would not do anything – dishonourable. I am certain of that.'

The Major-General agreed promptly. 'So am I, Miss Caverley, but a soldier has sometimes to do terrible things, and – probably – Mickeen Oge considered himself a soldier.'

'And a mighty good one – as I know,' put in Major MacDonald. 'No bid, partner.'

'Considers himself a soldier yet, doesn't he?' said Marcus Caverley. 'Keeping his Irregulars alive and all that – dumps of arms –'

'Under our feet, for all we know,' said the Major-General, his voice suddenly quiet.

His dark-haired niece twitched her shoulders in some irritation.

'Take your rank cigar out of here, uncle!' she urged. 'We want to get on with this rubber.' She looked up at him under curving eyebrows.

'And do not forget that you are an Irishman yourself, and not a very good one, some say.'

'I'm not ashamed of my Irish blood – and the Empire.' He turned and stumped straight-backed through the French window.

Kate O'Brien called after him. 'You should never fish *Poul Cailin Rua* unless Mickeen Oge is with you – and you never do. I am going three spades.'

Major-General Kelly Cuthbert stumped across to the veranda rail, and the smoke spurted furiously through the white brush of his moustache. But he was not a particularly choleric man, and the serene, silken-velvet sunset sheen of Lough Aonach, shining down below between the scattered trees, soon soothed him. Tomorrow, at last, might be a grand fishing day – with an occasional sunny shower – and a venturesome grilse or two up from Dunmore Bay in the lower river pools. His inner eye saw the two-piece greenheart curving to a lively five-pounder below the rocks at *Poul Cailin Rua* – and Mickeen Oge, poised on a rock, cursing his own bad luck. It was a grand world, and the retired soldier had his foot on its neck.

He was roused from his pleasant vision by the rattle of the hotel car coming round from the garage at the back. It slithered on the gravel below the veranda, and Big Michael Flynn, the hotel keeper, an immensely corpulent man, came nimbly down the steps from the porch to say a word to the driver. The driver was the Mickeen Oge Flynn – small young Michael – of the Major-General's thoughts, and he was neither small, nor yet youthful; his Gaelic by-name was merely used to distinguish him from his uncle, Big Michael, in a territory where Flynns and Michaels were as common as blackthorn bushes.

The Major-General took his cigar from his lips. 'Where are you off to, young fellow?' He liked Mickeen Oge in spite of his hellish brand of politics.

'Castletown Junction, General.'

'Damn! Who's coming?'

Mickeen Oge's face in repose had the quiet gravity of one of the great masks, but, when his mouth twitched out of its firm line, the antic mind peeped into the light of day. He jerked a thumb towards his uncle.

'The old thief there, General – ask him.'

The General looked down at Big Michael, undefined suspicion alive in his eye, and Big Michael looked up, frank guilelessness in his.

'A commercial traveller?' queried the soldier. He did not object greatly to commercial travellers. They stayed only one night, did not interfere in any way with the fishing, and, after the retiral of the ladies, brought forth a brand of anecdote astonishingly salacious and not without humour.

'A Mr O'Connor it is,' said Big Michael, not very informatively.

'An angler?'

'A Yankee,' said Mickeen Oge.

'An Irish-American! Hell's blazes!'

The French window was ajar behind him, and a brown, lean face appeared in the slit. 'Try the soft pedal, Munster Fusilier,' advised the quiet Highland drawl.

'The ladies don't mind, but I was brought up in a Calvinist battalion.'

The soldier strode to the window, shut it smartly and stamped back to the rail. The moment his back was turned, the window reopened noiselessly.

'What's this bloody fellow coming for?'

'To tell us how America won the War,' suggested Mickeen Oge.

'Sure, maybe, he won't be staying long,' said Big Michael hopefully.

'That's torn it.' The soldier knew his Big Michael. 'He'll be here all summer. Why did you let the fat old donkey do it, Mickeen Oge? That damned Yankee will have four steamer trunks, each as big as a hearse, plastered all over with hotel labels – from Trondhjem to Stamboul – collected in the ten days he has taken to telescope Europe. And he'll fish too – with those silly steel-core contraptions that never played a fish honestly. Oh Hell! I never met a Yankee who could work in low water, and he'll frighten every damn fish from here to Dounbeg.'

Neither war, pestilence, nor skin-flaying vituperation had any power to perturb Big Michael Flynn.

'I'll lave ye at it,' he said, laughed pleasantly and bounded up the porch steps lively as a rubber ball. 'You'll be fine and late for the train, Michaeleen,' he called and disappeared.

The engine roared, and the old flivver bucketed and scuttered down the short curve of drive to the main road that margined the long sweep of the shore.

'We've heard you do better, soldier man,' said the quiet voice from the French window.

And the sunset peace of Lough Aonach had to do its work over again on the irate soldier.

II

Mickeen Oge Flynn, as his uncle had told him, was fine and late for
the train – all of fifteen minutes, which is considered commendably
punctual in everyday Irish affairs, but not for train schedules.
Hurrying through the narrow-arched entrance to the platform at
Castletown Junction, he found it deserted, except for a solitary
porter who sat on a couple of oldish leather suitcases and fingered
a pair of canvas-covered fishing-rods secured inside the straps.

''Tis a greenheart, Mickeen Oge, but that one by the feel of it is a
split cane.'

'Whose, Jureen?'

'A Mr O'Connor.' The porter bent to the direction tag. 'Mr Art
O'Connor, passenger from Cobh to Castletown Junction for Lough
Aonach – your man.'

'Where are the steamer trunks?' He looked round the packed gravel
spread.

'Divil the scrap more.'

'A new type of Yankee! Where is he?'

'Yankee! Man, he spoke as quiet as yourself.' The porter gestured
with a thumb. 'Above at John Molouney's. He travelled up in the one
carriage with Kelty Murphy and John Tom Kissane – free an' aisy as
you like, and Kelty Buie tellin' them murderin' stories of his – you
know? I was to follow them across when you turned up, an' me sayin'
you wouldn't be much more than an hour late whatever.'

'Never told the truth in your life, Jureen.'

'Sure, what harm – an' what hurry? I was sittin' here, Mickeen Oge,
waitin' an' thinkin' to myself that when the hurry was on us it was
always Mickeen Oge Flynn was first in the gap – and his the gap at
hinder end. Them was the days.'

'Shut up, you dreamer, and bring along that baggage!'

And, looking at the grey-blue eyes grown suddenly bleak, Jureen
the porter shook his head and manhandled the bags.

They found the three men grouped round a corner of the high zinc-
covered counter of John Molouney's bar, and one was unmistakably
the visitor. He was drinking brown stout out of a pewter tankard and
listening to a short, flexible-mouthed man who was holding forth in a
marvellously rich and resonant voice.

'Shawn the Skillet we used call him back of Leacca, and coming on winter he used to be making a drop of poteen – moonshine ye call it beyant in the States, and a grand name to be sure! Wait a minute, Mickeen Oge, till I finish this one for Mr O'Connor; you'll be havin' a glass of stout – and a pint for Jureen, John. Well and fine, sir! at a certain season of the year, when the corn was all done and a man couldn't get a bag o' malt for love or money, Shawn the Skillet used to be thinking to himself that it was time to be making his peace with God and going to his Easter duty.' He looked interrogatively at his visitor.

'I know.' He nodded. 'Making his annual confession.'

'To be sure – you'll be a Catholic yourself, sir. Telling parish priest, old Father MacOwen, with the grating of the confession box between himself and the holy man, that at odd times, and the devil tempting him, he would be running a drop of poteen unbeknownst, God forgive us all! And sorry for it he would be, and promising God and Father Mac never again to build a turf fire under a still – barrin' the temptation was too strong and the price right. For ten, or it could be fifteen, years he told the same tale, and devil the tale else, and for the same length of time Father Mac put the same penance on him: five pounds to the Vincent de Paul Society and a decket of the rosary once a day for a week. He told me so himself. Faith, it was a poor day for the Vincent de Pauls when the police nabbed Shawn's still at the long last. They didn't nab Shawn, though.

'Well, sir! one Eastertide down comes Shawn from Leacca, and, without looking before him, pops into the old confession box and – cripes alive! – 'tisn't Father Mac was in it at all at the other side of the grating, but a young curate new-ordained from Maynooth College. "Murther!" says Shawn to himself. "My goose is cooked – me name is mud, but sure, God is good, an' I'll make sure of my man another year." So he ups and tells the young priest this and that, things wouldn't hurt a fly, and, when the well is dry, he takes a hitch on himself and tells about the making of the poteen. It was terrible, I tell you. It was a shocking thing. For in Maynooth College they do be teaching the young clericals that poteen is the ruin of the west, a depraver of souls, a curse out of the pits o' hell, made and retailed by servants of ould Nick himself – och, be japers! The young priest said all that and more, and when he couldn't think of anything else to say, he was in a quandary about what he would do to the poor penitent and him groaning – slap on a poultice of a penance that would hold Shawn on his knees till Lady Day in harvest, or send him up to the bishop himself. "Wait there, you old reprobate!" and out of the box with him and across to the side-chapel, where Father Mac was hearing confessions, one a minute. "Father Mac," says he, whispering, "there is an old scoundrel over there that confesses to making poteen. What should I give him?" "Give him, is it?" says Father Mac. "That robber Shawn o' the Skillet! Don't give him a penny more than five shillings a pint – and make sure 'tis the second run." Ay, faith!'

Under cover of the laughter, Mickeen Oge, who had been hearing that story since he was a boy, finished his glass of draught stout and turned to the visitor. 'Ready when you are, Mr O'Connor,' he said and went out to the car. He rather liked the look of that American. A good listener, and not given to 'shooting his neck.'

He was bending over the crank handle when the visitor's voice at his shoulder made him pause.

'By the way, I did not quite catch your name?'

'Michael Flynn, Mr O'Connor.'

'The hotel keeper?'

'His nephew. They call me Mickeen Oge.'

'Mickeen Oge Flynn! I thought so. You know, Mr Flynn, I have heard that name in the mouths of men far from here.'

Mickeen Oge's face, bent over the crank, gave no sign. It could be that, wherever Irishmen wandered, his name might be among the few not forgotten – but only for a little while.

'Whale of a fighting man!' murmured the American softly, as if quoting some remembered phrase.

Mickeen Oge's smile mocked himself only.

'Not much fighting left in us now. All it ever got me was half a year in jail – internment camp, if you like.'

Suddenly the engine roared to the kick of the crank handle.

'Care to sit in front, sir?'

'Certainly.'

As they rattled along the uphill road winding below the curving brown breasts of the hills, this American, Art O'Connor, was thinking to himself. So this serious-faced man in rough tweeds was the Mickeen Oge Flynn that his partner, Owen Jordan, talked so much about. Great guerilla fighter, hunger striker, incorruptible republican – and now driving a flivver for an angler's hotel! Some come-down in the world. Perhaps only a blind! For if Owen Jordan was right, the republican organisation was still underground. None of his business. He himself had an Irish name, but that was all. He wanted no labels

tied to him. He would see things for himself, discover the quality of
men for himself, sense for himself this Irish atmosphere before he said
one word of his friend in New Mexico. Perhaps the Irish blood in him
might respond to some things, but in no event would he lose his head
– and certainly not his heart.

Mickeen Oge was thinking too, considering the American in his
own mind. He had the marks of a sound man, and they were not
many: not blatant – calm; laughing in a middle register at things
worth laughing at, his voice cool and slow, taking its own time to
savour the run of thought in the mind of himself and others; and one
look at the brown neck and face above the loose-cut flannels showed
that he was no cave-dweller amongst sky-scrapers. The sort of man
who would be able to hold his own, even among a team of hard-shell,
jealous fishermen. All the same, it might not be a bad thing to give
him a small hint or two of the peculiar prejudices and atmosphere up
at the hotel.

He throttled the car down to its easiest pace, and his voice rose
above the rattle.

'You'll be for trying the fishing, Mr O'Connor?'

'Hope to.' He looked up at the high, clear sky, deepening for
twilight, and around him at the thirsty hillsides, grey-green in drought
below the purple of the bell heather. 'Not fishing weather, is it?'

'You may say it. Not a grilse or sea-trout landed in ten days –
honestly – but the trout-fishing on the lough is not bad.'

'Big fellows?'

'And shy – shy as heifers. You'll never fill a bag, but the ones you
land you'll be glad you landed.'

'Good fishing that!'

'And if we get a drop of rain – more than our share oftener than not
– there'll be grilse in every pool down to Dounbeg – ten miles.'

'Fine! The weather is due to give us a break some time.'

'And break all to hell when it does. One good thing, we are off the
beaten track here, and not many know the pretty fair fishing we have.
Those that do –' Mickeen Oge paused.

'Want to keep it to themselves. I get you. So would I. I guess I'll be
no welcome visitor?'

'You will not,' agreed Mickeen Oge.

'How many may I expect to pile me?'

'Four or five – and maybe four or five more when the weather
is right.'

'Just eight or nine too many.'

'Fishermen are the devil,' said Mickeen Oge. 'Major MacDonald would cut the liver out of you to get the first run of a pool, and there's no better man I know; and old Caverley would card you in one of his own mills before he'd tell you where a fish lies. Myself, I'd only bite your ear. The ladies are all right.'

'Snakes! Are there ladies too?'

'Miss Caverley and Kate – Miss Kate O'Brien – and she'll argue with you from dawn to dark and back again. She's niece to Major-General Kelly Cuthbert.'

'British general?'

'He is. We have him too. He will be of the opinion that you are of the opinion that America won the war. Would you rather be hanged or drowned?'

'Boiled. I'm in for a thin time, evidently?'

'There is no harm in him – the General. And there might be a bit of fun going too,' said the Irishman.

'I'll let you in on it. Thank you for warning me, Mr Flynn.' Already he was beginning to appreciate this man.

'Not a word,' said Mickeen Oge, and bore down on the accelerator.

III

A few minutes after ten, Big Michael Flynn, as was his nightly custom, came light-footed into the lounge.

Major MacDonald and Marcus Caverley were bending over a glass-topped table scattered with bright-coloured feathers, tinsel, silk thread, gut, and scraps of red and brown wax. The Highlandman was showing the Yorkshireman the only proper wing-set for a famous fly he called 'the Blue Charm,' in which the hackle only was blue. They were so engrossed that they took no notice of Big Michael, though they knew he was there.

Major-General Kelly Cuthbert was recumbent in a deep leather chair, his white moustache calm on his red healthy face, but the mind within glad of the coming of Big Michael, so that the usual night-cap be ordered – a particularly stiff Irish whiskey and small soda. His niece, Kate O'Brien, sat reading near the French window, which was wide open; and from the veranda outside came Betty Caverley's soft, almost sibilant English voice.

'Good-night, small Michael young! Will tomorrow be a fishing day?'

She had a quaint habit of translating directly Mickeen Oge's by-name, and Kate O'Brien noted that she was the only one that ever called and always called him by his proper name. She made Michael, as it were, her very own.

His voice, leisurely and mocking, floated up from the gravel drive. 'No, young lady. It will be the very devil and all of a fine day.'

'Major MacDonald says the trout might take on a night like this – on the lough, you know.'

'Not with thunder about. Tomorrow night, now, the moon would be about right.'

'That will be splendid, Michael.'

'Get off with you! Try the Major.'

'But –'

'Try him – he's tough! You try him. Out there in a boat – in the moonlight – you'd be tempting the Angel Gabriel.'

'I'd prefer to tempt someone else, Michael.'

'Very well so, small girl! I could give Gabriel points, anyway. Good night now and have sense – and say your prayers.'

Kate O'Brien smiled to herself. Mickeen Oge had a way of addressing this girl as if she still wore pigtails. She had been coming to the hotel with her father for a long time now, and, perhaps, he had not noticed her growing from friendly adolescence to a dangerous maturity. Watch out, Michaeleen!

His feet crunched away on the gravel, and Betty Caverley came back into the lounge. Her grey eyes were lustrous and frank under lashes that were darker than her hair, and her slim arms and neck were alarmingly lovely.

'Michael and I are going fishing tomorrow night,' she proclaimed; and her father turned and looked at her speculatively for a moment, and a small nerve at a mouth corner twitched half humorously, half anxiously.

'Betty Caverley,' said Major MacDonald, without looking up from the wings of his Blue Charm, 'I'm done with you – and I'm no Angel Gabriel either – nor is your young Michael.'

'May I come with you, Betty?' asked Kate O'Brien smoothly.

'Delighted, Kate, dear.'

The Irish girl's mocking smile held till Betty's colour deepened. 'You English are so equably kind-hearted.' She patted Betty's arm. 'Never mind, dear! You can't help being dangerous.'

Big Michael bent between the two men at the glass-topped table.

'Lift it, Major,' he urged. 'That back wing – just a taste! The water will do the flattening. I'm putting a small piece of ice in the lager.'

'Yes – small!' said MacDonald abstractedly.

''Tis a good drink – I'm having one myself.'

'On me, no doubt.'

The big man came across to the Major-General and placed a finger on the smooth-jacketed shoulder – an act of impertinence in any man but this big easy lord of his own domain. Through years of acquaintanceship there had grown some unassuming inner tie of friendship between the two.

'Well, General, another dry day over us, thank God! The same again?'

'Better if you have it.' He cocked a live blue eye. 'Your damn Yank arrived yet?'

'Ay, faith! And a cool lad. Wanting to know if the white trout he was having for his supper was honest caught.'

'White trout! Who caught it?'

'It was't honest caught, whoever caught it,' came the quiet Highland drawl.

'Honest as the daylight and the water,' protested Big Michael, 'and a coupleen more for the morning's breakfast.' He turned to the ladies and marked off an inch on a big forefinger. 'That much, young ladies – my own special compounding?'

'What is in it, Michael Big?' enquired Betty Caverley, laughing.

'Heather honey – so much, a leaf of mint, the drawing of two carraway seeds, the soak of a ripe sloe and the squeeze of a lemon.'

'And the kick?' Kate O'Brien wanted to know.

'Just a small flavouring of grain whiskey – as much as would blind your eye – and divil the hurt or harm in it.'

'Then we will have just so much – or a taste more. Are you letting the American in on us?'

'Sure, it would be good, but maybe not safe for any man to be looking at the both of ye,' said Big Michael, and took his big body nimbly to the door.

In the passage outside he met the American, Art O'Connor.

'Before I shut the bar, Mr O'Connor,' he enquired, 'would you be caring for anything?'

'On your life, Mr Flynn. What about some of your Guinness out of a pewter tankard?'

'Fine, sir! Try it out of silver. The lounge is in there.'

Big Michael ambled down the passage to the private bar where he found his nephew leaning on the counter, an account book under his eyes. He thumped him softly on the shoulder as he slipped inside the raised flap.

'Is it a drink you're after this time o' night, Mickeen Oge?'

'No-o-o – I don't think so.'

'You'll change your mind, maybe. I hear you're taking our Miss Betty fishing tomorrow night?'

'Not likely to catch anything either.'

Big Michael reached down a bottle here and there. 'There's fishing – and fishing,' he remarked carelessly.

'And there's only one kind that I do, Michael Mor.'

'Amn't I knowing it, *avic* – amn't I knowing it? But aren't you a bitter fellow, and you so young?'

'Young and bitter – am I?'

'You are then – sometimes. And small wonder, *avouchaleen*! Maybe it was wrong of me not to send you back to be a priest – and you with only two years to go.'

'Is it too late?' He smiled half cynically at the thought. 'Why not send me back to Maynooth tomorrow?'

'I will not, then,' said Big Michael firmly, 'unless the urge is on you – and I doubt it. If you must deny yourself, deny yourself like a man.' He looked at his nephew, solicitude in his eyes, still remembering this strong fighting man as the little lad he had reared. 'This place – the work – 'tis not fretting you, Michaeleen?'

'The only fret that's in it is a motherly old blether of an uncle.'

'Yerra, go to hell out o' that!'

Mickeen Oge straightened up. 'I will. What do you think of this American, Mr Art O'Connor? Queer name for a Yankee?'

''Tis. He'll hold his own, I'm thinking.'

'How did he find out about this place?'

'That's telling. He wrote a long time ago – you were off somewhere.'

'Where from?'

'Beyant. Montreal it was.'

'Montreal! That's Canada – that's the British Empire. We'll keep an eye on him.'

'Have sense, man! What the hell has the British Empire to do with us now?'

'As long as Ireland is not free – ay! and when it is – the British secret service will occasionally run its hands over us. A great empire, uncle, and its agents never sleep.' He moved across to the door. 'Leave the back door on the latch – I may be late.'

'Be careful now, Mickeen Oge!' warned his uncle seriously.

'Like a weasel,' said Mickeen Oge, and closed the door behind him.

Big Michael shook his head. The foolish lad! Hadn't he suffered enough for the old sod? Six months in jail, five weeks on hunger strike, a year hiding in the hills; and the spirit not yet broken in him. Pity now he wouldn't settle down and bring a wife to this house where a woman was wanted – and where she was not far away – not far away, surely. Och, well! God was good – and the young blood would work out its own urge.

IV

Art O'Connor, still in his loose flannels, slouched easily across the soft Dun-Emer rugs, his eyes quietly observant; and he noted that, after a single quick glance from all the eyes in the room, no eye again sought him.

'Good-night, ladies and gentlemen!' he saluted in an impersonal low voice and sank into a wicker chair near the open hearth.

Major MacDonald said something like 'Hugh-Hugh' affirmatively away down his throat, and went on whipping silk. And after a longish time gentle Betty Caverley murmured, 'Good-night.' That was all.

His eyes went over them one by one. There was the General, recumbent on his shoulder-blades, his face withdrawn with difficulty – no mistaking him; and the girl perched on the arm of the chair near the French window, who had returned his salutation in very shame, was fair English and daughter of the stoutish man at the side table – Caverley the name; and the dark girl pretending to read was Miss O'Brien – Kate O'Brien – dark Irish, pre-Celtic blood in her, proud as Lucifer and wanting the moon, of course! But my Lord! She had something in that grave, lean face of hers to set men marching. How was this Owen Jordan described her? 'A sexless patriot who would have nothing to do with men.' And a tarnation good job too! She would want all a man's soul to play with and ask for more. And there was Archibald MacDonald, tying a fly and not concerned with any American visitor; a cool, out-of-doors-looking customer with a family resemblance to his sister Margaid – though she had red hair. Hope she hadn't said anything about himself in her letters, for he looked the sort of man who could put two and two together.

So they were giving him the cold shoulder, sort of hoping to shoo him away from their own select little circle hidden in the hills. And it was out of these hills and valleys that his forebears had come, blood and bone and tough enduring spirit. Well, they would not shoo him away, and there was five cents on that. A small spark grew hot in him, and it was an Irish spark. Thunder! he would have to be careful, or this darned atmosphere would get him yet.

Might he smoke? Betty Caverley inclined a fair head. Kate O'Brien glanced at him for the second time. In that first quick glance, as he had crossed the floor, she had noted that he walked with the in-toed, slightly bow-legged slouch of the horseman; and now she noted his brown, weathered, strong-boned face, and his eyes – light-coloured eyes, as if they, like his eyebrows, had been bleached by sun and wind. This was no ordinary touring American in a hurry. He was lazy and tranquil and slouching, with a hint of some explosive reserve behind his eyes. Yes, his eyes interested her, quickened something in her. She looked at him a third time as he was lighting his pipe, and, even as she looked, his eyes lifted and met hers. Only for a second or two. He just looked, and then his eyes moved away, quite casually, without interest.

Kate O'Brien felt as if she had been detected – and ignored. The quickening increased to a tingle that was warm, almost angry, a shade resentful. And her face darkened over her book. She would get a little back on him presently.

Big Michael came in with the tray of drinks. The creamy head was rich and thick on the shining tankard he laid on a small table at Art O'Connor's side.

'A mouse could trot on it, Mr O'Connor,' he said.

'You should provide the mouse, Big Michael,' murmured the Major-General, without lifting his head.

'He'd be chasing the cat, General,' said Big Michael, and moved lightly towards the door. 'Good-night to ye all – and better luck tomorrow, with God's help!'

Art O'Connor sensed the prejudice behind the soldier's suggestion about the mouse, but he gave no sign. All right, soldier man! Cross swords if you want to.

They sampled their drinks, each in his or her own way, and Kelly Cuthbert reached for his briar pipe and leather pouch.

'Care to try mine, sir?' invited the American. 'A Virginian Cavendish.'

'No, thanks. I smoke Empire-grown.'

'I have tried it,' said the American, and the drawl of his voice condemned it as unsmokable filth.

'Good enough for me,' snapped the old soldier.

'No doubt,' said Art O'Connor smoothly.

The other looked at him with a cold yet choleric eye, turned to his whiskey, took a quick sip and then a deeper, cleared his throat as if about to retort, and thought better of it.

Major MacDonald grinned to himself. The General would be drawn like a badger in about two minutes, and deservedly so, but the exhibition would not be a pretty one. He rose to his long length, took hold of his crystal mug, came across to the fireplace and leant his shoulders against the high mantelpiece.

'You fish, Mr – O'Connor?'

'Darn you for a wily Scot!' said O'Connor to himself. 'I was getting his goat too.' And aloud he said, 'Some. The fishing is pretty slow about here, isn't it?'

'Not the best – just now. You fished in the States – California – New Mexico?'

A bright man this! Was he guessing who Art O'Connor was? Margaid might have written. After that careless question he was drinking pale lager, not greatly interested.

'Been fishing in Canada for a month,' Art O'Connor replied.

'Canada?'

'Yep. This very hour,' he looked at the ormolu clock under its glass dome behind MacDonald's shoulder, 'it will be only six o'clock over there, of course – but about this hour, two of my friends, with a net across the Gatineau and bricks holding it to the current, will be filling a canoe with twenty-pounders – if the game wardens do not catch them, which is part of the game.'

'Poaching! I see!' remarked the General to no one in particular.

'As ever was.' The American looked them over with a cool eye and smiled innocently. 'I've just had a poached trout for supper. Which of you caught it?'

Kate O'Brien laughed shortly, and it was a catching laugh for one who seemed almost saturnine. Art O'Connor looked at her accusingly interrogative, and she laughed again, shaking her head.

'I did not do it, but I might,' she answered that look.

'Why not? I do not blame anyone. If life here means killing fish, why not the stick of gelignite or bag of quicklime?'

'These have been tried,' said the Major-General, under forced calm, 'and fish have been caught – and six months in jail as well. You try it, sir,' he urged.

'I might not catch the reward, if I had a dollar or two handy.'

The other was at once the Irishman. 'Begad, sir! you cannot buy justice here as you can in America.'

'Possibly not.' He turned to his tankard and took a steady pull. He was getting something in on the fire-eater and would try a little more. But, when he laid down his tankard, he again found Kate O'Brien's eye meeting his.

'You are – Mr O'Connor, are you not?'

'Yes, Miss O'Brien.'

'Home to Ireland?'

'Hundred per cent American, I'm glad to say.'

'Irish descent?'

'Probably. One can't help that, can one?'

She looked at him steadily. 'One does not deserve it sometimes,' she said slowly.

'I mean,' he explained in his easy drawl, 'that Irish blood gets bred out of one in a generation or two – the dreaming stuff, the inhibitions, superstitions – all that Celtic twilight nonsense, you know?'

'I know – and one becomes a hard-headed, 100 per cent American.'

A sudden unreasoning hostility sprang up between these two. Not a dumb hostility, but one that had to be as vocal as steel blade meeting steel blade in thrust and parry.

'The dreaming stuff!' murmured Kate O'Brien. 'Do Americans never dream?'

'They wake up.'

'To say their prayers to the Almighty Dollar and grind the faces of the poor?'

'Not to export cattle and wheat – while a million Irish starved.'

'Touch!' She gave him the fencer's salute. 'You know your Irish history.'

'My great-grandfather starved in black '47.'

'Because he was a dreamer? And the 100 per cent American has not forgotten that. The Irish blood has not been quite bred out of you, Mr O'Connor.'

And so it went. By some subtle understanding they were no longer strangers to each other. They were frank, they were free, almost intimate, and oh! they were incisive. As Art O'Connor would put it in Americanese, 'they got each other's goat.' And though he had none the worse of it, deep down he was angry with himself for being drawn in drawing this vital dark woman.

The others looked on and listened. Somehow, they were outside the discussion, outside the ring, not considered at all by these two, whose spirits seemed to wrestle apart with a warmth not entirely engendered by the argument. Archibald MacDonald looked through the amber of his glass and smiled to himself. They were giving each other a lesson – and one deserved it.

And then the man, as if suddenly realising the heat in himself, finished the bout by drinking off his stout, rising to his feet, slouching his horseman's gait across the floor and calling a careless good-night from the door.

The Major-General kicked a rug with his heel and chuckled. The heat had gone out of him for some reason.

'A cool customer, dammit! He gave you hell, Kate.'

'He did quite well,' she said coolly.

Her uncle, aware of her political leanings, was sarcastic.

'Get Mickeen Oge and his Irregulars on to him.'

'You couldn't do that, Kate?' said Betty quickly.

Kate O'Brien laughed. 'Of course not. He got a trifle hot under the collar – and so did I. Did you see his Irish blood boiling? And I'll make it boil some more. One hundred per cent American, indeed!'

'Begad!' cried the Major-General. 'This damned hotel will not be fit to live in if you two get going.'

'But he must have his lesson,' said Archibald MacDonald, 'as a man who derides the blood in him. The only danger is that you'll exasperate him into going so far in self-defence that he'll attract the notice of your Red Girl. What?'

Kate O'Brien looked at him quickly and her eyes stayed on his. He smiled.

'Why not?' he enquired. 'If he was even half serious, I never heard a worse renegade. It might be worth while testing his reactions.'

She shook her head. 'No, Major! Who would dare conjure up the dead? He would never go that far.'

'He might.'

'If he does,' said Kate O'Brien and stopped.

Chapter Two

Art O'Connor was patiently and methodically working a shrimp, foot by foot, down the length of the run just below the outflow from Lough Aonach.

Behind him was a steep, short slope of grass with a low drystone wall at the head of it; and before him spread the shining shield of the lough, a league-wide reach into the recesses of Leaccamore Mountain. Below the run he was working was a still long pool, fringed with white-splashed limestone, and the grey ledges at the bottom showed through the clearness of the water. For ten miles, down to Dunmore Bay, the river went thus – pool and run, pool and run – and to bring grilse and sea-trout up to the lough called for a high spring-tide and plenty of rain water.

There had been a shower or two in the preceding night, and a spring-tide too, and, though the water was not even coloured, some game fish might have ventured the runs. And so Art O'Connor was doing all he knew.

Mickeen Oge Flynn had been fishing too and had moved down to the next run round a curve of the river. There he had grown tired of experimenting with lures – from prawn to what looked like an illegal stroke-all – and was now sitting on the top of a green bank on the edge of the footpath below the drystone wall, smoking a contemplative pipe.

Round the down-stream curve came Betty Caverley, neat and slender in a dress of blue linen. Mickeen Oge took his pipe from his teeth, waved her away with it and made as if to slide down the bank to his fishing-rod.

'Stay where you are!' she ordered.

'Very well so, ma'am,' he said meekly.

She sat on the grass bank near him, her slim ankles down the slope, and fanned herself with a wide-leafed hat.

'My, but it's a warm evening! I walked right down to old Castle Aonach.'

'And back again! Man, young lady, you English are the great people for walking without rhyme or reason!'

'And you Irish,' she mimicked, 'the great people for resting.'

'With the finest reason handy at our elbow – same as now.'

'Thank you, sor! Have you e'er a cigarette on you?'

He held a match for her in his cupped hand, and looked down at the face that was flushed so delicately, so rarely; and her soft hair in the evening glow was a spun halo.

'This is nice,' she murmured.

He turned away and relit his pipe with the same match, and teeth and lips were clamped on the pipe stem.

Betty Caverley examined his profile. It was aquiline and clean, and chin and jaw were outlined strongly as he drew in the smoke. There was a shading of grey in the black wave of his hair, and over the close-set ear there was more than a shading. Yet he was not old. But of course he had suffered. She knew of his fight in the Black-and-Tan war and the civil war, of his internment, his terrible hunger strike, his escape, his campaign in the hills. But she could never get him to talk of those experiences. He was a strange, calm, gentle man in a strange land – and the strangest thing of all was that a man might be working humbly, and yet be one of his land's chosen men. A man chosen! And he could be so deeply silent. But she, she herself, could always make him talk and laugh and exhibit a gay spirit deep down.

'Caught anything?' she enquired at last.

'Might as well be fishing in Simple Simon's pail.'

'Did Art O'Connor?'

'He will – if there's a venturesome fish in the river at all. As persistent a man as ever I saw.'

'He is,' Betty chuckled. 'And doesn't he keep the hotel alive? The night before last the General choked on his whiskey when told that England was on her last legs when America intervened in the Great War.'

'It was true for him,' said Mickeen Oge.

'And that was not the worst. I was certain the old soldier would have a fit when taunted with Ireland's lack of enthusiasm in the War. "Eighty thousand Irishmen died," he roared, "and every man a volunteer." "Better they died for Ireland," retorted the American.'

'Good man!' said Mickeen Oge.

'That is what Kate O'Brien said, and he bit off her nose. "The Irish who stayed at home," he told her, "weren't so keen either, I guess." "Had you ever ten thousand men under arms?" "We hadn't the arms," said Kate, her eyes flaming – you know how they flame. "Nor the heart," said he – but heart wasn't the word he used.'

'I know the word. Well?'

'Kate was furious. "Perhaps that is why you are 100 per cent American," she lashed him. "We had Irish Americans – like Owen Jordan – who were not afraid to fight. Were you?" And he went white below the tan and just looked at her.'

'It was a hard thing to say,' said Mickeen Oge. 'Kate shouldn't have said it.'

'She knew that, I think, for she went straight off to bed. But they were as bad as ever last night. They seem to lie in wait for each other and monopolise the talk.'

'It sometimes begins that way,' said Mickeen Oge.

'What?'

'What is in your mind.'

'You mean – love? But it does not always begin that way?'

'It has always its own foolish way of beginning,' said Mickeen Oge, gravely cynical.

They were silent for a space, and all round them was silence too. In a little while the thrushes would begin their evening song in the trees across the water, and the rooks go cawing homewards, but this hour, before the sun turned orange, all nature lay hushed, pressed under as by a taut wire. And the sheen on Lough Aonach was the sheen of a silken skin.

'I suppose it is the loneliness here,' murmured the girl, 'that makes one cynical – like – like wearing a mask.'

'I am never lonely, small lady.'

'Because you have something to live for?'

His face hardened. She watched him, and, suddenly leaning to him, touched his arm.

'I know, Michael – though you never tell me anything.'

'I would not give you any dangerous secret to keep – dangerous to yourself, Betty girl.'

'But I would keep it,' she cried.

'You would.' There was quick warmth in his voice. 'Never mind, Betts!' His voice changed and sombered. 'It could be that it is all foolishness; it could be that it is only keeping the breath of life in the dying, so that one shall remember, for yet a little while, the days when one was – a man.'

'It isn't – it isn't,' she comforted him, and then with sudden change, 'But is there danger, too?'

'A little – not much yet. A spy or two!' He looked at her with mock ferocity. 'Even you.'

She threw up her flaxen head and laughed. 'You know I am not a spy?'

'Why the questioning, then? The greatest spy in the world!'

'It is my right to question,' she proclaimed calmly. 'I have known you long enough. Don't you remember teaching me to cast a line?'

'The small girl that screeched blue murder when she hooked her first trout?'

'And you said, "Wheesht, colleen! he won't bite you." And he did.'

'''Twas the hook pricked you. My! but you've grown a big girl since.'

'And I've been here every summer. It would be nice in winter too, I think.'

'You would find it lonely.'

'No – I love this place.' She looked dreamily across the lough, her hands clasped over her knee and her body bent like a bow. 'I could live here all the time,' she said softly. 'What do you do in winter, Michael young?'

'Plenty. There is the shooting – and the farm – and a take-round amongst the friends, Hugh Forbes and Sean Glynn and Paddy Bawn – and my books all the time.'

'Yes, you are a great reader. I have been through your library, you know – travel, literature, sport, chemistry, and a great ugly pile of dry theology.'

'I am known as a spoilt priest – what the Scots call a "stickit minister."''

'I know, Michael.'

'And indeed,' he went on gloomily, 'I might join an Order yet – if Big Michael bids me. It is the final refuge.'

'Ah! you are lonely then. I knew it.'

'Not often, girl. But loneliness has its savour too. It is the source of all fine dreaming.'

She frowned. 'You would join an Order if your uncle bid you?'

'Why not?'

'But he wouldn't?'

'No.' He glanced at her obliquely. 'Just now he is bent on choosing a wife for me.'

She looked at him wide-eyed. 'Oh, Michael! You would never let another man choose a wife for you?'

'The custom of the country.'

'And all wrong. But I think you should marry, Michael,' she said seriously.

'Down to Gehenna or up to the Throne, he fares the fastest who fares alone.'

'And Kipling is all wrong too,' she said defiantly. 'If a woman cared for a man – and understood him, she would be a solace and a comfort in any crisis – in all crises.'

'You've been reading *The Iron Heel*. Very well so! If I change my mind I'll put it up to Big Michael. At the present moment he has a girl in his eye for me – and she is not a bad girl – as girls go.'

He got slowly to his feet, but she remained seated, staring across the lough at the blue bulk of Leaccamore. Yes, Big Michael would choose a plump country girl with a dowry – and the dowry would be more important than the girl – and Michael young would not be happy – he couldn't be – and she herself would not come here any more. She sighed and made to rise, a little listlessly, to her feet.

And at that moment a great shout echoed down the limestone banks.

'Saints-in-Glory!' cried Mickeen Oge. 'He's into a fish or he's in himself. Come on, Betts!'

He ran full speed along by the drystone wall, and, quickly as he ran, the girl came up to his shoulder.

'Wings to your heart!' he praised her. 'The foot of the roe is on you.'

II

Art O'Connor was into his fish beyond a doubt. He was backing carefully out of the thigh-deep water, the butt of the rod in his groin, and the point making a lovely deep curve out over the pool. The point nodded twice, and the taut line made a slow circle in the water.

'Give him his head a bit,' shouted Michael Oge, 'and keep your point up!'

He merely shouted that out of custom, for Art O'Connor knew his stuff and did a competent job of work, wearing his fish out in the heavy water and neatly coaxing him down-stream to the wide landing-net. In ten minutes Mickeen Oge had a clean-run grilse expertly on the gravel.

'Look at the neat prow of him!' Mickeen Oge pointed out to Betty, the two, heads together, gloating over the fish.

'Oh! the beauty!'

'As pretty a grilse as'll come out of the river this season! Five pounds, with an ounce or two spare, and clean as a new shilling! But how in thunder did the game fellow fight his way up from Dunmore tide?'

'Queer freak of luck!' said Art O'Connor. 'Hold that rod a moment, Mickeen Oge. I want to look at something.'

His voice was quiet, and there was a strange lack of enthusiasm in him. He turned away, crossed the gravel, scrambled up the slippery grass of the bank and climbed on top of the drystone wall. There he balanced himself and, hand shading eyes, examined the prospect before him. There was only a curving slope of brown-green pasture shining under the low sun, with thin dark streaks where thistles cast long shadows. Beyond it, on one hand, was a belt of trees, and, on the other, over the lifting curve, the chimneys of the hotel half a mile away.

The field was empty of any living thing, but, as he looked, over the slope from the hotel a woman came strolling easily.

She was Kate O'Brien. O'Connor waited for her on top of the wall. She was clothed in some thin, faintly yellow stuff, and the thoroughbred lines of her and the depths in her eyes might make any man's pulse stir. Her dark head was bare, and in her hand she swung an old panama. She must have been walking for some time, for there was the least delicate touch of colour under the pallor of her face, and she was breathing deeply.

'You are looking in the wrong airt,' she called to him. 'The bonny view is behind you. Here are only grasses withered by the sun and thistles not shaken by any wind. What stand you there to see?'

She had intoned the words for him. He stared down at her intently.

'A woman clothed in strange raiment,' he said softly.

She smiled at him. 'That woman is in the palace of a king – never in this place.'

'No. Thinner than that air shimmering above the trees, vanished like a dream – but the beauty of her stays in my mind.'

'Ah-h!' said Kate O'Brien. 'I was too hard on you last night, and your poor Yankee mind has given way. I am very sorry.'

'You may well be, if her blood is in you – and it is. She was of your race but ten times more beautiful – and nearly as wicked.'

She frowned up at him. 'What in the world do you mean?'

'Never mind! I have caught the nicest grilse in the river.'

'And it has gone to your head! But where – oh, where? And on an evening like this too! I must see it. Give me your hand!'

Her fingers grasped his, and with the ease of the country-bred she balanced on the wall and, still holding his hand, leaped to the path with him and slid down the grass to the gravel.

'My – oh my!' she said, bending over the grilse. 'Won't the others be jealous?'

'As the devil himself – and small wonder,' said Mickeen Oge. 'I'm surprised at you, Art O'Connor. Here you are with the first grilse of the season, and you as calm as a post.'

'Sorry! That fish gives me no kick.' He looked intently at the other. 'Tell me, Flynn, is there a woman in these parts – young and very beautiful – who goes round with a bare head of copper-red hair and a grass-green shawl on her shoulders?'

'My God!' Mickeen Oge's eyes widened in horror.

Betty Caverley drew in her breath sharply, and Kate O'Brien cried out, 'What have you seen, Art O'Connor?'

'I have seen her.'

'Where – here?'

'Up there – I'll tell you. Oh! I know the legend.' His voice was very serious, entirely hiding any emotion, and his words gave them a very vivid impression of what he had seen and felt.

'I was fishing out there in the middle of the pool, doing the best I knew, cursing myself for a mutt, wondering when I'd have resolution enough to give the darn thing up – same as you had, Flynn – and I decided to give it just one more whirl with a small lure Major MacDonald had tied for me, just ten last casts and no more. I didn't come out of the water. I stood out there, thigh-deep, and changed shrimp for fly, and as I was testing the last knot I noticed quite suddenly that everything was strangely hushed all round me. Queerly still! Like that pause that comes in summer when the sun sets – and the sun was not yet set. Weirder than that. I had felt the same hush once before – in a three-quarter eclipse of the sun.

A thrush had been singing in the trees over there across the water, and now no thrush was singing, and the murmur of the river down the run, though it had grown louder in the stillness, seemed to come from another world. It gave me a sort of forlorn feeling – as if I were a stranger in a lonely place under a light that never was on land or sea, and all that strange world watching me – and not caring – as I tugged at the last knot. I felt that someone was looking at the back of my neck – perhaps that was all.

'I turned round then and looked up – up there. And there, leaning on the wall, was the woman – no ghost woman; flesh and blood, or I have no eyes to see – the sun shining on her red hair, and her scarf green as grass on her shoulders. She was not looking at me. She was looking over my head at the far side of the pool, and, as I watched her, she raised a white arm and pointed. I looked where she pointed – out there under that rock – and I saw the tail-swirl of a half-risen fish. There it was – the first rise I had seen in all that afternoon. Half by instinct I pulled out yards of line and threw over it, saw the silver streak – and struck too soon. Missed it clean. I looked over my shoulder again, and the woman was still there and still pointing. I tried the fish again, and then again, and the third time he came and I gave it him good and hard. You know how the shock of the check goes up your arms and makes your heart jump? It was then I yelled. That is all. There is the grilse, and when I went to look, there was no woman any more only, after a time, Miss O'Brien came walking across the field from the hotel. Did you see any woman, Miss O'Brien?'

'I saw no one,' said Kate O'Brien gravely, 'but a woman could have reached the woods while you played the grilse.'

'That is so.' His eyes came round to Mickeen Oge. 'I know the local legend, Flynn. Was it a hoax, or was the woman she whom you inadequately call the Red Girl?'

'You have seen someone that I do not know,' said Mickeen Oge sternly. 'The game is hers and yours.'

'Very well! I will play it with her – flesh or spirit. But it is no game either. I only saw her over my shoulder, but she was fit to sit with Mona Lisa amongst the rocks – more beautiful by far and no less wicked. A woman I never saw before, yet a woman strangely familiar – like a face out of a secret dream, perhaps the dream of the race, God save us!' He took a stride down to the margin of the pool and threw his hand out. An odd harsh challenge was in his voice. 'If that woman's face appeared in the depths of that pool a man might be impelled to dive to it – and drown, as men have drowned in the legend.'

He swung from them without another word or look and stalked up the shore, ignoring his grilse, his rod, everything but his own concentration on something that had moved him deeply.

'He was touched to the quick,' said Betty Caverley, and then another thought struck her. She caught Mickeen Oge's arm. 'You must be very careful, Michael.'

He relaxed at her touch. 'All right, girl. I play no woman's games – dead or alive.'

Kate O'Brien looked gloomily after Art O'Connor, some secret anger in her eyes. 'Wicked as Mona Lisa!' she murmured. Then she smiled grimly. 'Yes, Betty! for a 100 per cent American, he was touched deeply.'

Chapter Three

I

Mickeen Oge strode slowly, but not aimlessly, down a small wooded glen that angled west from the hotel. A lively runnel of water flowed and fell and tinkled below the path and, two miles down, joined the main river. Some distance short of this junction the path turned from the stream and mounted amongst the trees, and Mickeen Oge went upwards with it.

At the edge of the trees, on the lip of the glen, he came suddenly on the grass-topped walls of the bailey-yard of ruined Castle Aonach. A jagged gap in the thick masonry let him through to what was now only an acre of ragged grass, scattered with clumps of wild raspberry canes and with big elder bushes growing out of the base of the walls. At the other side of this ragged acre rose the ancient keep, pierced by a bold, high arch and, to the right of this, a gaping doorway that led to the turret stairs and the broken battlements.

Mickeen Oge walked across the grass and through the gloom of the arch into the open beyond, and, surprisingly, there was the main river below him. The castle was perched on a promontory overhanging the water, and only a low shelter-wall fenced it from the steep rocky bank. He clambered over this shelter-wall and down the rocks to the shelfy margin of the river, here forming a long, curving, sheltered pool, famous for the big fish it held.

Seating himself on a jut of boulder, Mickeen Oge slowly filled his pipe with cut plug. His face, ever smoothly austere, had now an added cast of gloom. He was waiting here for Art O'Connor, who was working the river downwards, and the American was a disturbance in his mind. He was such a likeable man – and yet? What did Mickeen Oge know about him? He said he was from the States, yet he had come straight to Lough Aonach from Canada, and Canada was British territory. How did he know about an out-of-the-way place like this?

Very possibly, very naturally, Britain was interested in the underground republican movement in Ireland. She would use her own agents to find out what she could. Everyone knew that Mickeen

Oge Flynn was unchangeably republican; it was no secret that the old fighting organisation was still active; many suspected that he controlled secret dumps of arms and munitions. Did O'Connor want to place these dumps? He could try.

As he set match to pipe, a clink of shod shoes on stone came to his ears, and the man he was considering came round the curve of the shore, leisurely clumping along in thigh-waders, his long rod like a spear above his head. Mickeen Oge nodded shortly in salutation.

Art O'Connor nodded back, smiled faintly, and turned to the river; but when he turned, a troubled frown took the place of the smile.

'This the pool I should avoid?' he called over his shoulder.

'Why?'

'You know. *Poul Cailin Rua* – the Red Girl's pool.'

'You'll know,' said Mickeen Oge.

'Here's saying "How" to it at any rate.' His feet slipped smoothly through the shallow water, and his reel burred.

The lad could fish, sure enough, and had the fine, leisurely patience of the true angler. There, now, was a nicely timed flick of the wrist that, delayed a split second, would break a hook barb on the boulders, and the fly at full stretch came down on the water like a caress. A spy too must have the same leisurely patience and be acquainted of many arts – a man of indomitable hardihood, of infinite resource, his life on his sleeve and no weapon to guard it but his wit.

Mickeen Oge, searching through his own mind, could discover no least resentment against the man. As a matter of fact, Mickeen Oge was here at *Poul Cailin Rua* as a self-appointed guardian. He was no believer in superstition, but there was something sinister and fatal in the legend of the Red Girl; she had been seen and men had drowned in that pool; and Mickeen Oge, half believing, half doubtful, would make sure that no fatality would take place while Art O'Connor fished the river. That was all.

So ran Mickeen Oge's thoughts as he smoked and watched. So immersed was he in these thoughts that he did not notice the hush that came about him like a drift of cloud until Art O'Connor roused him by turning round in the water and staring at the high bank above his head.

Mickeen Oge turned and looked too, and goose-flesh ran up his legs and loins.

'It is herself!' he exclaimed, and the astounding shock made him realise that he never had believed.

She leant on the broken shelter-wall up there and looked out over his head at Art O'Connor. Her bare and shapely arms were over the green scarf that covered shoulders and bosom, and her red hair was like a flame. And she was beautiful – beautiful and tragic, her face like snow under sun, the light drowned in her eyes – a face that one has known in dreams, so familiar and so strange.

A splash in the pool behind made him turn hastily and in fear.

Art O'Connor was coming into action. He charged for the shore so furiously that the water splashed over the tops of his waders, and spatters leaped above his head. Mickeen Oge again looked upwards. The Red Girl was gone.

II

Art O'Connor never hesitated. He did not even take time to lay down his best rod but let it drop to shatter point across a rock. He faced the boulder-heaped bank and went upwards like a leopard.

The bank was steep and high, and the climb took him some time; his filled waders cumbered him too, so that, when he half-rolled, half-vaulted over the shelter-wall there was nothing to be seen. He stood there for a moment breathing quickly. Before him, in front of the keep, was a wide spread of grass, and, beyond that, the belt of trees fringing the small glen. No living foot could have reached the trees in the time he had taken to climb the brae. It was the ruined castle – or nowhere.

At a lumbering run he went echoing under the arch to the grass-grown bailey. It was empty. And then the black gape leading to the turret stairs caught his eye. 'Got you this time, my lady!' he said grimly.

In three minutes he came out through the ruined doorway, a puzzled frown on his face. In the broken-arched, roofless chambers there had been no woman hiding, there had been no place to hide in, and the dart of nesting swallows had told him that no living woman had climbed up there.

He stood and looked across the ragged bailey, estimating the distance to the breach in the far wall. Surely, not even the flight of a wood-nymph could have reached the gap before he had come through the arch? Slowly, now, he strode, the water swishing in his wading-boots, across the grass and looked down through the breached wall amongst the trees of the glen. No use scouting down there. Again he surveyed the bailey with trained western eyes.

'Ah!' He stiffened like a setter at point.

His eyes, practised in reading sign, narrowed on one spot. Down by the wall, not fifteen paces away, a thick elder bush grew out of the foundations, and there, on the ground below it, lay a freshly broken frond of green; and now those trained eyes saw where feet had trampled lightly over the grass. He walked evenly across and halted by the bush.

'Come out!' he invited quietly. 'Come out and let us have a look at you!'

There was no response. If any nymph had been changed into that plumed elder, no leaf quivered.

'Right! We'll take a pin to this periwinkle.'

He stepped quickly into the angle between bush and wall and pulled the branches aside. There was no one there.

There was a cavity in the wall behind the thickest of the foliage, and he bent forward and looked in. The cavity was barely a yard across and not more than half that in depth. The sides of it were grouted in the cement-tough mortar of the old builders, but the back of it was built up carefully of unmortared stones.

For a long time he stayed bent over, looking into the hole, and a small grim smile came about his lips.

'Well, I'm damned!' swore Art O'Connor.

'You have found it, then,' said a quiet voice behind him.

III

He straightened up and turned round.

Mickeen Oge Flynn stood within three strides of him, feet apart, hands on hips, head forward, not angry, not belligerent, just watchful.

O'Connor's eyes narrowed.

'Found what?'

'What you were looking for?'

'I see. Were you in this conspiracy against me too?'

'I am in no conspiracy against you, but, if you want to know, I am against what England stands for in this country.'

Art O'Connor was puzzled for a moment, and then illumination came to him in a flash.

'*Buenos dias!* I deserved it all.' He took a step forward and the Irishman's shoulders stiffened. 'Gently, Mickeen Oge Flynn! Take it easy for a moment!' They were close to each other now. 'You did not set the Red Girl on me, did you?'

'Did you set her on yourself?'

'By gum! I believe I did. But let that be. I wasn't looking for what you have hidden behind those stones. Let me show you what I was looking at. See!'

He turned and pulled aside the elder bushes, and Mickeen Oge looked over his shoulder into the cavity in the wall. He used exactly the same words that Art O'Connor had used:

'Well, I'm damned!'

'How nearly damned was I!' said Art O'Connor a little grimly.

Mickeen Oge leaned over and reached a hand into the cavity, but the other pressed shoulder against him.

'Wait! Leave them for the present. Two can play at this game.' He looked back at Mickeen Oge. 'Suppose we talk this over?'

'It was a dangerous game, whoever played it,' said Mickeen Oge. 'We'll do more than talk it over, by God!'

'Listen, Flynn!' The American caught Mickeen Oge by the arm and drew him away, and as they moved across the grass their voices went on murmuring interestedly. And, presently, Mickeen Oge stopped to chuckle, and Art O'Connor laughed.

Chapter Four

Kate O'Brien and Betty Caverley, the gloaming before them and the light from the French window shining on white shoulders, leant on the veranda rail and looked out across the silver of Lough Aonach at the big dim bulk of Leaccamore, where scattered points of light were beginning to gleam in cottage windows. They were silent, and when Art O'Connor came out from the lounge, pulling the window shut behind him, the silence still held.

In the lounge old Kelly Cuthbert sipped his whiskey and soda and remarked softly to the ceiling, 'Our friend has not been so insistent this last day or two?'

'No reason to regret that, have you?' enquired Caverley above his paper.

'Why not? A good chap to argue with – and as patient a fisherman as ever I met.'

Major MacDonald paced back and forth on the rug, hands deep in pockets, and looked under brows at the retired soldier.

'Getting to like him?'

'Well, dammit! He's an outdoor man and nobody's fool.'

'He says he has seen her twice – this Red Girl.'

'Pulling our leg probably – or some latent Irish superstition.'

'Don't you believe in her?'

'I have not seen her.'

'He says he has. You know the legend?'

'You would suggest he is spying on Mickeen Oge? I never could stomach spies.'

'Spying on Mickeen Oge, he would be on your side, wouldn't he?'

'Like hell!' snapped the soldier. 'Mickeen Oge may be a dashed young fool playing with fire, but he is a gentleman.'

'Scratch an Irishman and you'll find a rebel,' said Caverley, laughing.

'Begad!' cried the General. 'You fellows make me tired,' and he buried his bristling moustache in his tumbler.

Outside on the veranda, Betty Caverley pulled her white scarf on her shoulders and slipped down to the gravel drive. She was in a disconsolate humour this night. Her friend, young Michael, had been holding aloof from her of late, and she was disturbed about him. He had even given up the habit of drifting lazily across the gravel of nights and saying a few pleasant words as she leant on the veranda rail; and she now realised how she used to look forward to those few minutes. She felt dimly irritable against him, and, particularly, against his uncle, Big Michael, who wanted to marry him off to a wife chosen – she said bluntly to herself – like a milch cow at a fair.

She went out through the hotel gates to the main road and found Big Michael sitting on a stone stile overlooking the lake. His great head was bare, and he was peacefully smoking. A cheerful man, Big Michael, but a lonely man, too, and he was mostly satisfied with his own company.

'Good-night to you, *colleendheas*!' he saluted. 'Where 're you off to on your lonesome?' He had seen this girl put on womanhood, but, on occasion, he still treated her as a friendly small girl.

'I have arrived,' she said. 'I think I should be scolding you, Michael Big.'

'I would like to be hearing you. Go on now!'

'You keep the only order there is in this place, and bad order it is often.'

'Bad and worse, surely.'

'But I am worried.'

'So you should be – and me with you. And what puts the fret on you, small darling?'

'I am worried about Art O'Connor – and about young Michael.'

'Look now, my heart! You need not be one bit bothered about the Yankee lad – not one bit; but 'tis about Michael Oge I'm worried myself.'

'I know. There is something strange going on all about here, and Michael is playing dangerous enough already.'

'Not that at all. I am worried because he is a cowardly man.'

'You are either joking – or lying, Big Michael Flynn.'

'Neither one nor yet the other. Whisper! That fellow is afraid of a woman – a *girsha* – and she no warrior like Maeve or Helen.'

'Oh! is that it?' With that enlightenment came an increased touch of irritation.

'Yes, so!' said Big Michael firmly. 'And 'tis not me you should be scolding, but the young lad himself; for if there is bad order kept in the house above, the man to blame is the young and the strong man, who is leaving it without the caring hands of a woman and a wife – and a mother, by the grace o' God.'

She came close and peered into his eyes. 'Is it really true that you are urging him – that he would leave the choosing of a wife to you?'

'And, girl dear! wouldn't it be myself would choose him the bonniest, brownest cluster o' nuts ever grew on a hazel tree?'

'So you say – but what does he think of her?'

'That she is the topmost spray of blossom on a wild apple tree, lovely and pure and up above his reach.'

She drew back, and a little cold wave of desolateness flowed over her. It was true then that young Michael held a dream in his heart. 'Colleen,' said the big man softly, 'how did you know that I was coaxing him, and that if I had the choosing and knew the girl's heart – as indeed I do not – I would soon have young voices in this place?'

'Young Michael told me.'

He slapped his knee. 'And I after calling him a cowardly man! And was that the way he began? Cute fellow! What else did he tell you, and him whispering?'

'Oh!' Her heart had come leaping into her throat.

'Well, girleen?'

'That is all he said,' she whispered.

'Ah well!' said Big Michael resignedly. 'A bit of the coward was sticking in his gullet, but sure.'

'I do – do not understand you, Big Michael.' She turned and walked quickly towards the gate of the drive.

'How could you, indeed?' he called after her.

'You have no sense, big uncle,' she called back.

'And less I'd have and me twenty years younger, my bundle o' nuts.' And to himself he muttered, 'And I hope to God I haven't put my awkward foot in it this time.'

II

When Betty Caverley got back below the veranda, Kate O'Brien and Art O'Connor were still leaning on the rail, but they were now talking in unusually quiet tones. She slipped by on the gravel and up the steps of the porch and never halted till she reached her own room.

Kate O'Brien and Art O'Connor went on talking.

'You are afraid of her, then?'

'She haunts me even asleep – her beauty.'

'And her wickedness?'

'She must be wicked.'

'Why?'

'Because she will not forgive.'

'How could she forgive?'

'She might know – now, with the dross of living got rid of so long ago – that an Irishman might be loyal to another cause and yet be no traitor.'

'I do not understand you.'

'As the niece of a British Major-General you might.'

'Ah! Irishman, did you say?'

'Irishman, why not? There are two Irish parties in this island. Well? Is one traitorous?'

Her voice was not raised, but it grew bleakly cold.

'You need not be afraid of the Red Girl, Art O'Connor, but, if you are what you hint at, there is a man in this place that you should fear like judgment.'

'Young Flynn? I don't fear him or any man.'

'No? Yet I advise you to take the first train out of Castletown tomorrow.'

'Next day, perhaps. I hold Mickeen Oge in the hollow of my hand, and I can lay the other on one of his caches any time I want to – and not so far from here. Good night, dear lady, and don't worry!'

He turned carelessly on his heel and went through the door of the lounge.

She did not follow. She stood for a long time queerly still, her eyes staring out at the shining lough, and her hands grasping the veranda rail. Then, and suddenly, she turned, went through the main door and down a long passage to the private bar. There she found Mickeen Oge, a-lean on the counter, reading.

'What will it be, lady?' he enquired smilingly. 'A short one or a long one? And I'll tell your uncle.'

She ignored his facetiousness, leaning so close across the counter to him that he straightened up and looked with surprise at her serious face and troubled eyes.

'There is something we must do at once, Mickeen Oge. That dump we have at Castle Aonach – move it at once – tonight.'

He looked at her steadily, his face grave.

'Who is it?'

'You know. Tomorrow may be too late.'

'Do you think I did not take precautions, with the Red Girl showing herself – and to him?'

She threw up her head and laughed bitterly. 'The Red Girl! If she did not show herself, her spirit, her inspiration moved in one of her blood. He fooled us all, but not her. Is the dump safe, then?'

'The dump is still there,' said Mickeen Oge, 'but the man you have in your mind will never touch it.'

She slapped the counter with forceful hands. 'There is no need for – anything. He may be going tomorrow.'

Mickeen Oge smiled a little sadly, a little grimly. 'He is not leaving this place tomorrow – or next day – or –'

'Mickeen Oge,' she cried dangerously, 'If you – if anything happens to him, I will break my oath.'

'Things don't happen except they have to, Kate O'Brien,' he said. 'There will be no need to break your oath.' He gently touched the back of her hand with one finger. 'Leave it to me, girl.'

Without another word she turned and left him.

'Maybe we're damned fools, at that,' said Mickeen Oge doubtfully.

III

'I'll tell you what, General,' said Big Michael Flynn, ''tis going to rain in two days.'

'You cute old dog fox!' said the General. 'You guessed that I have a damned good mind to pack up and clear out.'

'I'm telling you. In two days – I feel it in my bones. And no use at all for you to go lashing the water till then, and less the use for you and me and others to be sparring with each other about the house day and dark. Two days – and what about that little bit of a picnic down at Aonach Well that we used to be having when we were all younger, glory be to God?'

'To the devil with you and your picnics!' cursed the soldier. 'Ask the ladies.'

So the picnic it was, down at Aonach Well.

'And that's that!' said Big Michael to himself, 'though why them

two fellows put me up to it you couldn't be knowing; they have some
devilment in their heads – but, sure, some good might come of it,
with the help o' God.' He was thinking of his nephew and the dear
English colleen.

Aonach Well was not within the bailey of the old castle, but in a
corner of the field some two hundred paces from the ruined walls. A
spring of limpid water with worn steps leading down to a small rock
basin, surrounded by a few ancient oaks, it had once been a holy well,
before that a druidic well, and many generations had made prayers
about it – not always Christian prayers for things commendable.

Early in the afternoon Mickeen Oge led a pannier-loaded pony
down there; and later the party followed leisurely, the men carrying
fishing-rods and tackle – in case a cloud came over the sun, or a
miracle of a shower rippled the water, or a gamesome grilse showed
the curl of a tail. And they had lunch – with champagne cider and
iced lager and a bottle of Paddy Flaherty.

Immediately after lunch Mickeen Oge led the pony across the
field and through the arch to the bailey-yard. Before leaving he
caught Kate O'Brien's eye and touched the empty panniers with his
hand. So he was thinking of clearing the dump after all! She looked
towards the castle arch and pointed to herself with a finger-tip, but
he shook his head and glanced at Art O'Connor. She was to stay
behind and watch.

A little later, Art O'Connor went off by himself, but in the opposite
direction: over the drystone wall to the river. And then Kate O'Brien
of the still poise was smitten with restlessness; she could not sit still,
and her anxious eyes went wandering to the black gape of the arch
and round to the low wall above the river.

The three men left were lazily smoking, peacefully digesting their
lunch, wondering whether they would have a snooze or set up their
rods. And Betty Caverley was wrapped in a silence where some
secret thought of her own brought the blood slowly to her cheeks.
She was wondering whether she might not make a flank movement
round by the small glen and come into the bailey through the gap in
the rear wall. But no! If Mickeen Oge held himself aloof she would
do likewise – until he found sense. But the temptation stayed.

Ten minutes later, Art O'Connor's head appeared over the wall.
It stayed there, moveless and watching, till Kate O'Brien's restless
eyes came round to it, when it hurriedly ducked out of sight as if
to escape notice. Ten seconds later his head again appeared for

a moment and disappeared, but this time twenty yards nearer the castle.

Kate O'Brien was to her feet in a moment, and her uncle swore.

'Dammit, girl! Can't you be easy for once?' He was comfortably on his back, his head on an upturned basket, and an infernal black cheroot at mouth corner. The dark ash was ready to fall down his neck, and he hoped to hold sleep at bay till he finished his smoke.

'That thing will choke you,' warned his niece and strode away.

Something in her voice made her uncle turn his head and watch her. She did not go across towards where Art O'Connor's head had disappeared, but skirted along the other edge of the field towards the castle.

She moved quickly, almost at a run, yet Art O'Connor suddenly jumped the shelter-wall well ahead of her and made straight for the arch. He was within ten strides of it when Mickeen Oge stepped out of the gloom and halted in the middle of the gap.

'Begad!' exclaimed the Major-General and propped himself on an elbow. Next minute he was scrambling to his feet. 'It's the real thing,' he cried. 'The Yankee is armed. Come on, MacDonald! We mustn't let him hurt the young fool.'

For all his years the old soldier made good time, Caverley flustering behind him, with Archibald MacDonald well in the rear, in no great hurry, rubbing his long chin, wondering a little. Betty Caverley came up to the Major-General's shoulder. Her heart was in her throat and her knees trembling. What she had feared had come at last: two men down to essentials, not concerned with her or with Kate O'Brien, not even concerned with right or wrong, ready to go any length each for his own side. All illusions of romance and glory receded before that stark reality.

Art O'Connor was poised on his feet, his right hand, at shoulder-level, holding a wicked flat automatic. A dozen yards away Mickeen Oge Flynn faced him in the middle of the arch, his hands on his hips, his head forward, eyes unwinkingly watchful.

The old soldier came on pantingly, and O'Connor pivoted a little, his arm stiff as a bar.

'Halt!' His voice whipped. 'You are on the dead line.'

Kelly Cuthbert halted, the others behind him. He was no coward, but he knew that this Western devil would jump into any game with desperate readiness.

'What damned folly is this?' he demanded.

'You are a fine judge of folly.' The other was flatly scornful. He threw his armed hand wide, embracing them all in that scorn. 'You are only people of illusion living idle days in a make-believe world. Flynn and I are the only real people – because we live for something that may break us – working in the dark, set against each other from the beginning. And you would play tricks with us, you and your Red Girl.'

'Leave the Red Girl out of it,' said Kate O'Brien bitterly. She was standing very still to one side, her eyes intent, but no fear in her face.

'I will not,' he cried at her. 'To whom did she point? What ghost will she now add to the many ghosts that haunt this place?'

He swung on Mickeen Oge.

'I'm coming through, Flynn,' he said.

'Private ground this,' said Mickeen Oge, and a sardonic humour added, 'and trespassers will be prosecuted.'

'Don't be a fool! I am going to make sure that nothing leaves this place – and I'm coming through.'

Mickeen Oge's right hand resting on his hip moved an inch towards his back pocket.

'Heeled!' said O'Connor. 'But I have the drop on you – and I'm coming through.'

'Move a step!' warned Mickeen Oge.

'Take your dare.' His arm poised, and he was in the very act of taking that fatal step.

And there Betty Caverley surprised them all. She darted forward quick as a flash between the two men, and faced O'Connor, her arms thrown wide.

'Get your gun, Michael!' she cried over her shoulder. 'Get your gun!'

She held herself to her slender height, her arms still wide, a flare in her eyes; and she moved backwards pace after pace towards Mickeen Oge. Five paces she went, and then a strong arm flung round her and she was lifted and whirled through the arch and out into the bailey.

Mickeen Oge looked down at the white face against his arm. There was a flare still in the big grey eyes staring at him.

'It's all right, bough o' blossom!' he comforted her gently. 'Only a foolish play on Kate O'Brien. She was masquerading as the Red Girl, and we planned to give her a fright. Girl, girl! don't be frightened of me!'

She blinked eyes rapidly. She stirred in his arms.

'I am not frightened – now. Oh! but I am ashamed. Please let me down – I can walk.'

'I will not,' said Mickeen Oge firmly. 'You will have to get used to this place where you are now – little fire-eater.'

The colour came warmly to her face before she turned it against his arm.

'That's it,' said he, and kissed her soft hair.

She turned her face up then.

'That's better,' said Mickeen Oge.

Art O'Connor, blank surprise holding his mouth open, stared at the empty arch. 'Well, I'm hanged!' he said, and drew a long breath. Then his face cleared and went into a pleasant grin as he turned to the dumbfounded group.

'The play is over, friends, and the curtain down. That last bit wasn't rehearsed. Hope you liked it.' He thrust the automatic out of sight. 'The dead line is wiped out, General. Step on the stage if you like.'

The Major-General's mouth hung open, and he was as nearly pop-eyed as a soldier could be. And then his white moustache bristled, his face purpled, his teeth clicked.

'You – you young jackanapes!' he exploded and, swinging on his heel, marched stiff-legged across the field. Presently a flow of adequate language would relieve him.

Marcus Caverley went too, but slowly, and his feet not too certain. There was a half-smile about his mouth, the small smile of one who has seen what he had looked for come to pass and is bereaved of his secret treasure.

Archie MacDonald, rubbing that long chin, looked across at Kate O'Brien with a pleasantly sardonic grin.

'They had me fooled for a bit,' he said. 'Had they you?'

'Bah!' said Kate O'Brien inadequately.

And the Major went across towards the river shaking his head.

'The silly young fools!' he murmured. 'The whole jing-bang of them – and not a thought of fishing in their heads!'

And then his lean face grew serious and a shade gloomy. Yes! people of illusion living idle days in a make-believe world. That described himself, he supposed. All his friends were getting settled – or unsettled – and himself a cranky old bachelor. Darn all this marrying and giving in marriage! And marriage nothing but a gamble! He was staring down at the pool in which Martin Kierley had drowned, and over there in that hotel he had seen Nuala Kierley, just for half a minute. Queer how she stayed in his mind! She had come in on them out of the night in her Irish cloak, her hair shining, her eyes drowned, her face white – and beautiful. Like the woman Ireland – wandering, broken, lost, worshipped. Lost! Where is she now, how does she live, what does she sell?

IV

Kate O'Brien had stayed where she was, and her grave white face showed no sign of bewilderment. Art O'Connor walked straight across to her.

'You dangerous fools!' she said in cold reprimand. 'You might have frightened that girl to death.'

'But I never dreamt –'

'Silly play-acting! Did you think you fooled me with it for a moment?'

'Did you think you fooled me with yours?' he stopped her hotly. 'And it was more than silly – it was almost sacrilegious. Your red mop and your green rag – and your white arms. Oh! they are white and shapely enough. Take these into them.' He thrust a crumple of red wig and green scarf into her hands, and she never looked at them. 'It was foolish of you to hide them in Mickeen Oge's cache. Did you think that I would not know your eyes below any disguise?' His glance was so compelling and angry that hers wavered and sank before it. 'Consider!' His finger was fiercely under her nose. 'Consider your wickedness! You made a mock of that woeful tragedy of the Red Girl – whose blood is in you. How could you do it? Why did you do it?'

She did not lift her eyes. 'To prove the Irish blood in you.'

'And now you know! What are you going to do about it?'

'Nothing, I suppose,' she said tonelessly, and half turned away. 'I was wicked – you said I was more wicked than Mona Lisa.'

He laid a detaining hand on her arm, and a sudden shade of fear and doubt went over his face.

'There were other things I said about you too, if you remember – and I meant them.'

She looked up quickly into his eyes and he caught her hand impulsively.

'Kate O'Brien, you and I were meant to be friends – with an occasional glorious row.'

She looked down and kept her smile secret.

'But you are leaving here tomorrow, are you not?'

'If you could think up something worth raising Cain about I would stay – say a year or ten.'

'That should not be very hard,' she murmured.

His face cleared. He took her arm and brought her round to his side.

'Come on, tigress, and let us think up something worth fighting about.'

They crossed the field together, and anyone could see they were of one mind. There was no one at Aonach Well when they got there; the spoils of the picnic were scattered about, and the men had gone about their own affairs. The two stood side by side looking down at the little crystal pool under the rocks. A thin rivulet of water tinkled down through drooping ferns and seeped away, gurgling through blue-green cress.

Quietly Art O'Connor placed arm across her shoulders.

'Kate, let us not fight just yet.'

'I do not want to fight any more.' Her eyes were deep.

The water tinkled as it fell, and gurgled as it flowed – carelessly, not caring, unconcerned, chuckling at some secret of its own. It was a pagan well, after all, and in its ten thousand years it had often seen what it was seeing now.

Bad Town Dublin

Clean Town Dublin, the Daneman built it,
Stone Town Dublin, the Norman walled it,
Bad Town Dublin, the Briton cursed it,
Our Town Dublin, we Irish hold it
        For weal or woe.

Flesh of our flesh, bone of our bone,
Our martyrs' blood on every stone,
In exile, broken, lost, alone,
In pain we won it, let pain atone
        To friend and foe.

———————

Chapter One

I

Major Archibald MacDonald yawned lazily and lifted himself out of the big chair. He was feeling drowsy, but it was too fine an afternoon to go to sleep in a hotel lounge. Last night, on the way over from Glasgow, he had spent most of the second watch on the bridge of the *Lairdshill* with First Officer Macgugan, and they had told each other some reasonably tall yarns; and afterwards in his own quarters, Mac and he had discussed Gaelic music over strong coffee – *Cruachan Beann*, which is a song of pure nostalgia, and that poignant song of warning before Glencoe, *Muintir a Glinne so* – 'people of this glen, this glen, this glen, if the stones knew what I know they would flee to the mountains.'

He reached his tweed hat down off a peg and strolled through the hall to the big front porch. He paused there, slowly filled a pipe, and looked across the wide roadway, over the roofs of taxis, at the dusty-foliaged trees of Stephen's Green Park. The head porter, a man even taller than himself, came to his side.

'Your friend, sir – when do you expect him?'

'Any time. He's coming up by car. Hot, isn't it?'

'Like hell, sir.'

'I think I'll strike down Grafton Street – and look for some German lager.'

'The pubs don't be open till 3.30; try Davy Byrne's in Duke Street, sir.'

'Very good! If my friend arrives – Glynn is the name, Sean Glynn – tell him I shan't be long.'

He lit his pipe with two matches, crossed the pavement, dodged a bus and a tram, went through the hand gate in the railings of the park, and strolled along the curving walks, hands in pockets, smoke drifting about his ears, eyes careless. Children were feeding ducklings along the concreted edge of the big pond, nursemaids careless whether they fell in or not; ancient men sat somnolently in the sun; young men, with apparently no more object in life than himself, moved just as lazily as himself. He liked this half-foreign

city of Dublin, half-foreign even here in Ireland, of which it was the
capital. An easy-going city, in no hurry about anything. Leisurely.
Hiding its currents under a smooth surface. Plenty of business too,
but, somehow, giving the impression that business was of secondary
importance to – something else.

Strange how this city of Dublin and nation of Ireland drew him! He
sensed the something else behind: the troubled discontent of dreams
that ever and again flared into action and moved an Empire to doubts
of its own permanence; because this nation retained its entity despite
all attempts to make it conform. His own mood was in tune – that
lazy detached mood that had a restless undercurrent of wondering
what was to happen next.

A tall man, this Major Archibald MacDonald, retired British
officer, but still in the prime of life; tall and lean under easy-fitting
homespuns; tough, indestructible, with a brown face and cool ironic
eyes. When he pushed back his tweed hat, his brow, in contrast to
the tan of his jaw, was startlingly white below black hair.

And now, at last, he was at a loose end. He was done with
soldiering. He had nothing to do – nothing worth while – and he
knew that contentment did not abide in idleness. Tomorrow, Sean
Glynn and himself would move off southwards, and he would fish
industriously for a month. And then? Back to Scotland for some more
fishing, till the shooting season came around. He had an income big
enough for all purposes, and not one foot of ground he could call his
own. He would go on fishing and shooting, like so many of his class,
until the years set him in a mould, and he became a sporting crank,
no earthly use to anyone, and greeted everywhere with a friendly
contempt.

Why not run across to New Mexico and see his sister Margaid?
Yes, dammit! And there he would do some more fishing and shooting
with his brother-in-law, Owen Jordan, and Art O'Connor who had
married Kate O'Brien. Or he might get married himself! And who
the devil would marry him? All his friends here in Ireland had taken
wives unto themselves – or the other way round. Hugh Forbes, Sean
Glynn, Mickeen Oge Flynn, Paddy Bawn Enright, all good men,
and all nicely tied up, with painfully pleasant little romances safely
behind them. Time some good, honest tragedy was introduced into
this cosmos.

He came out under a tall memorial arch raised to Dublin Fusiliers
who had died in the Boer War and paused to look at the long list

of so-Irish names. Died fighting for big business against the small republics, but it was a good fight at any rate! He crossed over to the top of Grafton Street and saw the portico of the Gaiety Theatre down on his left. That reminded him. Sean Glynn, up from the country, would like a show, and a couple of seats might be managed.

It was a popular English play, and circles and parterre had been booked out. But he could have two seats in the manager's box if he did not object to the owner of the show looking in once or twice. He took the two seats. And if Sean Glynn wanted to go to the Abbey instead, no doubt he had booked by wire.

Grafton Street was not yet crowded by the afternoon shoppers. A narrowish, twisting, wood-paved street, queerly intimate and leisurely even for Dublin; with tall houses of irregular architecture and plate-glass windows for the allure of women, who loved to hide or dissemble themselves behind silks and skins, corsetry and cosmetics – especially cosmetics. The cult of the Cosmetic! Sort of universal religion for women, older than Egypt, older than Crete, older than the last Ice Age. It did not beautify, it only typified – the art of the demi-mondaine. With the ideal of the demi-mondaine? Woman imitating the prostitute – but why? Religion, of course. Some pretty girls along this street – even below the cosmetic insipidity – but, at that, how insipid any of them would be placed beside one of the great courtesans: Aspasia, Magdalen, Elizabeth – even Mary Queen?

A cool entry down there on the left and people trickling in and out. A cross over an arched doorway, and a narrow concreted yard inside. There would be a church in there – a Catholic chapel. All the old Catholic churches in Dublin were in laneways and back streets; a relic of penal days, Mickeen Oge Flynn had told him, when no Roman church could be built on a main thoroughfare. Well, this was a half-foreign city, and in foreign cities one usually visited the churches. It would be cool in there too.

He followed a fashionable lady who dipped an un-gloved hand in a holy-water font and touched her brow with a dainty, practised, feline gesture. The interior of the church opened out wide and high, cool, serene, remote from the busy street not forty paces away; not as dark as Notre-Dame, not as lovely as Chartres, not as sombre as St Paul's, but with its own atmosphere all the same: something Byzantine, something foreign, a shade garish, but yet with a softly brooding, glimmering, withdrawn quiet. A brazen framework of votive candles flamed yellowly outside the sanctuary, and there was a lovely, fragile piece of sculpture under the high altar: Christ laid in the sepulchre – fine work, delicate work, lily-like, not tragic, not strong, just sorrowful only.

He moved softly on coir matting down the aisle and took a seat far back. It was pleasantly cool in here – even if he had no prayer to say. But one did murmur a prayer instinctively: 'Our Father' chart in heaven . . . forgive us our trespasses . . .' Was there no trespass that God would not insist on man forgiving? The traitor – the betrayer – the man who sold an ideal for vanity of power, as men had done, was now doing – even here in Ireland.

Women kept slipping in and out, kneeling, praying, asking for the moon, things beyond the moon: nurtured women, kept women, draggled women – women. Men too: workmen, unemployed men, men no man would employ, men who employed many men – for the love of God or the love of Mammon. Yes, this was a strayed bit of Latin Europe. Surely the Church held its grip and would keep on doing so – holding its grip – needing to hold it firmly – preaching Christ's ideal as prudently interpreted by a wise old man – and his wise college of Cardinals – who lived in a palace of eleven hundred windows. A damned Calvinist, Archibald!

A small cold air blew about the crisp hair at the side of his neck. He shivered. There was a draught from a door or window over there somewhere. He turned to look. There was no door or window for any draught to blow from – and there was no draught now. Just a little breath of iced air shivering through him, and it was gone. And then he saw the woman.

II

She knelt at the other side of the passage in the last seat of the nave, her hands clasped on the arm-rest before her, but her head not bent as in prayer. She knelt straight up, her shoulders back, chin lifted, staring before her at the far tabernacle on the high altar, sunk in some contemplation that might be beyond thought – beyond breathing. So might some saint commune unafraid with her God. Her profile in the diffused light was cut as clean as a cameo, and, like a cameo, it had no colour. She wore a wide blue hat, and under it her hair showed paler than pale yellow. And she was not old.

She came out of her absorption. Without any effort, without a lift of shoulders, a sigh of returning life, she turned, picked up a pair of gloves from the seat, and stepped out on the coir matting of the passage. And then she looked directly at Archibald MacDonald, as he was looking directly at her.

She was a lean brown face and eyes cool as still water: a man secure in his own poise and not afraid to look at any woman – or at any crisis.

She was not afraid either; she was merely detached. A natural woman with none of the smooth modern insipidity of woman about her. Her brow had a serious contemplative set that was almost but not quite a half-frown. Smiling rarely, laughing rarely, that serious, contemplative, faintly perplexed brow would still be there adding salt to her amusement. And though she was very fair, very blonde, she gave a strange impression of darkness.

So they contemplated each other for a second or two that had no hurry; and then, with that effortlessness he had noted, her head and eyes turned away from him, and she walked without haste down the passage and through the door in the aisle. Slenderly built and not too tall, she was wearing a bluish light cloak. That woman knew all about life.

After a time Archibald MacDonald came out of the chapel into Grafton Street and resumed his stroll. Presently he paused at a big plate-glass window, his glance caught by the flaming flimsy things that women wear. Cunningly and economically displayed, they caught even his male eye. He smiled at them, wondering – and gave up wondering. A woman stood at his side.

She was the woman of the chapel. They looked at each other, hers the same unhurrying consideration and then, unhurriedly still, she turned and moved away through the growing crowd.

He stayed where he was, looking in at the window, not seeing anything, meditatively rubbing his chin. There might be nothing in it. She did not look that sort of woman – or did she not? He smiled oddly. Back there in the chapel she had reminded him of a saint in her absorption and – he smiled again – saint – and sacrifice . . . and he was a dashed fool anyway!

He turned back then and moved up the pavement and by the west side of Stephen's Green to the entrance of Harcourt Street. There was the Municipal Art Gallery up there, and he had time to give it half an hour. There was a thing or two by Keating and Johns worth another look, and one extraordinary landscape of Constable's, where an immensity of sky made puny an immensity of plain.

He clicked through the turnstile into what was once the hall of a middle-class Georgian house and went through the almost empty rooms aimlessly; pictures all round him – good and middling, not too well arranged in that not-too-well-lighted house.

He was idly looking at the splashed colours of a modern Italian artist when a woman came in at the door. He glanced up quickly. There was an odd draining away in his breast, and after that his heart beat a little quicker – just a shade more quickly. He was a cool man.

As she passed him they looked at one another, and neither her face nor her eyes showed any surprise. But, darn it! she should have shown some surprise. His face must have shown some, and he was not a man of surface emotion.

He looked unseeing at the paletted colours before him and again rubbed his long chin. This was too much of a coincidence. This looked damn like an invitation, and he was a man never much amenable to that sort of invitation. Saintliness, my hat! A pity too. A beautiful woman and pitiful! Don't be a prig, Archie. Great saints, yes! Great courtesans – why not? Beyond a doubt. They needed to be great, and they were great: changing the face of Europe, Egypt, the world, making history alive. But ah! no longer was there room for such great ones. Not even the greatest could cause more than a flutter in the dirty little political dovecotes. This diffusion of Demos, the lordship of the bureaucrat, led to every silly woman painting her lips – courtesans in embryo, and never developing. And the great ones, instead of ruling kings, might follow half-pay soldiers round the streets of foreign towns. He grinned at himself. Hardly fair accusing a strange and beautiful woman even in his own mind. But, by the soul of Somerled! he would just see if there was anything in this business! and take a fall in the bygoing if he had to.

He walked slowly through the doorway and saw her in the statuary room, a well-lighted annex with a glass roof. He circled round, taking his own time, glancing at this and that, the torso of a Fenian, Tolstoi's beard, Rodin's head of Bernard Shaw, and so to where she was half-frowningly considering the bust of Lady Gregory by Epstein. He paused just behind her shoulder.

'The typical peasant woman?' He was addressing no one in particular.

'Yes, she thought she understood peasantry.' Her tone was as impersonal as his own.

'Did she not?'

'Ye-e-s! she did. But there is no Irish peasantry – that was the trouble – even in Kiltartan.'

'Peasantry?'

'The coarse rustic, of course.'

She was right. The Irish countryman was not a peasant. Someone had defined him as a strayed nomad tent-dweller, forced to till the soil and till it damn badly. A farmer by necessity, a saloon-keeper by choice, a politician by ideal.

'You know Lady Gregory's work?' That was more direct.

'Played it at the old Abbey.'

'One of the Abbey players?'

'In an amateurish sort of way. I wasn't a very good actress.'

She had not turned to look at him, and now, in her unhurried, unhesitating way, she moved aside from Lady Gregory and halted before the backless sardonic head of Bernard Shaw. It was not a dismissal. It was merely the interruption of a casual conversation.

This was a woman who knew the world and could remain herself. She had not started or bridled or shown calculated surprise. She just remained herself. But she could talk. He liked her voice. An Irish voice unmistakably. A man's voice similarly pitched might be almost harsh, but, though this voice could never be mistaken for a man's, it had the timbre and production very nearly masculine. Let this adventure develop. Again he moved up near her shoulder, rubbing that obstinate chin of his.

'We have been meeting rather often this afternoon?' he said.

She bent closer to Shaw's sardonic eyebrows. 'Why mention it? I haven't.' The voice was a casual murmur.

'Sorry – but I would be much sorrier –' he paused, and she finished the sentence for him without turning.

'If you thought I had been following you round?'

'Exactly.'

'It does look suspicious, doesn't it?' And then, 'You are not very complimentary, though.'

'Yes, I am. Would you care to come and have a cup of coffee?'

The fall was due him there. She turned round full and looked at him – that direct, half-frowning, faintly perplexed, cogitating look.

'Just a cup of coffee,' he said, his eyes steady on hers.

She smiled then, and, as he had known, her smile was faint, yet deep, slightly frowning, and with a small crinkling of the eyes. A man would remember that smile.

'Thank you,' she said. 'That will be nice.'

It was as easy as that.

They went out into Harcourt Street together, and an attendant looked after them with admiration – the tall, easy, brown man and the slender, lovely woman with the pale hair. She was not too tall, but a tall man would not have to bend to look under the widish leaf of the blue hat.

'There used to be a place – I think – at this end of Grafton Street,' she told him.

'You've been out of Dublin?'

'Some years.'

'And you were taking a look at some of the old places you knew?'

'It could be.' That was a southern Irish idiom.

'So was I. Incidentally, we seem to have followed the same route.'

'That's nice of you.'

'You are Irish, of course?'

'And you Highland?'

'Much the same, aren't they?'

'Are they?'

'The same thought processes – and the same idea of the things to see in Dublin of a summer afternoon.'

She smiled up at him again. 'And the same liking for coffee – or would you prefer beer? And, let me see, did you say the same prayer that I said in the Carmelite church – or did you pray at all?'

'Yes, I did. Our Father 'chart in heaven, never let me forgive a traitor.'

'I have never forgiven a traitor.'

Her voice had not grown emphatic, but it had grown deeper, and, while holding no emotion, held emotion curbed. He looked aside at her. She was looking straight ahead, and all expression was wiped off her face. He knew then that he had touched a nerve.

'No one should,' he murmured.

They were at the busy top of Grafton Street and paused, waiting for the traffic signal. And then:

'Hello, Nance!' came a strong English voice behind them. 'I've been waiting here twenty confounded minutes.'

The woman was not startled – or she never showed it.

'Sorry, Harry!' she said, without looking round. Instead she looked at Archibald MacDonald and smiled her faint deep smile. 'Sorry we could not have that coffee and a long talk, Captain MacDonald,' she said. And then, over her shoulder, 'See you later, Harry.'

She stepped off the pavement, moving quickly but not flurriedly, and swung on to a tram just moving out for Terenure.

The man Harry – a well-built, well-dressed, handsome fellow – said, 'Damn!' explosively, and strode off the pavement too. And a taxi did its best to kill him, though an unusually humane driver clapped on all the brakes he had. In return the humane man was called an ugly name, and in reply, being Irish, told the 'mealy mouthed Jew man' his final and immediate destination. Archibald MacDonald left them at it.

For a moment he had thought of making a run for the tram-car, and then some inspiration of Highland insight warned him that that was not the way. He felt disappointed, robbed, a little forlorn, but something that underlay consciousness had a confidence that curiously stood apart from himself. He shrugged a shoulder, turned his back, and proceeded down Grafton Street.

'May the devil sweep Harry!' the Highlandman cursed with Irish warmth.

III

He leant an elbow on the counter of the lounge-bar and ordered his pot of München Spatenbrau. He had the lounge to himself, for the evening exodus from the nearby government offices had not yet begun.

He started to go over the last hour in his mind. It had been interesting, exciting in a way, and, in spite of the disappointment, that same confidence still held – just as if something were leading up to something else more important. A striking, cool woman, and she knew him! 'Captain MacDonald,' she had called him. He was a Major now, and had been for five years. Someone that had known him more than five years ago? But if he had ever met her, how could he have forgotten? One could not easily forget her. He straightened up then and his mouth opened. It stayed open for five seconds, and shut then with a snap.

'My God!' he said, and hit the counter with clenched fist.

The swing-door swished behind him and a man came to his side at the bar, so close that MacDonald moved a little away without looking up.

'You knew that lady?'

It was the cultivated voice of an English gentleman, and there was a bold autocratic eye behind the formal smile: the man that she had called Harry at the corner of Grafton Street. And Archibald MacDonald was rather glad to see him. The astounding thought that had made him hit the counter was racing in his mind, and here was a man who might help to elucidate it. But he would have to move cautiously.

The barman came to the counter, and, as the stranger ordered a British beer, the Highlandman looked him over. He was no Jew, though he was very dark, and his nose was not so much fleshily hooked as shoved slightly flat; good-looking in a smooth-faced, big-jawed way; not tall, but very well built, beginning to put on flesh, and with the set of shoulders of a man who had gone in for severe physical training.

MacDonald put down his pot of lager.

'What did you want to know, sir?' he enquired.

'You know that lady?'

'She knew me?' suggested the Scot equably.

'Please do not misunderstand me, sir.' He was still smiling, but there was a certain coldness in his eye. 'I do not accuse you of importuning the lady.'

'I know.'

'I am aware that Nance – Miss O'Carroll – has acquaintances in Dublin, but there is one thing I would like to point out: she is no longer interested in Irish affairs. She is here on her own business – and on mine, I might add – and she and I want to have nothing more to do with – all that past nonsense. You understand, I hope?'

'You followed me in here to impart that information?'

'Exactly.'

'You speak for the lady too – explicitly?'

'I do, sir. She is my fiancée.'

'You do not fear the lady's Irish friends, I hope?'

'Fear has nothing to do with it. Just a matter of choice.' His voice had remained diplomatically cool, but his eye gave warning. The man was certainly not afraid.

MacDonald looked through the amber of his beer, and there was tranquillity in his eye and in his voice.

'I have been told – I don't know myself – but good men have told me that one should hold the reins not too tightly before marriage – and a little looser thereafter. Might I assume that the lady's Irish friends might object to you as her husband?'

'The lady's Irish friends can go to hell, sir!' said the other warmly.

'A risk every Irishman runs – closely,' said the Scot.

The swing-door again swished behind them, and a brown-faced, dark, wiry man came through.

'The hall porter told me where I might find you, you thirsty devil,' said Sean Glynn, and stopped.

He had glanced at the Englishman, and his eyes had concentrated for a moment. Only for a moment; then he frowned, turned his shoulder, and shook hands with his friend.

'What's that you're drinking, Archie? Oh, thin lager! Order me a pint of Guinness – and how are you keeping, my poor fellow?'

'Having quite a pleasant time,' said Archie.

The Englishman drank his beer, but not too quickly, laid down his glass and walked to the door without looking at the two friends. Dublin *was* a sinister town still; for a flash there had been menace in the newcomer's eye. Pity they had come to Dublin at all. He had tried to persuade Nance not to, but she would come 'for the last time,' she had said. Only three days more, and then on to loyal Belfast and royal Edinburgh – and damn Ireland!

Sean Glynn looked frowningly at the swing-door swaying behind the man.

'Cool nerve that fellow has to be seen in Dublin,' he growled. 'But, of course, he is safe enough now.'

'He might not be,' said MacDonald. 'You know him?'

'I do, but he does not know me.' Sean was serious, almost gloomy. 'Six – let me see – seven years ago, he and I played a life and death game here in Dublin and he lost – and I am not sure that I won. His name is Hanley – Sir Henry Hanley, Bart. – and he was a British secret-service agent during the Tan war. He's half Irish.'

'I was unfair to the English half,' said the Scot.

'You were, whatever you mean. If the truce of '21 had been delayed another week, Hanley would have left Ireland like my mother's black hen. You've heard of my mother's black hen?'

'No.'

'It walked in the door dead to her one fine day. But let him be –

he leaves a bad taste in my mouth. I may be at liberty to tell you about it some day – you know some of it already.'

He imbibed deeply from his polished tankard. But the Scot would not let Hanley be just yet.

'What does he do now?' he asked.

'Hanley – Sir Henry Hanley! Surely you've heard the name? No? You've been abroad, of course. He keeps pretty well in the public eye in these islands. Racing motorist, speed merchant, fined half a dozen times and his licence suspended: first-class amateur middle-weight when I saw him first – putting on weight now. He's a well-plucked one too: DSO in the war, and took his life in his hands over here in the "bad times" out of sheer devilry and nothing else. He has plenty of money and loves to ride on the narrow edge of things. I believe he is interested in some theatrical company at present.'

'A theatrical company?' said MacDonald musingly, and tapped the counter softly with a finger.

'Yes! And last year he divorced Eleanor Carluke, the well-known music-hall artiste.'

'He divorced her?'

'Yes! In his way he is rather particular about his women – I know that much.'

'He is thinking of getting married again,' said MacDonald.

Sean opened his eyes. 'How the devil?'

'I'll tell you later. And, speaking of theatres, we are going to the Gaiety tonight.'

'Like hell we are! We are going to talk all night and take in the Curragh Races on the way down tomorrow.'

'We'll do that, but we'll go to the Gaiety too. I've booked two seats, and if you think a Scot is going to waste two seats you are jolly well mistaken. The play will astonish you, I lay odds.'

'Very well so! Time is long.' Sean knocked on the counter. 'The same again, or will you try something stronger? Damn Hanley!'

Chapter Two

I

Archibald MacDonald and Sean Glynn came to their box rather late in the first act. Sean had so much to talk about before, during and after dinner that they did not trouble to dress. They sat well back in the box, not caring, not much interested in the play. The man in evening-dress, already in possession, looked over his shoulder and stilled in that attitude. He was the man of the afternoon, Sir Henry Hanley. He frowned, made as if to rise from his seat, thought better of it, and faced round to the stage. One could see that he pulled his hardihood together.

Sean Glynn said, 'Damn!' under his breath, but the Scot only grinned to himself. This mere coincidence of occupying the same box would, almost certainly, look sinister to the man, who, as a one-time British agent, had no reason to feel secure in Dublin town.

The play was a popular English one and, like the English play, started slowly. The friends had not missed a great deal and, at best, they were only mildly interested.

But near the end of the act Sean Glynn got the shock of his life.

The woman that Archibald MacDonald had talked to that afternoon walked on to the stage. She had only a secondary part, and she acted it efficiently, adequately, not brilliantly.

'Great God!' Sean was leaning forward suddenly.

'Steady, son!' warned his friend, shoulder against him.

Sean caught his arm in a tight grip. 'That is Nuala Kierley,' he whispered, and shook the held arm. 'You know? Nuala Kierley.'

'I know.'

'But Nuala Kierley! My God, Archie!'

'Leave it now, Sean – leave it!' and he nodded towards the man in front.

Sean fixed his eyes on the man's back, and there was real menace in them this time. He was beginning to grasp things.

And then the curtain came down.

Hanley had sat still, taking no notice of the whispering behind

him. Now he rose quickly to his feet and brushed by them out of
the box without a glance.

Sean was on his feet too. 'Nuala Kierley!' he said excitedly. 'Her
eyes, her voice, just the same! A miracle, I tell you! I have been
looking for her for six years.'

'I met her this afternoon,' said Archibald MacDonald calmly,
leaning back in his chair.

'You what?'

'We talked. That man who was here, Sir Henry Hanley – she calls
him Harry – speaks of marrying her.'

Whatever Sean Glynn's impulse was, this astounding information
did not inflame it. He was a resolute man at bottom, and he was at
bottom now. He sat down slowly.

'You had better tell me about it, Archie,' he suggested quietly.

And MacDonald told him, baldly, clearly, with no sententious
philosophising. And at the end, all that Sean said was, 'I must
see her.'

'After the play?'

'It must be after the play – I must talk to her. She cannot marry
Hanley. I tell you, he is the one man she must not marry.'

Archibald MacDonald sat back in his chair and laughed with an
odd bitterness.

'Don't be dramatic, Sean. I am saying that to myself too. You
know, that woman has been in my mind since I got a glimpse of
her that night when you brought her to Lough Aonach – that time
I was a prisoner.'

'And on mine,' said Sean. 'The thought of her nearly drove me
mad once, as you know.'

'Because we dramatised her – from the very beginning. That was
why I did not recognise her at once this afternoon. She was the
wandering woman, Erin – wandering, forlorn, defeated, but never
lost. And she is only a minor actress in a second-rate English play.
What else?'

'She is Nuala Kierley,' said Sean steadily. 'I will see her.'

The orchestra was tuning up and the audience drifting back from
foyer and bar. But Hanley did not come back to the box. He did not
come back at all.

Sean Glynn could never tell what that popular play was about.
Neither could Archibald MacDonald. They were interested only in
Nuala Kierley, and her part was not important enough to give a

meaning to the play. And, between long intervals of silence, Sean spoke in whispers half to himself, half to his friend. 'No change in her, hair or eyes, or that voice. The stage does not suit her style. She is too static – cannot lose herself in her part – but doesn't she make the leading lady look tawdry when they are on together? Six years – and here she is – and here I am – and here Hanley is – and the old hellish game is beginning again. But she can't marry him.'

In the interval before the last act they went out to the bar, and there Sean had a revulsion of feeling. He laid a hand on MacDonald's arm.

'You're right, Archie! I see your point of view. Here am I, a douce married man happy to carry on as a staid householder and farmer, and there are you, a tough bachelor keen on your sport and the vagaries of wind and wing and weather. We don't want trouble.'

'What have I got to do with it?'

'Begad, that's right! A queer thing – I never thought of that. Somehow, I felt that you were mixed up in it too. But, of course not. This is my pidgin. You know, Archie, a thing once done will never let you go. Nuala and I once did a thing together, and it holds us still – here tonight its claws are in us.'

'In you only, perhaps?'

'Even so. I must see her and talk to her. Must see her alone. We were a good team, and she would always listen to me. We liked each other.'

He seemed to clamp his teeth close down on the need for that interview, and MacDonald knew that there was bound to be trouble with Hanley.

Well on in the third act, after Nuala Kierley had made an exit, a thought struck the Scot. He touched Sean's knee.

'She may not have any more lines – and Hanley will want to slip her away as soon as he can.'

Sean was at once on his feet.

'You'll go to the hotel, Archie, and secure a table. I'll try and get her to come to supper.'

'I am coming with you,' said his friend.

Sean looked at him and nodded. 'I suppose you will. But leave it to me, old man. Don't you go looking for trouble.'

'I'll leave it to you, all right, my son,' said the prudent Scot.

II

They were only just in time. There was a taxi at the stage door.

'Engaged?' Sean enquired.

'A gentleman in there, sir.'

'You might be needed,' said Sean.

At that moment the gentleman came out: Hanley. Nuala Kierley was with him, wearing a light wrap and her hair bare – bound for supper somewhere. Sean Glynn went straight to her.

'Nuala, you darling!'

'Sean!' she said, a little breathlessly.

He caught her hand from her side, held it in both of his, squeezed it.

'It is good to see you again. You are having supper with us.'

She shook her head, not smiling, but Sean, holding her hand, tried to dominate the situation.

'You must, Nuala, you must!'

Then she smiled that faint, serious, small smile, and answered what was in his mind.

'No use, Sean – no use at all.'

'Look, Nuala – an hour.'

'I'm having supper with Sir Henry Hanley.'

'I'll never let you go,' said Sean desperately in his teeth.

Hanley's hand came on his shoulder powerfully.

'What do you mean?'

Sean wrenched his shoulder free.

'Hanley, if you want a rough house you can have it.' Archibald MacDonald was a law-abiding citizen after the fashion of his countrymen, but at a pinch he could shed his law-abidingness as quickly as any Irishman – and retain his head. He saw that a rough house was inevitable, a rough house that would lead nowhere, and that he was the only man that might turn it to his friend's purpose. He was very prompt for a man who had proposed to leave it alone.

'Gentlemen!' his voice was shocked. 'Sean, I'm surprised at you.'

He caught his friend's arm and pressed it. 'Have sense, man, and show the lady to her taxi.'

'All right,' said Sean.

MacDonald held the door open and the lady entered, Sean letting her hand go at the last moment.

'To the hotel,' MacDonald whispered in his friend's ear. 'I'll hold him. Go on, blast you – if you must have it so!' The shove he gave Sean sent him asprawl on the floor of the taxi. The door slammed. 'Go on,' he roared to the driver.

He did not see the taxi go. He had more than enough on his hands for the next minute or two.

As Hanley tried to thrust him aside, he got a grip of the white evening-vest. Whereupon the other gave him a straight, hard lunge on the breast-bone, and the buttons of the white vest tore away. Hanley dived for the taxi as it moved, but MacDonald snatched the flying tails of a light dust-coat, brought the wearer sitting on the pavement and stumbled on top of him.

The man was astonishingly strong and energetic. He heaved himself to his feet in spite of all that MacDonald could do and threw him off savagely. The taxi was gone.

'Now then!' said MacDonald.

I'll smash you, you smooth hound!' said the other.

The moment Hanley put up his hands the Scot knew that he was in for it. He might do his part in ordinary rough-and-tumble, but against a trained boxer he was bound to get the worst of it. His only assets were his fitness, his toughness and some skill in Scots wrestling; his only hope was to get close in and stay there. He dived for Hanley's hips, and the other hooked him with both hands to the side of the head as he came and chopped him painfully on the back of the neck as the long, tough arms got a purchase. Then they were on the pavement and the Scot on top. But not for long. The other rolled him over with frenzied vigour, and MacDonald could do nothing but cling tight.

The taxi should be clear away now – no taxi man could gainsay Sean Glynn in a hurry. A nice business this . . . street brawling . . . a respectable half-pay soldier. Why in thunder did he intervene? . . . A hell of a town Dublin . . . A five-pound fine . . . but maybe Sean had a pull somewhere . . . cling on, lad.

There was a shouting, and a big voice spoke above them.

'Now then – now then?'

Hanley was wrenched to his feet. MacDonald scrambled to his and saw a towering Dublin policeman grasping his antagonist by the back of the neck. They were the centre of a jostling crowd – newspaper boys, loiterers, and the disemboguing audience from the parterre. The play was over.

Hanley had gone berserk, and small wonder; he had been badly used. Now he wrenched free from the policeman and launched a furious right hand at MacDonald, who jerked his head back so nearly in time that the blow landed but lightly on his cheek-bone. But the policeman was active for his size and secured a fresh grip. And then Hanley made his fatal mistake. He struck the policeman: a sound swinging punch that made him grunt.

Sir Henry Hanley was unlucky – had always been unlucky in Dublin town. He had always done his best as he saw it, and always had the worst of luck. And his luck was at its very worst now. For that policeman happened to be one of the world-famous heavy-weight boxing team of the Dublin Civic Guard. And a warm-tempered man besides. It was as good a little bout while it lasted as any gay Dublin crowd could wish to see.

Archibald MacDonald only saw the bare beginning of it. Someone thrust his hat into his hand, and a rough voice urged him, 'Get out while the goin's good.' The Dublin crowd, bred to years of feud with the old British police, had not yet learned to take the side of law and order. He was jostled into the crowd. He saw where two others of the Dublin Guard were ploughing towards their colleague – who did not need any help – and he edged away. It was the only thing to do. The crowd of theatre-goers swallowed him.

He got out of King Street, down Grafton Street, across into Anne Street, and so round again into Stephen's Green. As he went his wind returned to him; he pulled down his vest, straightened his tie, got the dust off his knees. One eye felt hot. But out in Stephen's Green he was no worse than a reasonably respectable loiterer, hat pulled down, Irish-fashion, over the doubtful eye, and the dust not showing on the shoulders of his grey homespun. Lucky thing he had not changed into blacks. And as he went he was wondering how Nuala Kierley would take her abduction. It was abduction, and a heinous offence.

III

Nuala Kierley and Sean Glynn were in a corner of the almost empty hotel lounge, at right angles to the door, and she was much the cooler of the two. She sat upright in a wicker chair, her long fine arms resting on a small glass-topped table, her hands easily clasped, and her eyes looking up at Sean Glynn. Sean was not looking at her; he stood biting his fingers, his eyes on the entrance. He would just stand about one minute more of this anxiety. And there Archibald MacDonald came through the door and walked across to them. He was as cool as ever.

At once Sean's spirits leapt sky-high.

'You got away?'

'The play was over, so I came away with the crowd,' said the cool man, and looked at the lady.

'Where is Sir Henry Hanley?' she asked him in a voice as calm as his own.

He smiled at her equably. 'No need to worry about him, Mrs Kierley; he has probably secured lodgings for the night.'

'Well, I'm – sorry, Nuala!' apologised Sean. 'For a prudent man, Archie, I'll put my money on you every time. This is Archie MacDonald, Nuala – but you've met him. He's a major now.'

'A policeman or two will be looking for us in the morning,' said the Major.

'We are in the one hotel where they will never look for a Highland thug,' said Sean.

Nuala Kierley retained her wonderful composure. 'What do you think you – gentlemen – are doing with me?' she enquired without heat.

'We don't know yet,' said Sean.

'Any reason why I shouldn't get up and walk out of here?'

'We'd come with you – we'd tear Dublin apart – we'd burn the Custom House. Wouldn't we, Archie?'

'And the Four Courts,' added his friend.

Sean shook a finger under her nose. 'If necessary, I'll ring up,' he named a man high up in the Free State Government, 'and he will not allow Nuala Kierley to make a fool of herself.'

'You think I am doing that?'

'We are taking the quickest way to find out, are we not?'

'I'll say you are.' And then she leant back in her chair and laughed. Her laughter was nearly as deep as a man's, and there was only that small crinkling about the eyes. 'Oh, Dublin! I might know that I am back in you. You are a lawless people, Sean, and you make your friends as bad.'

'Worse,' said Sean. 'A lot worse.'

The lady did not ask any more questions. She showed neither surprise nor anger – nor that indignation that a woman should show at unmerited disaster to a man who proposed to marry her.

She sat very still, the men watching her, her eyes half-closed in some cogitation of her own. Then she drew a long deep breath and looked up at Sean Glynn.

'All right, Sean! I will play this silly game out with you, but I warn you that I will take my own way at the end. What comes next?'

'Supper,' said Sean. He looked at his friend. 'Go and change your jacket, Archie, and plunge your head in cold water. You'll have a fairish black eye by morning.'

'He deserves it,' said Nuala Kierley.

They had supper at a secluded table behind a pillar, and for a while the talk was commonplace and easy enough. But very carefully Sean was leading it in one direction – getting Nuala to tell something about the past years. She did not seem to mind. She was frank but brief. She had been to Paris for a while, in the States, Canada, back to London and the Provinces: at best only a medium success on the stage.

'I was never a versatile actress, as you know, Sean.'

'But, my Lord! some things you could do,' said Sean. 'All the same, there is not a thing on the stage for you, Nuala.'

And then it came.

'I know. That is why I am thinking of getting married.'

'Thinking?'

'Your conduct tonight has put it beyond that stage, probably.'

'Who is the man?'

'Sir Henry Hanley.'

'Where did you meet him again?'

'He owns the show.'

'But not you. You cannot marry him, Nuala.'

'Why not?'

'You can't. He is the one man –'

'If you will look at it in another way, Sean,' she stopped him, 'he is the only man.'

'You can't, Nuala,' insisted Sean.

'Would you prefer me to be his mistress?' she asked him baldly.

'You will be that if you marry him; he is divorced, and you are a Catholic?'

'Does religion matter so much, Sean?'

He leant across to her. 'Tell me, Nuala, do you want to marry him?'

'I do not want to marry any man.' She said that in a slow, toneless voice that was more convincing than any emphasis.

'Well then?'

'Harry Hanley is not a bad man – and he is sincere. And, as you say, there is nothing for me on the boards. Well?'

'But you have your friends – all of us – and a pension due you from the State.'

She shook her head. 'I will never touch it. Ireland is still in serfdom.'

'But not for long. Look, Nuala! Come down with me to Leaccabuie.'

'You are married, are you not? I saw it in the press.'

'But Joan –'

Again she shook her head very definitely. 'I am not coming. No use, Sean. I told you that already.'

Sean looked at Archie MacDonald, hopelessly, desperately. He would be angry in a minute, and anger would lead nowhere with that woman. A silence, slightly tense, settled on the table while she poured coffee for them.

The Scot offered the lady a cigarette, held a match for her, lit Sean's and his own, took one or two meditative pulls, and spoke in his calm way.

'Might I say a word, Mrs Kierley?'

'Well, Major MacDonald?' She sat forward in her chair, leant her elbows on the cloth, her chin in her hands, the cigarette smoke drifting about her hair, her contemplative eyes steady on him. It was exactly as if she said, 'You may have something to say, but I am watching you carefully.' And he did not want her to have that antagonistic feeling.

'I am interested in Sean's point of view,' he began, 'but frankly I do not see – well, why he importunes you. You see, I know nothing.'

'I understand his point of view, Major MacDonald, but, really, there is no need for his anxiety. Well?'

'I would like you to know that I am quite disinterested in this.'

She smiled faintly. 'You did not act as if you were, Major.'

'I was only interested in giving my friend a hand.'

'Then you are not disinterested.' She was going to make things as hard as possible for him.

'I am quite disinterested as far as you are concerned,' he said, bluntly firm. 'You must accept that. Before today I saw you only once – for a minute at Lough Aonach.'

'I saw you two or three times, Major, though you did not see me. I recognised you at once today, and you know, I did follow you

round, trying to make up my mind to speak to you. You made it
easy for me.'

'I owe you an apology, Mrs Kierley.'

'Never mind! You were quite nice. How are you going to help
Sean out?'

'I would like to help you too – if I could.'

'I do not need help.'

That was a challenge, and he accepted it.

'Very well! there is no reason why I should say anything.'

He tapped his cigarette in the ash-tray and leant back in
his chair.

There was a silence for a while. Sean understood his friend and
kept hold on himself. Nuala Kierley, her chin on her hands, her eyes
steady, thought her own thoughts.

'I would like to hear what you have to say, Major MacDonald,'
she said at last.

'It is not much,' he said in a low voice, almost indifferently. 'I
am not pleading. You have seen enough of life not to have any
illusions left.'

'Just one – the greatest illusion of all.'

'Yes, Mrs Kierley! I think I understand how you feel towards
Ireland.'

That touched her. That brought her out of her uncompromising
attitude towards him – an attitude that had in it something of
self-defence.

'Quick of you, Major! Yes, Ireland has its pull; it may hurt us –
but no matter, more was lost on Mohacs Field. Go on, please!'

'I would merely ask you to consider your own attitude. You say
that you do not want to marry any man, and that you are thinking
of marrying Sir Henry Hanley. If that means anything it means that
you have some difficulty in making up your mind.' He paused there,
but she remained still, her eyes on his. 'And you will have to make up
your mind, you know. Perhaps I am old-fashioned in thinking that a
decision on marriage is an important one. As a hardened bachelor, I
think it is. A man of the world might say that it is not, that one should
act on impulse and kick over the traces when one has a mind.'

'Or a man of the world might say the very opposite?'

'Quite so – seeing the many horrible examples. My point is that
if you have difficulty in making up your mind, you might cultivate
the detached attitude, get out of the ruck, make up your mind in

surroundings where your decision will not be swayed by anything – or anyone, slip away by yourself for a few days, or a week, or a month, let no one know, and then – that's all.'

That was clever pleading. It seemed so entirely without bias, without any apparent calculation, pressing on her what was a secret urge in her own mind.

'You would advise me to go away by myself?' she said musingly.

'I would.'

'Not Leaccabuie, then?'

'No.'

'Glounagrianaan?' murmured Sean. His mind had leapt to Lough Aonach, but that place had tragic memories.

She shook her head. 'I know Hugh Forbes. He would tell me to go to hell, and make sure it was a heaven of his own choosing.' She looked at Archibald MacDonald and smiled. 'Do you suggest any place, Major MacDonald?'

'Oddly enough a place has come into my mind this moment, but I would not advise you to go there.'

'What kind of place – where?'

'Forty miles from Leaccabuie – or any place you know – and off all roads; up on the shelf of a hill with the heather all round it. I was only there once, but I remember the great plain spread out below it, with the distant wall of the mountains, and the sea over there. But what I remember best is the quiet, the quiet that underlay the songs of birds and the humming of the bees.'

'The quiet!' said Nuala Kierley. 'The quiet! You serpent!' but she smiled. 'Why, my mind would be swayed there every hour of the day and night.'

'That is why I advise you not to go there.' And then he went on in that remote and reasonable way. 'But after all, if anything sway you, why not let your own land do it? Nothing – no one else would. There is a place where you could stay, and you need see no one.'

'I will go to that place,' she said, as if she did not want to give herself time to change her mind. 'I will arise and go – when?'

'Now,' said the Scot.

'Now – tonight?'

'Why not? It would save a lot of explanations – and Dublin will not be a wholesome place tomorrow for some of us. Sean has the car here, and we could have breakfast in Limerick, or beyond it.'

'And buy a bit of raw beef for your black eye,' said Sean, breaking his wise silence. He knew where they were going and the man that was there, but he said nothing to Nuala.

MacDonald thought it strange, in his own mind, that no least consideration had been expressed for Sir Henry Hanley: where he was, or what he might do, or what he would feel?

'This finishes me with the whole business,' he told himself definitely.

IV

Paddy Bawn Enright tumbled handily off the bay colt and patted the glistening neck.

'Good boy, yourself!' he praised. 'Never a foot wrong, and eleven stone on top of you.'

A nice bay colt, on the light side, a finger under sixteen hands, with one white stocking and a small star, and the long, ugly, indomitable head of the Irish hunter breed.

Ellen Roe, Paddy Bawn's wife, lifted young Sean into her arms and came across the corner of the paddock where her husband had been exercising the colt. The child crowed and reached hands to his father, who hefted him with one hand and set him astride in the saddle.

'Mind him, Paddy Bawn,' warned Ellen Roe. 'You had your breakfast well shaken in you this morning. I thought you were off at the double ditch beyond.'

'He is weak at the double ditch,' agreed Paddy Bawn, 'and 'tis the only place he is weak. Man, Ellen Roe, if Joan Glynn wasn't riding ten seven I'd put her up on him for the Lady Cup at Dublin Horse Show, and get a hundred and fifty for him. As it is, I'll show him in the ring and get eighty, maybe. In two years' time he'll be carrying twelve stone at Punchestown – and I bred him.'

'Sh – listen!' said Ellen Roe. 'There's a car coming up the lane.'

An open touring-car topped the rise and bucketed slowly along the rough road leading to the cottage.

'That's Sean Glynn's car,' said Paddy Bawn, 'and early he was up this morning. He has people with him – Joan, I think, and another man. Come on, girl!'

Holding their proud bantling on the saddle, they led the bay across the paddock and into the yard before the cottage. The car arrived at the same time.

'Happy day!' cried Paddy Bawn joyously. 'If 'tisn't the Major himself – and who is the lady?'

The colt was restive facing the car, and Paddy Bawn lifted his son down and handed him to his mother. When he turned round to the car the lady had alighted.

'Glory be to God! Look – I say, look who's in it!'

The greetings were very friendly. Paddy Bawn, from past experience, had an almost idolatrous admiration for the Scot. 'He'll do to take along,' he used say in one of his quaint American idioms.

'Ellen Roe,' said Sean Glynn, 'this is my cousin, Nuala Kierley. Paddy Bawn is one of the old team of dog-stealers, Nuala.'

'God bless her!' said Paddy Bawn.

Nuala Kierley liked these two folk, the shy-smiling, red-haired woman, and the strong-shouldered, smallish man with the steady eyes below strong brows. She went across and touched the child's chin softly. And then her eyes came to the horse, and interest was alive in them.

'A nice young hunter, Mr Enright! Does he jump?'

'He'd lep the side of a house, ma'am. Rising five, and never saw a hound. You ride yourself, ma'am? He's a lady's horse.'

'Stop it,' shouted Sean Glynn. 'Stop it now! I won't have you two talking horse – you'll have enough time to talk horse.' He placed a friendly arm across Ellen Roe's shoulder. 'Ellen Roe, I want ten words with you and your husband. Give me hold of my namesake, and come across to the stable. The ladeen is growing more like his da every day, God help him! Come on, Bawn!'

They went across to the stable, Sean carrying the child, whose godfather he was. Paddy Bawn remarked, ''Twasn't you pegged the Major in the eye? You couldn't do it, anyway.'

'The man that did that could knock your block off.'

'It has been done before now, but all the same I would like to see the lad that struck the blow. I might?'

'I hope not. I'll tell you about it – and a lot more.'

Archibald MacDonald and Nuala Kierley looked at one another.

'This is nice,' she said inadequately. She swung full circle. 'This *is* nice.'

'Care to take a look round – you're not tired?'

'Not a bit.' She drew in a long breath. 'This air has a kick – I can smell the heather and the sea.'

She did not look tired after the long drive through the night. There was even a faint colour in her cheeks under the creamy tint, and her lips were not wan as after a sleepless night. She had pulled her hat off, and the soft morning air moved lightly in her wonderful light hair. And that strange aura, as of darkness, persisted and abolished the insipidity of the blonde.

They strolled together across the paddock. A pleasant sense of ease had grown up between her and this equable man – equable but explosive, as she knew. That sense had developed during the night. They had sat together in the back of the car, not talking much, dozing a little, waking up to say a few words, lapsing again into a silence in which, perhaps, their minds touched.

'There is the view I wanted you to see,' he said.

They had come to a clay fence at the end of the flat paddock, and the shelf of the hill steepened below them. They looked down over the great vale of North Kerry, verdant with pasture, dark with woods, shining with ribbons of running water; and over there, far beyond, were the smoky, tall ramparts of the mountains; and the gleam of blue-green that caught her eye made her turn to the lifting plain of the sea shining between the promontories of Shannon Mouth. The air from the sea spun the flax of her hair on her brow, and all about her was the hum of Ellen Roe's bees busy with the nectar of the bell-heather that bloomed along the margin of the ditch.

'And I stay in this place!' she wondered.

'As long as you please.'

'That will be longer than I may stay. These two nice people, Ellen Roe and Paddy Bawn – they won't mind?'

'They won't mind. They will spread green rushes under your feet. And Paddy Bawn will let you ride the bay. Get him to talk. He has a quiet way of talking and some good stories of his fighting days in the States. But you must be careful not to make his wife jealous.'

She laughed. 'Poor me!'

'Perhaps you can't help it,' he said.

'Help what?'

'Oh, nothing!'

She considered for a space, her eyes staring out over the great plain. Probably it was his reference to Paddy Bawn as a fighter that recalled to her mind the man left in Dublin.

'We were not very considerate,' she said. 'I mean to Harry – to Sir Henry Hanley – you and Sean – and myself too. Street-brawling!'

'And abduction. But we had not much time to work in.'

'You did not need a great deal, did you? I suppose it was your plan to rush me right off my feet – and you did.'

'We had no plan at all. Act quickly and consider slowly – an old maxim. Plenty of time to consider here.'

'No, I won't think about that. I'll ride the bay colt – if I'm let – and be a vegetable the rest of the time.' She looked directly at him. 'Where will you be?'

'Fishing the Ullachowen or Lough Aonach – there, beyond the mountains.'

They smiled at each other, and the same idea was in both their minds.

'If I were to come over once or twice,' he suggested, 'sort of to wipe the blood off your nose – the bay might throw you?'

'That would be nice,' she agreed. 'You have done a good deal of my considering already, and you might do some more. I like your detached attitude, Major. You can be so quiet – and you knew that I wanted quietness – I always did.' She smiled again. 'But you can be explosive too.'

'I would prefer that you remembered the quietness,' he requested.

'I will.'

'You had better be careful, my lad,' said Archibald MacDonald to himself.

Chapter Three

I

Nuala Kierley and Archibald MacDonald sat on the clay fence and looked over the plain and the sea. The woman held small Sean Enright on her lap, and the little fellow sat very quietly, his head against her breast.

It was a warm day in late July with a translucent heat haze veiling the woods, dimming the mountain wall, fading pearl-blue sky into pearl-blue sea. But up here on the shelf of Knockanore a cool flow of air tempered the heat and moved softly in the woman's hair. She was in riding-togs and looked supple and boyish. Out in the paddock Paddy Bawn walked the bay colt up and down to cool off. The horse was after a hard schooling and was perspiring freely.

'Isn't he a good 'un!' she said.

'With a crackerjack to ride him. Not once have I had to wipe your nose.'

'I wish I could afford to buy him.'

'I'll buy him for you.'

She opened her eyes at him. 'You couldn't – it would not be right.'

'You mean that I have not the right?'

'I do.' And she went on quickly, 'Paddy Bawn is tempting me to ride the colt for the Lady Cup at the Horse Show in August. I would like to.'

'Why not? You are not afraid to adventure Dublin?'

'No – yes, I am. I would have no excuse to come back here.'

'By the way – are you?' He paused, finding words difficult to choose.

'I have decided nothing,' she answered him. 'One doesn't – one just drifts along. Probably that means that the decision does not interest me.'

'I know what you might decide.'

'Well?'

'You might decide to marry me. Then I could buy the colt for you.'

He made the astonishing proposal in that tranquil voice of his. As he made it he rubbed a match briskly and held it to his pipe, not even looking at her.

But she gave him a sudden intent look, drew in a long breath, and her arms tightened about the child. Then she shook her head slowly, sadly, and a small, sad smile came about her eyes. Her voice was as cool as his.

'You are not a marrying man, Major.'

'Think not?'

'I know. I even know what is in your mind.'

'Marry me, then.'

'You have seen all your friends marrying all around you, and that has worried you. You are wondering if you should not follow precedent; and here is a poor lame dog with a few good looks left and – you know? I have a certain appeal, I suppose, and – well! no harm is done in being gallant.'

'Will you marry me, then?'

'I will not!' She shook that sad head again. 'Do you not know that I am unlucky – that tragedy –?'

'Dammit! Couldn't we dare that bogey like sensible people?'

'You know what happened to my husband – Martin Kierley?'

'He was drowned?'

'It that all you know?'

'Only surmises.'

'He was betrayed – I betrayed him – and I knew what I was doing.'

'The circumstances –'

'You ask Sean Glynn. It was a woman's work, and done in the only way a woman can do that work. You ask Sean Glynn how I betrayed my husband. No, Major, we are not marrying people. Mind you, I do like you, and I am glad we can talk so reasonably about it. But I will not marry you – and after a week or two we may never see each other again.'

'We are darned reasonable about it,' agreed Archibald MacDonald gloomily. And then, with some vigour, 'but I do not believe for a moment we are not marrying people. I did think I was a pretty tough specimen, but I have been coming up to see you every week, sometimes twice a week, and – I am a man – a male, if you like. That's putting it reasonably too. And I think you are wasting your life also.'

He looked at the child nestling in her arms, and she understood that look. Colour came into her face.

'Don't let us have any romantic illusions,' he went on. 'The sense of tragedy – of loss – does not persist. You will marry, you must marry – you will even fall in love – though I may not be the man. But, all the same, I will not take this as your final answer. Don't make it that. I will ask you again, some time.'

'Ask Sean Glynn.'

Emotion was very near the surface with him, and to hide it he got to his feet and turned away.

'Very well,' he said, and walked across the field to meet Paddy Bawn.

She looked after him steadily. Her face did not change, her look did not change, but her eyes darkened. Then her head sank, and her mouth whispered in the soft hair of the child:

'He was too cool, Seaneen, and I am not used to that. I must be getting old; but, Seaneen boy, I would hate to be married calmly.'

II

Archibald MacDonald, in the long July evening, drove across from Lough Aonach, where he had been fishing, to Leaccabuie, and had supper with Sean and Joan Glynn.

After supper the young matron left the two men to talk and smoke; and they talked a little of haymaking, and a good deal of fishing, and in time worked round through horses to the subject that was in both their minds. Sean was the first to introduce it. He had been quietly observing his friend for a month and was beginning to hope that a miracle would happen.

'Been up to Paddy Bawn's lately?' he enquired.

'Yesterday.'

'Nuala still training the colt?'

'Yes.' MacDonald set match to pipe and took one or two pulls. 'I proposed to her,' and took another pull or two.

Sean Glynn sat up and stared at him. The matter-of-fact tone made him wonder if he had heard aright.

'Say that again!'

'I asked her to marry me.'

Sean's eyes narrowed, but he copied the other's coolness.

'From your tone I gather that she refused you.'

'She did.'

Sean tapped the arm of his chair. 'I have known you a long time, Archie, and there is one thing I have noticed about you.'

'Yes?'

'You always insist on getting your own answer.'

'An egotistic hog?'

'To be sure. You will not take no for an answer?'

'She referred me to you.'

Sean nodded. 'She would do that.'

'She had some notion that I must ask you how she betrayed her husband.'

'She did not betray her husband.'

'It does not matter. I am not interested.'

Sean threw himself back in his chair and ran his hand through his black hair. 'It was a bad business,' he said gloomily.

'She said I must ask you, but I do not want to hear it – really I don't, Sean.'

Sean considered that for a long time while the other smoked. At last he drew in a long breath. 'You had better hear it from me, Archie, once and for all.'

'Please yourself.'

The two men lay back in their chairs, and Sean put down his pipe and did not again take it up; but the Scot went on smoking, hand over bowl, chin on breast, eyes fixed steadily on his outstretched feet.

Sean told the story of Nuala Kierley as it has been related at the beginning of this chronicle.

At the end he looked at his friend curiously, but MacDonald never looked up. His pipe, clenched in his teeth, was out now, and his brow was propped in his hand so that his eyes were hidden.

'Let me explain,' said Sean.

'Nothing to explain,' the other stopped him, a harsh note in his voice.

'But you do not understand.'

'I understand very well. There's no need to grow sentimental over what the woman did. She did her job, and her husband destroyed himself – or was destroyed. Dramatic enough, I admit, but sordid as hell. We might have left her to the man Hanley.'

'Don't be a damn fool, Archie!'

'I suppose I am – I suppose I was.' The Scot seemed to have kicked over the traces and was brutally destructive. 'A blasted fool! When I saw her in a Dublin church I thought of her as one would think of a great saint, but another name was under the surface of my mind. Perhaps there is not much difference in your patriotic circles. The woman Ireland, worshipped – and despoiled.'

'Shut up, blast you!' Sean, equally mad at himself and his friend, was on his feet pounding the table, his voice raised. 'Listen to me!'

MacDonald was on his feet too. 'I have listened. You sold a woman for your cause – and you would explain it away!'

'You deserve your teeth down your throat for that. Damn you! you are not fit to touch the hem of her garment.'

They glared at each other. And at that moment Joan Glynn, having heard the raised voices, came in.

Archibald MacDonald turned, bowed to the tall and lovely lady, and walked straight out of the room and out of the house.

Chapter Four

The first Thursday in August was Lady Day at Dublin Horse Show – the big day of probably the greatest horse show in the world. The ladies, with a carriage dowered them by some ancient subtle devil and arrayed accordingly, make that day their very own – even in spite of the grand horses. They move lazily around the covered band-stand, lean on the backs of chairs, gather and move apart, stroll about the oval promenade below the huge stands, glide up the wide steps, come pacing down again, no evidence of a hard bone in lissome bodies. Tinted sunshades bob and whirl, arms gleam, eyes glisten or grow slumbrously speculative, red mouths smile or grow serious; and the men of Ireland and Britain and the world admire, and are diffident and awkward and restless as proper men should be.

It was three of the afternoon and carriage horses were showing their paces in the ring; all types, all sizes – fourteen to seventeen hands – high-steppers, long-reachers, smooth-pacers, harnessed to gigs, traps, tubs, sulkies, phaetons; and as each spun by the grand-stand a man might say, 'Damn! you couldn't get the beat of that one!' Only the judges knew better.

The promenade was not yet crowded – as it would be when the big jumping event came on – and three men were able to walk abreast well away from the rails and below the grand-stand. The three were Hugh Forbes, Sean Glynn and Paddy Bawn Enright; lean, hard, brown men from the country, strangers in this half-foreign town, but at home here where horse was king. They were not greatly interested in the pacings of the women.

Moving slowly below the grand-stand, pausing now and then, their eyes went over it tier by tier, carefully, searchingly, looking for someone. Suddenly Paddy Bawn stopped dead.

'Got him, be the powers!'

They looked where he pointed.

''Tis himself, sure enough,' said Hugh Forbes. 'I told you he'd be here.'

Half-way up and to the right of the royal box, Major Archibald MacDonald sat slumped on the wooden bench, gloom in his very attitude. Paddy Bawn pulled off his tweed hat and waved it about his head, but the Scot was staring aimlessly out across the ring. And there Hugh Forbes, as unconcernedly as at home in his own Glounagrianaan, threw up his head and from his strong jaws came forth a brazen bellow that boomed and rolled in the girders of the roof.

'Archie MacDonald! Hullo there!'

The Major started – hundreds did the same – looked down, and saw Paddy Bawn's waving hat.

'Come down, we want you. Come down out o' that!' the great easy voice ordered him.

The Major came down hastily and in some embarrassment, for people laughed all round him, and some remnants of Scots dignity still stuck to him.

'Take him easy,' Sean Glynn warned his friends. 'Take him easy! He's as stubborn as a mule – and we daren't make a mistake.'

The greetings were warm, though possibly there was a small shade of restraint between Sean Glynn and the Highlandman; but both knew it for the merest shadow on a lasting friendship.

'We were looking for you,' said Hugh Forbes. 'Where've you been?'
'Scotland.'

'And you thought you'd come over to see the show?'

'Why not?' There was a little challenge in his voice.

'Were you here yesterday?'

'No. I only arrived by the evening boat.'

'You missed some good leppin',' said Hugh. 'Come over here to the rails, all of us. Never mind your seat amongst the quality. They'll be singing "God save the King" in a short while – and I like to feel my hair bristle. An' I wouldn't condemn the king – or any man – to an hour in purgatory – well, maybe one or two men, and to hell I'd send them.'

The rails were not yet crowded for the jumping, and the four, moving round, found a place to line up opposite the grass bank. MacDonald leaned on the rails between Hugh Forbes and Paddy Bawn. They idly watched the judging of the horses and talked desultorily but with some undercurrent disturbing the idle flow.

'Are you all well at Knockanore?' MacDonald enquired presently, his tone almost casual.

'What's left of us,' said Paddy Bawn heavily.

'Mrs Kierley has left, then?'

'This week – she's not coming back.'

'No?'

'No. She was quiet on us the last couple of weeks.'

The Scot said nothing to that.

'She was as quiet as God,' said Paddy Bawn.

The Scot said nothing to that either, but it was a sore saying. If he thought it over long enough it would bring a lump into his throat. She was a woman who would take all hurt quietly; and she would know that Archibald MacDonald had judged her and had found her wanting.

'H-s-s-h! Here come the jumpers,' said Hugh Forbes. 'Will ye be quiet, now?'

But no one had said a word for two minutes.

The judges had chosen the winners in the harness class, and the three, sporting their rosettes, had paraded proudly to the applause. A military band had blared forth the lively air of *The Kilruddery Hunt*, and in from the barrier sidled and pirouetted the jumpers for the Lady Cup. There were two dozen horses of the young hunter class, mostly raking sixteen-handers with long heads, powerful shoulders and barrel ribs. All the riders were ladies, and quite half of these – the more experienced half at that – rode the orthodox side-saddle: hard-bitten, tanned women with wrists of steel. The girls riding astride were inclined to sit down hard in the saddle.

The horses paraded and took a breather outside the jumps, and a coming 'lepper,' here and there, was pointed out and discussed. There was one young horse rather out of its place amongst the big-boned hunters: a nice bay colt with a white stocking on the off fore and a small forehead star, long in the leg and light in the waist for class jumping, but with the smooth, nervy action that told of jumping ancestry. He was ridden by a slender boy-like woman, riding American style with long stirrups. She wore no hunting-cap, and the wind of her going tossed back from her brow a spray of short, fine hair whiter than pale yellow. Loping easily down by the side of the jumps, she stood in the stirrups, her body alean like a slip of whalebone over the horse's withers; and men clapped her as she swept by; for it was good to see a woman ride like a jockey – a toughened old steeplechase jockey giving his mount a breather down the straight.

'A nicely matched pair?' said Hugh Forbes, and nudged the Scot in the ribs.

'They are.' He leant well over the railings, his eyes following horse and rider, and his face still – almost too still.

'She was placed second yesterday in the young class,' Hugh told him, 'and if the judges knew better she'd be first. A cob thing got by with trick jumping. Any chance today, Paddy Bawn?'

'No. He's out of his class,' Paddy Bawn decided soberly. 'He won't be named even. I was offered a hundred and eighty for him last night, but I wanted to see how he went with the six-year-olds and a lady up.'

The horses disappeared into the waiting yard; the megaphone blared forth its announcement; and the first couple of jumpers came pacing out. They jumped well, of course, but over that exacting circuit – hedge, hurdle, in-and-out, single bank, stone wall, double bank, water-jump, pole, and gate – they did not approach perfection.

The bay colt came out in the fifth couple, tossing his starred head and prancing sideways.

'Easy – easy, you devil!' reprimanded Paddy Bawn. 'That's no way to face a hedge! Hold your hands down on him, my darling – and over he goes. Nice – oh, nice! and did you see him change feet like a hound? Oh, murder!'

'Only a small bowler of a stone with the near hind,' said Hugh Forbes, 'Nothing at all . . . Change 'em, boy, change 'em . . . and over with him like a bird . . . and only for that lump of a stone sticking up.'

'And a bit of a cat scramble at the double bank,' judged his cool owner. 'He's weak there – and I'm not sure but there was a spurt of sand at the water. He'll maybe not be named for the second round.'

'I'll bet you a pound.'

'You will not. I wouldn't bet against her to win a million,' said Paddy Bawn.

The loud-speaker spoke out of the sky. Seven horses were called for the second round, and the bay's name – *Cnucanor* – was announced third.

'A pound saved is a pound won,' said Paddy Bawn. 'He'll go kinder this time with the temper cooled in him.'

He was too sanguine all of a sudden. But, indeed, *Cnucanor* might

have jumped better that second round if his rider had held hand
and mind on him. For two days her eyes – when they had time
– had been looking over that sea of faces for one face; and now,
when she was not looking for it, she saw it. If she had once
started for the green bank she would have seen nothing, but
in that moment before she steadied her mount she saw that
looked-for face with the tail of an eye – just beyond the bank
and to one side, low down, leaning far over the railing, set on her
like a magnet.

She could never tell what happened after that.

A touch of knee, a jerk of the off-rein, the least thing – perhaps
the horse's natural weakness at a wide bank – would do it. The
colt came slew-ways at the jump, rose gallantly, rapped his forefeet
hard, bumped his nose into the grass top, kicked for a hold under
firm rein, came down somehow on four feet on the right side, and
pecked disastrously forward on his head.

A deep lifting moan went over the crowd.

The rider had been jarred loose in the saddle by the first jolting
bump and had no time to recover balance and knee grip before that
disastrous peck. Instinctively her feet were clear of the stirrups; she
sailed in the air, turned a clean somersault and came down clump.
But barely had she touched the ground than she rolled away from
the trampling hooves and in the same movement came to her feet.
Only for a moment. She swayed, drooped, crumpled down on her
side and lay still.

'God Almighty! her back!' said Hugh Forbes, and placed a
holding hand on MacDonald's shoulder. 'Steady, son – wait till
we see!'

The Scot threw back his shoulders stiffly against Hugh's hand.

The Saint John ambulance men were already at Nuala Kierley's
side and lifting her carefully on a light canvas stretcher. Sean Glynn
spoke for the first time.

'See that! She kicked her legs straight then. Nothing wrong with
her spine – only a wrench. Come on!'

'Right!' said Hugh. 'We'll go down to the dressing-station end.
Paddy Bawn has the entrance to the ring, and will bring us
out word.'

But already Paddy Bawn was gone.

On the way down Archibald MacDonald slipped his friends in
the crowd. He could not face Nuala Kierley.

II

Archibald MacDonald spent a bad evening, as he well deserved to.

As soon as he had left the show grounds, he knew that he had acted in a churlish manner, but could not summon up enough self-discipline to go back. Nuala Kierley was nothing to him, but as, in a way, he was responsible for her riding the colt that afternoon, he might at least enquire after her. He must do that – but not just yet. His friends would know, but to find his friends in the crowded Dublin hotels might take all night.

His dissatisfaction with himself drove him round to the City of Dublin Hospital not far from the show grounds. Nuala Kierley had not been brought there nor to any of the nursing homes in the vicinity, nor to St Vincent's across the Green from his hotel. She might be anywhere in a city of half a million people. He even went into a phone-booth and rang up the show yard, but the officials had already left and the attendant knew nothing. Finally he cursed himself heartily and plodded heavily across Stephen's Green Park to his hotel.

The first man he saw in the foyer was Paddy Bawn Enright. He was alone and sitting forward on a leather couch outside the door of the lounge, his strong brown fists clenched between the knees of his riding-breeches, one shoulder hunched in that characteristic fashion he had, and his brows down over his steadfast fighter's eyes.

'Sit down here,' he said shortly. 'I want your advice.'

Archibald MacDonald sat down. He felt a strange little glow of warmth in him. These Irishmen who were his friends would never let a friend go. They understood, and stuck by him.

'How is Mrs Kierley?' he enquired at once.

'All right. 'Tis about her I want your advice.'

The Scot frowned. 'Not badly hurt, I hope?'

'Nothing broken. A twist to something with a long name that'll keep her on her back for a week. Listen to me! You and Sean Glynn took her down to Knockanore and put her in the hands of me and Ellen Roe. And what am I going to do now?'

'Is there anything to be done, Paddy Bawn?'

'That is what I want to know. If Ellen Roe were here she'd know, but I want to know now, before the night falls. Listen! When I went to the dressing-station after the fall I couldn't get in to her for a while, as the doctor was with her, and, when I did get in, there was another man with her. A strong-built man, a dark-complexioned man, with a nose that was hit hard some time or other. You know who he was?'

'Hanley?'

'That's him. I know about Hanley – Sean Glynn told me. And I might as well tell you that she had dinner with him last night. But the two of us had a walk by ourselves down to O'Connell Bridge after that and had a cup of coffee at a place. Look now! All that Nuala Kierley said to me today and she lying there was, "Good-bye, Paddy Bawn, and give my love to Ellen Roe and small Sean." And after that Hanley took her away in a big car with a nurse.'

Archibald MacDonald's chin was on his breast, and he felt nothing but an utter sense of depression.

'What could I do?' went on Paddy Bawn. 'I could do nothing, but I wasn't the least bit satisfied – not one bit. So I galloped a hack after the car, and we hadn't far to go. Listen! This fellow Hanley has never left Dublin since that night at the Gaiety – I know about that too; he has taken a service flat in Fitzwilliam Street, and Nuala Kierley is there now. Are we to do anything about it?'

'Have you put it to Sean Glynn and Hugh Forbes?'

'Leave them out of it. They have a dislike to Hanley – and you are a cool man – as I know.'

'Not very cool, Paddy Bawn.'

'Cool enough at a pinch. That girl was placed in my charge, and I liked her – and Ellen Roe – and she liked us and small Sean. She was nice in the house and had simple ways; and she would make you laugh and you with the toothache. You wouldn't think that now, but she has the light heart in her if she had a chance to show it. Like a lad she was. Sure, 'tis her heart kept her alive. And one thing we noticed, and it used to make Ellen Roe cry. It was the way she held that life in her arms as if she was saying, "Oh God! 'tis only for a short time." Are you listening to me?'

'I am listening, Paddy Bawn.'

'Is there anything to be done?'

'She said good-bye to you this afternoon?'

'She said good-bye to me, her face gallant.'

'She went away with Sir Henry Hanley?'

'He took her away.'

'She went with him. There is nothing to be done, Paddy Bawn.'

'That is your advice?'

'I can see nothing that you can do – that anyone can do.'

They sat silent then, and slowly Paddy Bawn's face changed. MacDonald had never really seen the small man's fighting face, and it gave him a cold shiver. All expression was wiped off it, a glaze washed over the eyes; and the cheek-bones were blenched and hard as stone. His hands were clenched over his knees at the end of stiff arms, and his voice, not raised, had a strange even harshness.

'By Christ God! I will not have it that way. She will be lying there waiting for a word. I will go and see her now.'

'Better be careful. Hanley is exceedingly tough.'

'I hope he is,' said Paddy Bawn, and rose to his feet.

Archibald MacDonald rose with him.

'I am coming with you,' he said.

'I know you are,' said Paddy Bawn simply.

III

Sir Henry Hanley's flat was the top floor of a converted Georgian mansion overlooking the trees of Fitzwilliam Square. The sky-lighted passage outside the door had originally been the topmost landing of the stairs. Inside was a wide hall, also sky-lighted, with four doors opening off it.

Propped on pillows, with pillows all round her, Nuala Kierley lay on a white bed in the middle of a big room. The bright bars of evening sunlight came level over the trees of the park, through two tall windows, and lay across the white coverlet. A uniformed nurse moved some things about on a dressing-table between the windows, and Sir Henry Hanley sat aside on the bed and looked at Nuala. Her fine light hair was about her face, and her face was entirely colourless. But it was not a weak face. It was set in some steady inner strength of its own, and the eyes, slightly frowning, were considering the man dispassionately. Her smooth long arms lay outside the coverlet.

The nurse turned from the table. 'I'll want a few things for the night,' she said. 'If you'll excuse me for half an hour, I'll go out and get them.'

When the nurse was gone Hanley took Nuala's hand, brown after the sun of Kerry.

'I knew you'd come back to Dublin, old girl,' he said half playfully.

'You knew where I was?'

'No.'

'But you knew who took me away?'

'I could have found out, no doubt, but I did not want to incur any danger – for you. You see, I knew you'd be back. That is why I took a risk and stayed on in Dublin.'

'I don't think you run any risk in Dublin, Henry, nor was I in any danger. I left Dublin of my own free will; are you not afraid that I may leave it again as soon as I can put my foot under me?'

'So you will, my dear – with me. We will cross over to Holyhead and get married. You surely see at last that that is the thing to do?'

'I suppose it will come to that – unless your pride saves you.'

'Pride?'

'Yes. You have a certain attraction – a force – but I do not love you.'

'That will come.'

'It is worse than that. I love another man.'

He said nothing, but a dour obstinacy darkened his brow, and his big jaw stuck out.

'And yet you would marry me?' she wondered.

'I will. This other man?'

'It does not matter, Henry. I will never see him again – and he does not know. Queer, is it not, that this disaster of love should come to me again?'

'And it will come again. I know enough of life to know that. Give me time, Nance.'

She nodded her head, her eyes considering him curiously. 'I understand. You must have your own way. Since that night – your mind has been set on one end – and I felt the force in you even then.'

'From the very beginning – from the first hour we saw each other – I knew I had to have you for wife. Anything else did not matter – does not matter. It is inevitable, my dear.'

'I suppose it is. We brought disaster enough upon each other from the beginning and seem fated to go on. That sense of fate has been always on me.'

'Then you will marry me?'

The front door bell rang and went on ringing, as if a finger remained pressed hard down.

'Damn!' exclaimed Hanley. 'My man is out for the evening. Just a moment, Nance.' He bent quickly and kissed her and went out, shutting the door behind him.

Nuala Kierley listened to the racing bell. Her heart had started racing with it. She kept her eyes fixed steadfastly on the closed door.

When Sir Henry Hanley opened the front door, a smallish, hunch-shouldered man placed a foot on the threshold. Behind him stood a tall man in loose tweeds. Hanley knew that man, and a flare came into his eyes. There was little need for parleying here.

'We came to ask for Mrs Kierley,' said the small man mildly, but that firm foot remained inside the threshold.

'She is all right. Get out of here!'

He looked contemptuously at the mild man. He did not attempt to thrust the door against him. Instead he threw it wide to the wall.

'If you do not get out I'll throw you out.'

The small man lifted a deprecatory hand.

'Now, sir – now, sir! No need to be rough. Mrs Kierley knows me. She rode my horse today.'

Hanley gave no further warning. Why should he? He, himself, had been manhandled without warning, not so long ago. And prompt action is half the battle. He launched his right from the hip, a hooked, stiff-armed drive, with enough power behind it to knock Paddy Bawn heels over head. That was its intent. Then the tall man would get thrown over the banisters, with this fellow kicked downstairs after him. A reasonable and probable conclusion – if that powerful first blow had landed.

But it did not. The small man was not there when it arrived. He had no time to guard it, no time to jerk back out of distance, but he fell inward on the other's breast and the fist grazed the back of his neck. At the same time he might, as he well knew how, have brought his right devastatingly into the short ribs. But, instead of that, he thrust the big man back and held up an open hand protestingly.

'Have sense, man, and listen to me,' he implored.

Hanley might have guessed by that quick forward duck that he was up against a skilful professional, but his Dublin luck pursued him, and he held fast to the intention of tying up this small country man with one solid blow and getting his hands on the man he really wanted to manhandle.

'I'll get you, you little thug!' he growled, and came on.

Paddy Bawn threw three quick words over his shoulder.

'Look for her!' and dodged quickly sideways into the hall.

But Archibald MacDonald did not look for anyone for a space. He stepped in, shut the door and stood with his back to it.

The bigger man was in a hurry. But so was Paddy Bawn. That says almost enough. Well then! Hanley, once a first-class amateur, was now out of training, going to flesh a little; Paddy Bawn, once known as Tiger Enright, the most explosive welterweight in the American ring, had been kept in good condition by the life he led. Surely that says enough. Hanley, confident of an easy task, was a little more than astounded. He was hit quickly, from all angles, very hard and two or three times too often, crowded into a corner, brought down solidly, sat upon, dragged up, trundled through a doorway. Tiger was the right adjective. And Dublin was Sir Henry Hanley's unlucky town.

Nuala Kierley, lying still, her eyes steadily on the door, had heard the voices, the angry tones, the movement of feet, the sound of struggle, the thud of blows and bodies, and then a bump and a lull.

And there the door opened and Archibald MacDonald stood looking in at her.

'A small argument,' he said calmly. 'It's over now.'

The bars of sunlight had moved an inch along the white coverlet and glowed on the hands clasped closely. That was the only sign of agitation she showed. Her eyes were steady as ever.

He did not stand long in the door. He shut it softly, walked slowly across to the bed and looked down at her sternly.

'The colt threw me at last,' she said in a quiet small voice. 'Are you coming to wipe my nose?'

'I am coming to take you away,' he said, 'and it will be for all the time.'

'All the time,' she whispered, and that faint crinkle of a smile came about her eyes. But then her mouth quivered and her eyes, grown strangely dark, filled up.

'Nuala, girl!' He caught her hands firmly, lifted them, and pressed them down on her breast. 'No nonsense about this! You are marrying me.'

'Why?'

'Because I want you – because I'll never let you go.'

'Did Sean –?'

'I don't care a damn,' he said fiercely. 'You must marry me.'

'I must,' she whispered. 'I am very tired. Please take me away, Archie.'

A quiet, deep voice spoke behind them.

'Paddy Bawn can't sit on his head all night.'

That was Hugh Forbes. He grinned at them pleasantly.

'There's no hurry in the world, but, if we don't make haste, we may have to fight our way out. We have a big saloon car down at the door, and a nurse of our own. If you would leave the lady's bedroom, Archie, the nurse would be getting the girl ready. Dublin is too hot to hold you more'n a day at a time. Come on, son!'

'Hugh, you darling!' said Nuala.

''Tis what the ladies call me always,' said Hugh.

Out in the hallway Sean Glynn caught Archibald MacDonald by the breast and shook him.

'We'll apologise to each other, Archie,' said he.

'It does not matter now, Sean.'

'It does. You are a pig-headed Scot.'

'Please, Sean! It does not matter.'

'Listen, damn you! You need not be ashamed.'

'It does not make the least difference, Sean,' persisted Archibald MacDonald.

No one at all had a word or thought for Sir Henry Hanley, who had done only his best and had found Dublin a bad town.